fall in love again

serendipitous love
book three

Christina C Jones

Fall In Love Again

Copyright © 2015 Christina C. Jones

chapter
one

Charlie

I *NEVER* CLAIMED TO BE HIS "RIDE OR DIE".

Really, I couldn't understand why he would expect such a thing from me. I mean... it was never a secret — at least not between *us*— that *love* was the very last thing on the list of needs we met for each other. An educated, successful, good-looking, brown-skinned spouse, check, check, check, and *check*. And just to make it even, we could throw occasional hot, albeit *meaningless* sex in there to round things out to an even five "checks". But... considering us anything more than good friends who decided to get married because it was convenient was honestly laughable. That's why it was baffling to me that Adrian actually thought I was going to wait around for him while he served a sentence in *federal prison*.

Like... real ass prison.

That negro was out of his mind.

He waited as long as he possibly could to tell me he was under investigation for securities fraud. He was sweaty, and nervous, and stuttering, and not at all the cool, collected Adrian I knew. I could accept that I'd committed my life to a man who wasn't my "soul mate". I could *not* accept that I'd married a criminal... until the FBI started showing up at the house and freezing our accounts, and news vans started popping up in the front yard. I couldn't really be in denial after *that*, which is why I was preparing to sublet an apartment thousands of miles away, where hardly anybody knew Adrian's name. Here I was, leaving in disgrace, to go back home.

Back home.

Guess how I left home in the first place?

Yep.... *in disgrace.*

I didn't *want* to go home. What I *wanted* to do was throw a fit. *You get what you get, and you don't throw a fit.*

I had no idea why *that* kept coming to the forefront of my mind, because if *anybody* deserved to throw a fit... *I* deserved to be throw a fit. And I don't mean a sitting around pouting for a few hours with ice cream and a glass of wine kind of fit. No, I mean a snotty-nosed crying, rolling around on the floor, black auntie at a funeral kind of fit.

FBI, SEC, IRS... I'd dealt with enough abbreviated government agencies to make my head spin by the time they were done tearing our life apart. But once I finally got the news that *I* had been cleared of any wrongdoing... only one acronym mattered.

POS.

No, not *that* one, even though as of late, Adrian was frequently a piece of shit in my thoughts... and words, and emails, and texts, etc. No, the *POS* I refer to is the cute little saying I'd run across in various groups online, for women trying to conceive a baby: peeing on a stick.

I had to make sure that bastard hadn't gotten me pregnant.

Please God, don't let me be pregnant.

That sentiment was a big difference from six or seven months ago, when I actually *wanted* a little blue plus sign to pop up on a plastic stick. I needed *somebody* around here that I could love on. Now, as I stood in the bathroom, furiously washing my hands to pass the time, I wanted nothing more than a big, fat, minus.

If Adrian had finally succeeded at getting me pregnant, after months of trying... I was *gonna* throw that fit.

I somehow found the self-control to not look at the test until the two minutes had passed, then I snatched it from the counter and held it in front of my eyes.

My heart slammed to the front of my chest.

Halle-freakin'-lujah.

I tossed the test into the trashcan with a flourish, and pranced into the bedroom I'd shared with Adrian for the last three years. Before all of the bullshit, this had been a beautiful room, decorated in lush summer blue, gray, and white. Now, all the accessories I'd painstakingly chosen — gorgeous bed linens from Paris, one-of-a-kind paintings commissioned from black artists... everything was packed away in boxes. One set of boxes for the storage building I couldn't really afford, one set marked as "evidence", and one set tagged for auction — to pay restitution to Adrian's victims.

Victims.

I'd married a man who had *victims.*

Kelis' *Caught Out There* cycled through the speakers, and I cranked it up louder. "*I hate you so much right now*" was a more than appropriate sentiment for the onerous task of clearing out the house — to be sold as well.

"*I can't believe you're bailing on me Charlie. I thought we were in this thing together— forever.*"

Hmph.

The look on Adrian's face when I had to explain that he'd *thought* wrong was comical.

This *entire thing* was.

I almost laughed as I pulled the boxes of ovulation prediction kits from under the bathroom counter, tossing them into the bin marked "purge".

Almost.

Because it wasn't funny, not even a little, that instead of happily planning a baby with my husband, I was packing the wreckage of my life into as few boxes as I could. There was nothing amusing about the hassle of settling massive bills, talking to lawyers, and keeping a tenuous hold on the only thing I had left.

It was messed up.

I was messed up.

Maybe I should be sticking by my husband.

So what that he was kinda... vanilla. He was good to me, and he made me laugh. In general, he was a little on the quiet side, but *so what*? When prodded, the man could talk people, politics, and pop culture, so we were never hard up for conversation. *So what* that we didn't love each other "like that"? Before the decision to get married, we were friends. So maybe... maybe I did love him a little. It wasn't possible to live with someone for three years and not develop a certain level of fondness. Repeatedly, the thought that I could *really* use one of Adrian's firm, delicious-smelling hugs ran through my mind... but, oh, yeah.

Adrian was a POS.

Yeah. *That* kind.

When I boarded that flight to Morocco for our ridiculous, bougie-overload destination wedding, I had no idea that three years later, the man I married would be sitting in a federal prison awaiting trial. *Real ass prison.* Nothing tipped me off that "investment banker" — at least in Adrian's case — was just code for "white collar criminal". There were zero hints that he'd funded our luxurious life on the backs of little old ladies living off their husband's pensions.

His pleas of innocence meant nothing to me when I — and my clients, friends, hell, the *mailman* — was watching dateline-esque probes by the local new station, with my husband's face — and sometimes *mine* — constantly flashed across the screen.

No.

No.

He could talk to me when he'd won an appeal.

My music stopped.

A text message notification interrupted the stream, and I pulled the last of the things under the cabinet out, dumping them in the trash before I went to collect my phone. When I saw the name of the person who'd sent the message, I lifted an eyebrow.

When I *read* the message, I played *Caught Out There* again.

It was even *more* appropriate for *lost his mind negro number two*, on the other end of this text.

I took a deep breath, and ignored his message. I could deal with *that* later. For now, my priorities were getting this house cleared, and not missing my flight.

The next several hours were devoted to packing the last of our things. Once they were securely taped, and tagged with a prepaid shipping label, the boxes with my personal belongings would go to my cousin's apartment, where I would be staying until I found a place of my own.

Almost too late, I remembered that I needed clothing for the few days it would take to get the boxes cross-country. I found my luggage in a — luckily not-yet-taped — box, and filled my carryon with a random assortment of tee shirts, jeans, and underwear. I didn't anticipate needing or feeling like putting in the effort into looking cute.

The way I saw it, I was in mourning. For my lifestyle, my house, my dignity... and my marriage. None of this was easy for me. I didn't feel brave, or free, or relieved, I felt... like a failure. My grand plan to marry someone who made sense, versus someone who affected my sensibilities... wasn't so grand.

As a last act of wifely benevolence, I packed as many of Adrian's treasured belongings as I could fit into two large boxes, and slapped on a shipping label that would take them to his mother's house. If you wanna talk about a ride-or-die, *that* lady was it. When it came to the men in her life, Sandra Richards believed the sun rose on their whim, and set on their command. She was beyond scandalized that I wasn't visiting Adrian every day, weeping, and lamenting, and decrying the injustice of it all, because *didn't I know her son was innocent,* and *don't you know what you won't do, another woman will*.

Uh, no girl.

The alphabet soup of agencies with Adrian's name at the top of their lists, the fact that even my *personal* assets were frozen, pending investigation, and the fact that he was sitting in federal prison — *real ass prison* — all told a different story about his innocence. I couldn't, and *wouldn't* put my life on hold for that. And as far as another woman taking my please?

Hmph.

She could have his ass.

***

BY DESIGN, NO ONE WAS WAITING FOR ME AT THE airport. I didn't want to see *anybody*, I wanted to get to my new apartment, take a long nap, and wake up to realize this was all just a horrible nightmare.

My cousin, who I was subletting from, had already sent me the key, so I let myself in and took in my surroundings. Being back in this city, back in this neighborhood... I'd expected to feel anxious, and maybe even a little afraid. The people I considered my friends before... would they still feel that way? But somehow, as I stepped up to the large window that looked out over familiar streets, I just felt... *home.*

I knew my mother would be ready to kill me for not being the first to know I was back in town, but I wasn't ready to deal with her dramatics. Between her and my aunt Morgan, they probably already had a list of potential *new* husbands waiting for me, and I wasn't quite rid of the first yet.

Instead of calling her — or anyone else — I texted my cousin to let her know I was there, then stripped down to nothing and took a hot shower. It was late, and I was *tired*. After my shower, I crawled into the bed and closed my eyes. *Starting over* could wait until tomorrow.

chapter
two

Charlie

WHEN I OPENED THE DOORS AND STEPPED INTO POT Liquor, — the cozy, eclectically designed modern soul food restaurant I was *so* proud of — I felt a warm, welcoming sense of *home*. When I stepped into the *kitchen* of said restaurant... this first thing I heard when my heels hit the tiles was "So I heard your high-class husband went to *federal prison*. Like... real ass prison. *Damn*, that's... hilarious."

Mugshots aren't cute, girl.

I hadn't even been back for a full day yet, and here I was, already trying to talk myself out of a murder. One would think I'd try my best to stay away from any and everything related to ending up behind bars, but... bodily harm seemed like the only *proper* reaction to a bullshit statement like that.

Nostrils flared, I stopped walking to take a cleansing breath. Around me, it seemed like everything had stopped. The cheerful banter, running water, sizzling skillets... all of the normal noises of a commercial kitchen were replaced by apprehensive quiet, leaving behind the sounds of Grown Folk's Music — the only radio station we played — in the background.

My eyebrow twitched as I turned to face the source of the ugly remark that had my cheeks burning, fists clenched, and shoulders full of enough tension to crack pecans.

Lost his mind negro number two, in the flesh. Nixon Graham.

Or, as I think of him more often than not — a thorn in my side.

My irritation faltered — just a little — and the heat in my face intensified as his gaze took an unhurried, appreciative expedition from my head to my toes. Inexplicably, I was glad I'd managed a cute outfit from what I had in the hastily packed carryon bag from my flight.

We communicated on a professional level almost daily, but I hadn't seen Nixon face to face in years.

On purpose.

Unfortunately for me, those years had been *very* good to him. Like... crazy good. Like, *went through the line twice* good.

Nixon was nobody's pretty boy. The last traces of *boy* were gone from his face, replaced by a sculpted hardness that spoke very strongly of *all man.* He wasn't even the kind of handsome that was universally agreed-upon, but *lawd, have mercy,* the confidence in his walk as he swaggered up to me screamed sexy. The top of his faded haircut was left a little longer than I remembered, but it suited him well. The self-assured way he held his broad, athletic shoulders, those dark hazel eyes against that deep, golden-brown skin, and his newly-acquired, velvety-thick beard... I was a *fan.* I would purchase tee-shirts, tickets, follow him on a world tour... if only there were a different *person* in the body.

But there wasn't.

It was... *ugh...* him.

"Screw you, Nixon. Will you trip and fall into the deep fryer already? *Please?*"

Nixon chuckled — a warm, robust sound that sent vibrations through my chest. When his eyes met my face again, his lips turned up in a grin as he took the last few steps to reach me. For a moment, he just stared, then without a word, he pulled me close, enveloping me in the aroma of cardamom and sweet potatoes, blended with the woodsy scent of his cologne.

Don't close your eyes, don't close your eyes.

Screw it.

I closed my eyes and inhaled, taking advantage of the fleeting opportunity to revel in a man's embrace, something that hadn't happened in a while. Too late, I remembered that he and I weren't alone in the kitchen, and I opened my eyes to find part of the kitchen staff pretending not to stare.

Clearing my throat, I shoved my way out of Nixon's arms, tugging at the hem of my fitted tee to straighten it. "Aren't there customers waiting for their food?" I posed the question aloud, to no one in particular, but it was enough to snap the sous chefs' attention back to their jobs, instead of Nixon and me. To him, I said, "I need to talk to you. Privately."

"Lead the way."

He winked, and I sucked my teeth. Nixon thought he was slick, talking about "lead the way". I knew exactly why he wanted me to walk in front of him, but I turned on my heels to head to my original destination: his office.

The whole way, I felt his eyes caressing my jean-clad backside. When I glanced back, he was wearing a lustful grin as he ran a thumb over the swath of hair under his lip.

Shaking my head, I pushed open the door to the tiny office, stepping in far enough that Nixon could enter as well. He grabbed me at the waist, lingering against my ass longer than necessary as he squeezed past me to get to the other side of the desk.

"Nixon, seriously? Could you not?"

He shot me another of those lecherous smirks, bringing his dimples into full view. "Could I not... what?"

"*Feel me up.*"

"It's a small space."

"You had room."

Nixon chuckled, running his tongue over his lips as he sat down, then leaned back, kicking his feet up on the desk. "You're looking damned good these days, Charlene... but I didn't do nothin', I swear."

"Whatever. Can you not call me that?"

"Call you... what?"

"*Charlene.*"

"Ain't that what your mama named you?"

I sighed, running my fingers through my close-cropped curls.

"Can we get to the point, please? We have something important to discuss, if you don't mind."

"I don't mind at all," Nixon said, propping his hands behind his head. "I would *love* to know the whole story behind your precious *Adrian* getting the book thrown at him."

"That's *not* what I'm here to talk to you about."

He smirked. "Okay. We can talk about you ignoring my text yesterday about hiring a new chef. What are you even doing here? Had to fly down and tell me how to run things?"

I lifted an eyebrow, and crossed my arms. "Pot Liquor is *my* restaurant too. We're fifty-fifty here — you don't run things by yourself. Besides... there's no need to hire a new chef."

Cutting his eyes toward the ceiling, Nixon let out a deep, exasperated huff, then responded in a tone edged with annoyance. "Charlene..." — I narrowed my eyes — "We agreed that with Paul leaving, we needed another executive chef. Jordan and Amina are good, but neither has the experience to help me run this kitchen."

"I *know* that."

"Then why—"

"Because *I'm* going to be Paul's replacement," I interrupted, shrugging. "We'll run the kitchen together, like we did before."

Nixon cocked his head to the side, scrutinizing me for a moment before he shook his head. "No."

"No?"

"Did I stutter?" he asked, raising his brow.

With a dry laugh, I took a step closer. "What makes you think you can tell me whether or not I can come back?" I challenged, sitting down on the edge of the desk.

He scoffed. "What makes you think *I can't*?"

"The ownership documents. *Why* don't you want me in here?"

"*Why* do you want to be back here?"

"Can you stop answering my questions with questions?"

"Can you answer the damned question?"

I briefly shut my eyes, running my tongue over the smooth surface of my teeth as I tried to repress my annoyance. I didn't even have to wonder at how Nixon knew about Adrian's legal troubles.

My mom knew, which meant *his* mom knew, which meant *he* knew. And *I* knew what he was aiming for.

He wanted to hear that technically, I was broke. He wanted the words "I have to move back here" to actually leave my mouth. Nixon wanted me to plead with him not to make it more difficult than it already was to admit the fact that I couldn't give the executive chef opening to someone else because *I* needed it.

Hmph.

I would *never* give him the satisfaction.

"I'm just... homesick. I'm going through a hard time, and I want to be back in a place that's familiar for me. Is that so hard to understand?"

Nixon gave a quick shout of laughter, shaking his head. "You expect me to believe that?"

I lifted an eyebrow, leveling him with a glare. "I *expect* you to mind your damned business. Do you have a question about my professional ability?"

"Should I?" He shrugged. "You're the one who ran away from here to get married. I don't know what you've been doing since then."

"I didn't "run away". What's with the running references?" I asked, propping a hand on my hip. "You tryna' make a point?"

I knew I'd put on a few pounds since he'd last seen me, but I'd *always* been a curvy girl, and Nixon had *always* liked it. A few days a week at the gym kept the cellulite at bay, but other than that I let the ass, hips, and thighs flourish — and never got any complaints.

"That's bull, and you know it. Stop deflecting, and answer the question. *Should I* have a question about your professional ability? You haven't lost your hot-shitness have you?"

Despite my irritation with him, I grinned at *that*. "Never. I was a private chef out in Cali." — What I *didn't* mention was the fact that because most of my clients came to me through Adrian, there were questions about whether or not my business was legitimate. — "I've been keeping the wheels oiled and in motion."

Nixon nodded, chewing at the corner of his lip. "We'll see."

"We'll see? Negro what, you think I can't cook anymore?"

"Oh, I'm not worried about your cooking, not really," he said, pushing himself up from his chair. "I'm worried about our ability to cook *together*. Memba' this?" He came to stand in front of me, pointing to the lingering scar I'd given him with the hot end of a frying pan.

"You deserved that."

"Says you."

"Says the whole neighborhood."

"You asked them?"

"I can," I replied, trying to grin and hold my breath at the same time. Nixon stood close enough that his leg was touching mine, and the intoxicating aroma of brown sugar and cinnamon lingered around him. I *loved* Nixon's sweet potato pancakes, and he just *had* to be making them the day I came back. *Of course.* "I can call up Grown Folks Music, get Vaughn or Leah on the line... I'm sure they'll let me broadcast a message."

"You wouldn't."

"I *so* would."

"After everything I've done for you?" he asked, placing a hand to his chest as if I'd wounded him.

"Like *what*, Nix?"

"I got you back in town, girl!"

Biting my lip to keep from giving in to his infectious smile, I gave him a playful roll of my eyes. "And how exactly do you think you did that?"

He sucked his teeth. "You didn't hear me singing for you? *Come on home... to... me... Charleeeene.*"

"Oh *God*," I giggled, teasingly shoving his shoulder. "Are you *ever* gonna stop doing that?" I looked down at my hands, trying to hide that I was blushing. *Damn...* he even still sounded good. So much for my distant hope of a permanent vocal cord strain.

Nixon moved closer, and when I looked up, he pinned my gaze with his as he nudged my knees apart to step between them. "Nope. Never."

Keep it together, Charlie.

"What are you doing?"

He dropped his gaze to my lips, then shifted forward, just slightly, but enough to make my heart crash to the front of my chest and stay there, racing like it was late for work. "I'm not doing anything," he declared, hovering not even an inch from my face. "Unless... you're feeling something?"

Oh, I was *feeling* something alright. *Throbbing* between my legs, from where his hardness nudged my softness. I knew I should probably smack him for such a brazen act, but my kitty was purring a little too loud for me to hear my common sense over it. *This* was the kind of thing Nixon did to me, and exactly why coming back here was probably an awful idea. But... there were bills to pay.

"Ain't nobody feeling nothing."

"Oh you're feeling *something*," he said, speaking into my short, springy curls before he placed a kiss against my forehead.

I had to bite my lip to get myself in order, then swallowed *hard*. "Yeah, I'm feeling grossed out by you taking the liberty of putting your lips on me, after they've been God knows where."

"*You* know where." Nixon grinned, gently gripping the soft flesh of my thigh before moving his hand to run a finger along the inside seam of my jeans. "I bet you're thinking about it now."

"It's been five years, Nix. Do you really think I remember that?"

He chuckled, placing his palms flat against the desk on either side of me. "If you've been counting the years... you remember."

"I don't."

"You're putting off pheromones, Charlie... *you remember*."

Of *course* I remembered. It wasn't like I hadn't had good sex in the five years since we'd broken up, but yeah... even if I *didn't* remember, my body certainly did, and I didn't doubt for a second that I *was* emanating *fuck me* vibes, because... I kinda wanted him to.

"What's your point?" I asked, in a breathless whisper I barely recognized as my own.

He got closer, his minty-cool breath tickling my ear as he responded. "I'm sayin'... your little husband is out of the picture...right?"

Right.

"Why?"

"Maybe I can refresh that fuzzy memory of yours."

Mmmm, I'd be lying if I said that wasn't a tempting offer, but I could *not* go back down that road.

"Uh-uh," I said, pushing him away so I could slip down from the desk. "You and your damned voodoo dick will *not* pull me back in. *Not* making that mistake." I wagged a finger in front of his face to emphasize my point, then headed for the door.

With my hand on the doorknob, I turned to face him again. "Email me with how you want to set up the schedule, and we'll work it out. I'll probably need to shadow you for a few days to get back into the swing."

Nodding, Nixon slipped his hands into his pockets. "The schedule will be in your inbox within the hour."

"Thank you. I... I'm gonna go now. Have some... other things to do." Even though I said I was leaving, I stood there for a moment longer, keeping my eyes locked on his face, even though my peripherals were *all over* the imprint at the front of his pants.

He lifted an eyebrow at me, breaking my trance, and I turned and opened the door. Just before I stepped out, he spoke up again.

"Charlie?"

I let out a little breath before I turned to face him. "Yeah?"

Nixon's lips spread into a grin, dimples on full display as he winked.

"Welcome home."

chapter
three

Charlie

I couldn't get my ass out of there fast enough, and didn't fully breathe until I was back on the sidewalk in front of the restaurant. Outside, the sultry late-summer air laid heavy on my skin, and leaving the air-conditioned restaurant in such a hurry didn't seem like such a good idea.

Pot Liquor was like my baby, a love child between Nixon and me. The *only* successful thing to come out of our relationship. It started with us hosting tasting parties, then slightly larger catering jobs, and developed into the cute little modern eatery I stood in front of now.

Back when we first started, we didn't have anything but immature love, a feeble bank account, and a dream that the little rundown space in a mostly abandoned part of town could be the start of something beautiful. Nine years later, it was. Slowly but surely, our community cleaned up our city, and turned it into a place where *our* businesses could flourish.

Instead of languishing on my heels in the sweltering heat, I headed next door. I smiled as I entered the space, breathing deep. The place had been renovated since my last visit, but the warm, inviting aroma of good coffee that was uniquely Urban Grind would *never* change. I glanced around, and didn't spot the owner, Roman, but I *did* make eye contact with another handsome business owner from the block.

His face spread into a smile as he walked toward me, balancing a cup of coffee and pushing his wallet back into his pocket. "Yo, what's up pretty girl?"

I grinned as Carter pulled me into a hug, squeezing me tight before he released me and took a step back. His barbershop, Fresh Cuts, predated *all* of the businesses on the block. It was his inheritance, started by his grandfather, before factory closings and economic downturns killed the vibrancy of the neighborhood.

"How have you been? You good?"

"As well as can be expected with... everything." I shrugged, then glanced over his shoulder and around the coffee shop. "I heard you've got yourself a gorgeous new girlfriend..."

Warmth bloomed in my chest at the way Carter smiled about *that*. Carter was already a good looking guy, with his neat, shoulder length locs and smooth pecan-colored skin, but the mention of the woman he — so *obviously* — loved brought a light to his face that made him exponentially more handsome. So friggin' sweet.

Wonder if Adrian ever smiled like that when people asked him about me?

"Yeah... so you've been hearing things too?" he asked, trying in vain to tone down his grin.

I smiled. "Yessir, I have. And... I have to admit, I was glad to hear it."

I'd known Carter a *long* time. Before we were business owners, Carter, Nixon, and I attended high school together, just a few blocks away from where we stood now. Carter was, without question, a nerd, with just enough swag from playing basketball that he avoided bullying. Now, he'd outgrown his "nerd" label, and was, from what I'd heard, quite a charmer.

"Does Nix know you're back?"

I rolled my eyes. The fact that I'd expected the inquiry didn't make it any less annoying. It wasn't a problem that *Carter* asked, but he was just the first in a *lengthy* string of people with the same question: *Does Nix know you're back*, as if we were high school sweethearts from a sappy movie, and he'd been pining away, waiting for me to return.

That *wasn't* us.

Nixon and I had been over, no backsies, for five long years. I'd gotten married, and Nixon had... done whatever he'd been doing. In our constant communication, which was necessary to run the business, there had never been any awkward declarations of continued love, no desperate pleas to take anybody back. *We* had moved on, and I couldn't understand why everybody else wouldn't.

"Yes, Carter, your friend, who I speak with often, because we own a business together, knows I'm back in town." I twisted my mouth to the side, raising an eyebrow at him to highlight my annoyance.

In response, Carter laughed. "I know, I know, Nix *ain't your goddamned man*," he said, mimicking my voice.

"Carter..."

"*Okay*, I'll leave you alone. I'm sorry."

"Yeah, you oughta be," I said, rolling my eyes. "First full day back, and *already*, y'all are—"

"Ah, hush girl." Carter draped his free arm around my shoulder, pulling me with him as he headed outside. "I know you've got a sweet tooth, let me take you by the chocolate shop as a peace offering. My treat."

I lifted an eyebrow. "It doesn't count as "your treat" when you're getting booty from the owner of the shop."

"Of course it does," he chuckled as he led me across the street. "Nixon was right, you're kinda ungrateful."

I skidded on my heels, no longer moving willingly on the sidewalk as I shoved Carter's arm away from me. "He said I was *what*?"

Carter let out a shout of laughter as he shook his head. "I'm playing, Charlie, damn. You know Nix didn't say that shit."

"He better not have," I said, eyes narrowed. "Both of y'all play too much. Since you wanna be funny, I'm telling on you, how about *that*?"

The smile slid from Carter's face. "Wait a minute, what?"

"Mmhmm," I smirked. "You aren't the only one with a hookup at the candy shop, *remember*?"

I laughed as I pulled open the front door to Guilty Pleasures and headed straight for the back, bypassing the counters full of gourmet chocolate confections. The owner of the shop, Vivienne was at her desk, poring over something on the computer.

"Viv, your boyfriend is being mean to me," I said, turning to stick my tongue out at Carter as he walked up to stand beside me in the open door to the office. When she looked up, her pretty face spread into a smile, and she stood from her desk to walk over.

"Carter," she playfully scolded as she looped an arm around my waist. "You know that Charlie is family, and I expect her to be treated with the utmost kindness and respect, no?"

"Yes ma'am." He pulled her away from me to gather her in his arms, then dropped his head to give her the kind of kiss that would likely have turned into a *lot* more if I hadn't cleared my throat, reminding them that I was there. Carter was slow to release her from his grasp, and they both looked a little dazed as they stepped apart. They stared at each other for a few seconds, silently communicating before Viv bit her lip and looked away, shooting me a grin that was half embarrassed, half delight.

"I'll see you later tonight baby," Carter said, finally taking his eyes off of her. "Charlie, it was good to see you... I'll be sure to tell Nix—"

"Carter..." Viv and I warned at the same time.

"*Okay.*"

With a final wave and a chuckle, Carter exited the office, leaving Viv and I alone.

"Sorry about that," she said, running her thumb over her lip. "Got a little carried away. He just got back from dropping his little brother off at college. He was gone for a week, and then yesterday was Roman and Simone's wedding, so we are a little..."

"Horny?"

Viv blushed a little, then nodded. "Is it obvious?"

"Very," I said, laughing. "But hey, nothing wrong with that, especially when you're in love. You should have seen his ass light up like a Christmas tree when I mentioned you."

Shaking her head, Viv closed the door to the office, then sat down on the edge of her desk, motioning for me to take one of the chairs. "It certainly was not easy, but we made it, and I am... elated."

I grinned, reaching forward to grab her hand. "It shows. Love looks good on you. On *both* of you. I'm glad it all worked out," I said, thinking back to the heartbroken phone call with Viv a few months back. She and Carter had started as friends, then turned into friends with benefits. As usual, those benefits turned into feelings. *Unreciprocated* feelings. Or... so she thought.

Viv sighed. "So am I. But I must say, it would have been nice to have my cousin here with me at the time. But, you are now, so all is well."

I sucked my teeth. "Girl, I would have killed Carter. It was better that I stayed where the hell I was."

Brushing her mass of curls back from her face, Viv laughed. "You know... maybe you are right about that." Her smile lingered a few moments longer before her expression sobered. "So... how are *you*?"

I shook my head, pushing out a little breath as I leaned back in my chair. "I'm... surviving. Got a negative pregnancy test yesterday, so thank God for *that*. Still waiting to hear about when and if they'll release the hold on my personal money, so I can pay you back sooner."

"I am not concerned about that," Viv said, scowling. "You are *family*. When that mess happened with Thierry, you were the only person who did not treat me as if I was stupid. You have always treated me as a sister. Anything I can do for you, let me know."

Nodding, I swallowed past the lump in my throat in an effort to hold my tears at bay. "Thanks Viv, but you're already doing more than enough. Letting me crash at your place..."

"You are doing me a favor. Consider it *your* apartment. It is usually empty, since I am basically living with Carter."

A slow smile spread across my face, and I leaned forward to prod Viv's leg. "Mmhmm. Nasty asses think you're grown, huh? Maybe I should have given *you* those extra pregnancy tests instead of throwing them away."

I sat back in my chair again, waiting for Viv to laugh.

I waited.

And waited.

And waited.

"Viv! Are you..."

"*No*," she said, shaking her head. "But... I did think that I might be. You and I may have been taking pregnancy tests at the same time."

She dropped her gaze to her hands, and I sat up, trying to get a glimpse of her expression. "How would you have felt about it if you were? Have... have you guys discussed that?"

"We have." Viv looked up, wetting her lips with her tongue before she continued. "Carter would be thrilled. He has been campaigning since we made things official, but I prefer to wait. After... everything that has happened, I need to be sure that Carter can handle the commitment of *us* before working toward the even *bigger* commitment of a child, you know? I do not want to have a child if I cannot be absolutely sure he and I can surround it with love — not just for the baby, for *each other*."

Yeah.

I *did* know.

That declaration hit me right in the chest, dredging up a wave of guilt about my eagerness to have a baby with Adrian. No way would my home have been filled with the kind of love that *oozed* off of Viv and Carter. It was all over them, all in the way they looked at each other. The *child* would have been loved, without a doubt, and that was a large part of why I wanted one so bad. I needed *somebody* around that I could feel that variety of deep, tangible emotion for. I hadn't experienced love like that since...

Since Nixon.

And he screwed it up.

"Charlie? Are you okay?"

I gave a slight shake of my head. "What? Yeah...yeah, I'm good. Just thinking about everything I still have to do. I haven't even gone to see my mom yet, still trying to mentally prepare."

"Yes, I know the feeling," Viv laughed. "But... you know that your mother is in Paris with mine right now, no?"

My expression dropped into a scowl. "*No*. She didn't tell me that!"

"You did not receive the group text aunt Melissa sent last night?"

I lifted an eyebrow. "The picture of her and Aunt Morgan in their little 50+ club gear, captioned "Turn down for what?" yeah, I got that, but I didn't realize it was from freaking *France.*"

Viv's moms and mine — Morgan and Melissa — were not only sisters, but best friends. Twins in more than once sense of the word. M&M were beautiful, fun, nosy, and *loud*. Aunt Morgan moved to France, got married, and had Viv. My mom globetrotted, and had herself plenty of fun exploring cultures, food, fashions, and... men. As a result, my paternity was... ambiguous, at best.

Giggling, Viv climbed down from the desk and went around to the other side to collapse in her chair. "Yes, my mother talked her into it, and they left yesterday morning. I may have dropped it into my mother's ear that you would probably need some time to settle in before Aunt Melissa got ahold of you."

"Bless you," I said, giving her a playful salute. "How much time did you buy me?"

"However long it takes my father to shut off the credit card... so probably about two weeks."

I let out a relieved sigh. "So at least I'm not dealing with her *and* Nixon at the same time."

Viv shook her head, sympathy lacing the smile she gave me. "I did what I could."

"I definitely owe you one. *Another* one. Where are we now, like a hundred?"

"I have told you about that already."

"I know, I know, family, schmamily. *Still.* I *owe* you. And your man promised me chocolate for teasing me about Nixon."

Lifting an eyebrow, Viv crossed her arms over her chest. "Is *that* what you were tattling on him for when you two came to the door like children? I should have known. How *did* your meeting this morning go with Nixon?"

"So anyway, you said Roman got *married*? To *who*?"

"Ah, changing the subject now are we?"

"We are," I nodded eagerly, *not* wanting to get on the topic of Nixon. Viv wasn't living in the neighborhood back then, but she'd certainly heard every detail, good and bad, of the relationship. "Back to Rome. Tell me who locked down his sexy, dark roast ass. I was trying to come home and see what he was talking about. You didn't mention *nothing* about that."

Viv laughed. "Well, you were *married* when he and Simone started dating, and then you were a little busy with federal investigations and such. But you'll really like Simone. She owns the flower shop next door, and she's a sweetheart."

"If you say so."

"Oh, whatever. Besides... I am quite sure that Roman would not have crossed such a line with you, considering..."

I huffed. "Of course. Considering Nixon is his homeboy." I rolled my eyes. "Anyway, if you say Roman's new bride is a sweet girl, I believe you. I'm jealous, but I believe you."

"Mmhmm. Speaking of Nixon..."

"*Oh God.*"

"Stop it. I just want to know how things went, how he responded to your going back to the restaurant."

After a heavy sigh that earned me a glare, I gave Viv a rundown of the meeting with Nixon, leaving out that I'd been ready to leave my panties on his office floor.

"So do you think you will be able to work together?" she asked, propping her elbows on her desk.

I shrugged. "I don't know. But, I *think* so. We're both professionals, and we've worked together really well before. If we can put the personal stuff behind us..."

"*Can you* put the personal stuff behind you?" Viv raised an eyebrow, not looking all that certain.

Scratching my head, I let my fingers linger in my curls for a moment as I thought about it. After a long moment, I gave another non-committal shrug. "I mean... Nixon and I broke up *five* years ago. We should both be over it, right?"

"There's no certain time frame Charlie. You get over a breakup... when you're over it."

I sucked my teeth. "I'm not talking about *me*, I'm talking about *him*. He's the one with the flirting, and the touching, and the—"

"Touching?"

Crap.

"What?"

"You said Nixon... *touched* you."

"I said no such thing. Are you hungry?"

Viv rolled her eyes. "You are very good at changing the subject, cousin, but yes, I *am*." She paused for a moment, then gave me a wicked grin. "Do you want to go to Pot Liquor for lunch?"

***

Forty minutes later, Viv and I had patio seats at Honeybee, one of the few restaurants I would sit down in within a fifty-mile radius of Pot Liquor. It was a larger restaurant, much further into the hustle and bustle of the big city than my place, but the food was always impeccable.

I'd seriously considered cursing Viv out when she suggested that we eat outside, but the patio was shaded, and cooled with large, gentle-breeze producing fans, so it was actually nice. The warm weather, good food, and the sounds of the city were relaxing to me, unlike the stuffy suburban life I'd fallen into with Adrian.

Despite my trepidation, it *did* feel good to be home, to a place that I knew well. It didn't hurt to surround myself with familiar faces — even Nixon's. Being around the people I still considered family took the edge off the pain and loneliness of a failed marriage, even if it *was* something I'd done out of desperation to get over the botched relationship with Nixon. Funny thing was... I wasn't even sure it worked.

"Excuse me."

My breath caught in my throat as I looked up, into a pair of brown eyes warm enough to melt butter. A quick perusal of the rest of the face gave me deep chestnut skin, a straight nose, full lips, and a clean-shaven jawline.

"Yes?" I said, almost choking on a too-quickly-swallowed mouthful of lemonade once I pulled my lips from my straw. "Can I help you?"

His mouth tipped up into a charmingly crooked smile. "You can, actually. I think I know you from somewhere, but... I can't quite place it."

Shaking my head, I smiled back. "Look," I said, taking advantage of the opportunity to scan the rest of his body as he stood over our table. He was dressed in a button up and nice slacks, with a tie loose around his neck. *Corporate brother.* "You're a really nice looking guy. You don't have to use a line to approach me."

"It's not a line," he laughed. "I swear. What's your name?"

"Charlie. Charlie Bennet."

He propped his elbow in his hand as he stroked his chin. "Charlie Bennet... Charlie Bennet... as in, *Charlene* Bennet?"

I lifted an eyebrow. "Yes..."

"I *do* know you, we went to high school together. *Trent Ellis.*"

Is there something in the damn water?!

My mouth slacked a little, eyes wide as I finally recognized him. He'd changed, but I still recognized a little of the boy who used to wait for me outside of Biology to walk me to my next class — until Nixon found out, and threatened to kick his ass. (Sidenote, Nixon and I were *not* dating at the time.)

I stood up with a smile, wrapping my arms around his neck as he pulled me into a hug. He held me a little longer than necessary, squeezed a little tighter than required, but he was fine, and he smelled good, so I gave him a pass.

When he stepped back, he looked me over with obvious admiration in his eyes. "*Damn*, those fifteen years since we graduated have been *mighty* good to you."

I blushed, biting my lip as I shot a glance at Viv, who was pretending to be *very* interested in the shrimp and pasta on her plate. "Thank you. You don't look so bad yourself. I see those braces were well worth it."

"Yeah, you know. I got teased for it, but..." he smiled, showcasing a mouthful of beautiful white teeth as he shrugged.

"Look at you now, right?"

He nodded. "Right. So... what, are you just back for a visit? I heard you got married, moved to Cali, all of that..."

"Um... I'm back permanently, I think. For now," I said, returning his smile.

"With your husband?"

I dropped my gaze to my hands, then returned it to him. "No, actually. I'm... divorced."

Or... *would be,* soon, but he didn't need to know all that.

"Wow... I'm sorry to hear that."

Of course you are.

He *said* he was sorry to hear it, but his eyebrows shot up, and I could practically see the mental high-five happening in his head.

I shrugged. "Hey... stuff happens, usually for a reason."

"Yes, it does. Including us running into each other like this. I... I hope I'm not being too forward, but maybe we can have dinner or something, since you're back in town. I'd love to catch up."

Butterflies erupted in my belly. My cheeks grew hot, and again I glanced at Viv for a little hint on what I should do, but she was still acting as if those shrimp were spelling out the cure for cancer.

"Uh... sure. I'd love to."

Trent smiled big as he pulled his cell from his pocket. "Cool. What about this Friday, if you're available?"

"Let me check," I said, knowing *damned* well I didn't have anything better to do on a Friday night as I reached for my purse and pulled out my phone. For a few seconds, I pretended to check my calendar, then nodded. "Friday works for me."

My heart raced as we exchanged numbers and agreed on a time, then with a final parting embrace, Trent walked away, leaving me to swoon into my chair across from Viv.

She glanced over her shoulder to make sure he was gone, then leaned over the table and whispered, "Details. Give me every single one."

chapter
four

Nixon

Thicker than a goddamned snicker.

My mouth went dry when I walked in my office to see Charlie standing by my desk, in slim black pants and a rich blue sports bra, looking like hot sex, first thing in the morning. Bountiful breasts, curvy hips, thick, supple thighs... blood rushed straight to my groin. When she and I were together, her body was easily top five in my favorite things on the planet, and right now, those lush curves were calling my name.

"Good morning," I said, closing the door behind me and dropping my things into the chair in front of the desk. Charlie's head popped up, and I noticed then that she had earbuds in, with the cord draped behind her. Her eyes went wide, and she turned her back to me, snatching what appeared to be a tank top from the desk.

"Good morning. I wasn't expecting you to be here so early," she said, with a hint of strain in her voice. She glanced at me over her shoulder, then pulled the shirt over her head. When she turned back, I saw that there was a large coffee stain on the front, and a soiled towel on the desk where she'd obviously been trying to clean it.

"I always get here early. If the schedule says nine, I'm down here by eight."

She picked her chef's coat up from the desk. "You didn't used to. You avoided me, for a while."

"I do a lot of things now that I didn't used to do."

Charlie's fingers paused over the buttons to her coat, and her eyes flickered up to meet mine. "Yeah. I see." She gave a slight shake of her head, then continued the task of donning her coat as I stepped forward.

"You have a little accident?" I asked, pointing at the stain on her shirt.

She let out a huff of air, rolling her eyes. "Yes, because I had a full cup of coffee in my hands, and ran into a table on my way in. Luckily I hadn't buttoned up yet, so it just got on my shirt. You didn't say anything to me about changing the table layout," she snapped as she finished closing her coat.

The hell...

"I didn't realize I needed to run every little decision by you first. I've been running this place basically by myself for the last four years, and it *has* survived... you *do* realize that, right?"

Charlie took a deep breath, then bit down on her lip as she gave me a little nod. "Yeah... sorry. I don't mean to snap at you, I'm just feeling a little... stressed."

"I can tell," I said, approaching the desk. "What's up... you not happy to be back home? Do I need to do something to make you feel a little more welcome? I know what *always* used to make you feel better..."

She rolled her eyes, but a little smile danced at the corners of her mouth. "No thank you, Nix. I *am* happy to be back, it's just..." she stopped to sigh, then shook her head. "It's... other stuff. Stuff from back in Cali."

"Stuff meaning... your husband?"

Bingo.

From the way her shoulders tensed, and the tightness in her jaw, I knew I was on to something.

"Yeah," she mumbled, avoiding my eyes. "He called yesterday, wanting to talk about the divorce."

"Wanting to *change your mind* about the divorce."

She scoffed, then nodded. "Yeah."

"But... you don't seem open to that."

"I'm not."

"Why?"

Raising a neatly shaped eyebrow, Charlie eyed me for a second before she licked her lips and looked away. "Personal reasons."

I kept my eyes on her, wanting her to look my way again so I could see her face. Those pretty brown eyes of hers never could hide how she was feeling. She kept her gaze averted, so instead of pressing the issue, I sidled past her, taking care *not* to touch her. She wasn't in the right mood to let it slide this time.

"So, is that all? That's what has you on edge this morning, your ex getting on your nerves?" I asked, reaching into the closet behind the desk for my own chef's coat.

"More than one ex getting on my nerves, actually." She shot me a sweet smile, and I chuckled, shaking my head as I shrugged the coat on. "But, no, that's not all. My boxes, with all of my stuff were supposed to get here yesterday, and I find out this morning that they won't be here until Friday."

"That's just tomorrow."

"Right... but they were supposed to be here *yesterday*. I had to borrow a coat to cook in from Viv and it's not exactly the best fit. I've got a couple of pounds on her."

I cocked my head to the side. "A couple?"

Bad time for a joke, dude.

Charlie's face immediately dropped into a scowl, and her hand went up to rest on her hip. Even with that mean expression, the only thing ran through my mind was how damned *gorgeous* she was. Golden-bronze skin, cute little nose, and those juicy, perfect lips. She'd cut her hair off, into a short, curly, tapered cut that gave her a little edge to what would have otherwise been just a whole lot of "pretty". *So damned pretty.*

"You *know* I'm playing with you, come on. You're banging, baby."

"*Baby*?"

I grinned, reaching forward to grab her hand. "What, I can't call you that?"

"Uhh... no..."

"You didn't *used* to mind when I called you that."

She gave me that syrupy-sweet smile again as she pulled away. "I mind a lot of things I didn't *used* to mind."

"Oh, so you're a changed woman, huh?"

I took a step toward her, and she took one away, backing herself against the desk. She met my gaze with a mischievous twinkle in her eye as she countered. "Actually... yes. I am. We broke up five years ago, Nix, and haven't been around each other in four... I hope you've changed too."

There.

Just like that, the dynamic of our teasing conversation changed... or did it? I didn't know exactly what she was getting at, but if she wanted to be cryptic... I could do that.

"I have. Changed, grown up, evolved... all of that. Spent some time figuring out what and who was—no, *is* important to me."

By the time I finished my sentence, Charlie and I were almost touching, and I had her *full* attention. From the expression on her face — eyes wide, lips parted — she'd caught *exactly* what I was saying. Not that it was supposed to be a secret. If Charlie was: 1. Back in town permanently, and 2. Single, I had no problem letting it be known that I still wanted her, past bullshit aside.

She cleared her throat, then finally tore her gaze from mine as she edged between me and the desk to get away. "Good to know," she said, tugging at the hem of her coat to straighten it. "Now, I believe we have some prep to do for brunch service... we should probably get on it."

Chuckling, I ran a hand over my chin. "Whatever you say, Charlene. Lead the way."

Charlie rolled her eyes — at what I called her, or my instructions, or maybe both— and turned to head into the kitchen.

Damn.

Her chef's coat was too long to see her ass as she walked away.

***

"Y'ALL HAVE A GOOD AFTERNOON NOW, ALRIGHT?"

I held the door open for two pretty women as they left Pot Liquor with smiles on their faces after their meals. One of them turned to give me a last smile, along with a look that let me know if I was *trying* to get it... I could've had it.

I made it a habit that at the end of each service, once the rush died down, I would go out and shake hands, talk to the customers, kiss babies, so on. I did it because I enjoyed it, but stuff like that was also good for business, and there wasn't much that was more important to me. Pot Liquor was *right* behind Charlie's thighs in the rankings of my affection.

Anyway, because I was out in the crowd, and highly visible, it was only natural that a little bit of flirtation would happen when a beautiful woman crossed my path. Okay, maybe a lot of flirtation, but never anything too serious. Except that one time.

I fucked that *all* the way up.

But I was a single man now, and that had pretty much been the case since Charlie. Yeah, I dated, and had even gotten close enough to call a few people my girlfriend, but... it never *quite* worked out. I don't exactly wanna say that nobody since Charlie really measured up, but.... yeah.

And *topping* her?

Forget about it.

No chance.

Not that I wasn't looking. I mean... the girl went off and got married to some dude she'd only known a year, *if* that long. But... he offered her what she was longing for, so... what the hell was I supposed to do about that? She moved on, I moved on, everybody moved on... but why did I still feel a twinge of guilt, knowing that she could see and hear me flirting with a customer?

When I turned back to the dining room, there Charlie was, her pretty face set into what, at first glance, seemed to be a nonchalant expression, but I knew her too well to for that. The slightly lifted chin, eyebrow damn near about to pop off her face because she was trying *so* hard not to raise it.... She was.... Was she *jealous*?

Grinning, I sauntered over to where she stood observing the dining room. "Hey."

Her gaze flicked around in confusion. "... Hey."

"So... what's up? You getting in some good analysis? See anything interesting?"

"Oh I saw something *interesting* alright," she chuckled, shaking her head.

I leaned against the wall beside her perch at the kitchen door. "What's wrong, Charlie? You're not salty about me doing a little harmless flirting, right?"

"*What*?" Charlie broke into a laugh. "Why would I feel any kind of way about that, Nix? I mean... other than it being a little unprofessional, I really don't care. I hope you don't think I'm jealous, Nix. I have a date tomorrow night."

Ouch.

She looked *so* smug about telling me that, and I had to admit— hearing it set off a dull, irrational little anger headache at my temples. "A date?"

"Yeah, a date," she nodded, looking me right in the eyes as she smirked.

"With *who*? You've been here two damned days, and you're already going out with some stranger?"

Charlie's eyes went wide, then her smirk spread into a full-on smile. "Whoa... *some stranger*? You're not... *salty*, are you Nix?"

"*Hell no*. I'm just saying... you don't think it's a little fast?"

"Not at all... he's not a stranger. You remember Trent Ellis, don't you?"

That dull, irrational headache? Sharp and rational now.

My my face screwed up into a scowl. "With the pimples and shit? And the thick glasses?"

Charlie waved a hand. "*Oh ho ho*, the power of contacts lenses and a good dermatologist. Trent is *fine* now. Not just regular *fine* either. Capital F-A-H-N type fine. Ugly duckling to a swan type fine. Might give up the panties on the first night type fine. I may need to go stand in the cooler cause I'm getting *so hot* thinking about him type fine," she said, with a big grin on her face.

"Whatever Charlene, you're selling this dude *way* too hard. Must be another one of those boring pretty boys you used to like."

"Are you including yourself in that crowd?" she asked, poking a finger into my chest.

Grabbing the hand she'd used to poke me, I scoffed. "Come on, now. I'm not pretty *or* boring."

She opened her mouth to deliver a comeback, but I eased her toward the wall, then stood in front of her not saying anything — just looking, until she began to squirm under my gaze.

Mission accomplished.

"Nix, *what*?"

"Nothing. I'm just looking at you."

"For what?"

Her breath hitched as I lifted a hand to her face, grazing her cheek. "No reason, really. I just... missed you. You're so damned *beautiful*." I cupped her chin, tipping her head back as I closed the space between us, to the point that her chest pressed against mine. "And... I still remember," I murmured, lowering my mouth until my lips were nearly brushing hers, "that you taste *so* good."

"Nix," she whispered, biting her lip as she met my eyes. "You *do* realize we're in full view of the customers, right?"

I chuckled. "I've never been shy about public displays of affection, you know that."

"Is that what this is?"

Her expression was calm, tone measured, but the way her heart was racing — *that* was something she couldn't hide.

"What... you think I've lost my fondness for you, Charlie?"

She shrugged, then averted her eyes. "How should I know?"

"You never should've doubted."

That got her attention back. Her gaze shot back to mine for a fleeting moment, then she pushed me back, so she could walk away.

Shit.

I caught up to her just on the other side of the kitchen doors. Gently grabbing her arm, I tried to get her to look at me, but she aimed her sight anywhere except on me.

"*Charlie*... baby, I—"

"*Don't* call me that."

"It's a habit, I'm sorry."

"I haven't been your *baby* in five years, Nix. You're not sorry."

Releasing my grip on her, I ran a hand over my head, then scrubbed my face. "You know what... nope. I'm not. We were together for *six* years, Charlie. It's gonna take at least that long to not still think of you like that, especially when I didn't even want—"

"Save it, okay?" She held up a hand, self-consciously glancing around the kitchen for listening ears. "I don't need a history lesson. Let's just... can we be professional? Just coworkers, business partners... nothing more?"

Wow... it's like that?

*Nothing more...*like a double shot to the gut.

Wow.

I ran my tongue over my teeth as I inclined my head, processing her words. "Uh... I guess I just didn't realize our relationship had devolved *that* much. But, yeah. If that's what you wanna do... yeah." I paused, to wait for her response, but she had this wide-eyed look, as if she was shocked I wasn't giving her any push back. Hell, *I* was shocked I wasn't forcing the issue, but... what was I supposed to do about it if my chances with her were looking as likely as snow in the summer?

When she was still wearing that same deer-in-headlights expression a few beats later, I continued, "So... with that said, we should probably get started on the prep for dinner service. It should go faster since we've got you back now, but I like to make sure it's done in plenty of time in case anything goes wrong."

Without waiting for a reply this time, I turned and headed for the walk-in fridge to start pulling the vegetable and herbs for our *mise en place*. Charlie was close behind me to help, and soon, between the two of us plus Jordan and Amina, we had everything for the dinner plate options cut, prepared, and ready to cook.

When the kitchen was clean and restored to order, I sent everybody home. There was a three hour window between lunch and dinner service, so I liked to give our small staff that time to be off of their feet, take a nap, whatever, so they could be fresh for the chaos of the dinner rush.

I rarely left. Instead, I used the time for the other side of the business. Accounting, inventory, maintaining the website, marketing, — all of it needed to get done, and whenever I could, I avoided staying up late at night to do it.

Charlie disappeared with the rest of the staff, so I was surprised when she approached me in the large walk-in pantry, an hour after I'd sent everyone home. I felt her presence before I saw her, but I didn't turn around until she reached for me, placing a hand against my arm.

The first thing I noticed was that her nose and eyes were slightly red, as if she'd been crying. Immediately, any little animosity I felt melted away.

"*Not* nothing more," she said, meeting my gaze.

I lifted an eyebrow. "What?"

"Sorry." She shook her head. "I... I'm all mixed up, but... what you said earlier, about not realizing that our relationship had devolved to a place where we couldn't even be friends... you're right. It hasn't. We've known each other for what... more than twenty years? And we were intimate for six of those. I mean, yeah, that part didn't work out, but the other times, we were the best of friends, and... I'm at a place right now where I can use every friend I have. I mean... we've been apart long enough that we should be able to go back to that... right? Back to being friends?"

"Ah..." I scratched my eyebrow. "Um... yeah. Yeah. I'm cool with that, Charlie... I thought we had been getting along pretty well the last few years."

She tipped her head to the side. "You... *did*?"

"Yeah," I chuckled. "I'm guessing your perception has been different?"

Charlie laughed, sending a wash of warmth through me. "Uh, yeah. Nixon, we're *constantly* going back and forth, always trading jabs... the first thing you did yesterday was tease me about my locked up husband. You thought that was friendly banter?"

Shrugging, I leaned into the pantry table. "Yeah, I did. I don't know.... Maybe I've just gotten so used to it that it felt natural to mess with you. And it's a *definite* improvement over..."

"When we *first* broke up." She dropped her gaze for a moment before she nodded, then looked at me again. "Yes, it's better than that, for sure."

"Right. So... what's up? We're homies, or nah?"

Charlie let out a big puff of air, then propped a finger against her chin. She looked up at the ceiling with her lips pursed. "Well... let me think... um..." She gave a shriek of laughter when I wrapped her in my arms, lifting her off the floor as I pulled her into a hug. She giggled until I put her down, then draped her arms around my waist to return the embrace.

If we were gonna talk about what felt natural... *this* felt natural. So I squeezed her a little tighter. Having Charlie in my arms was like... the default setting. *Everything else* was a subpar modification that I'd just been living with for the last few years.

Several seconds past "friendly", I dropped a kiss on her forehead that was quick enough to pass off as innocent, then loosened my hold on her. A moment later, she released me as well, stepping back with a little smile and some unspoken, unintelligible emotion in her eyes.

Neither of us said anything.

We ended our communication with nods as she left, and I tried to focus again on the task of the weekly inventory, to no avail. The only thing my brain seemed to want to process was the fact that when it was time to end that hug... Charlie wasn't the one who let go first.

chapter
five

Charlie

TRENT WAS GENEROUS WITH THAT SEXY CROOKED smile.

He smelled good enough to lick, and he was dressed as if he'd just stepped out of a magazine shoot. He was funny, and smart, and easy to talk to, and flirted just hard enough to make me blush, without crossing the line of impropriety. He was a *perfect* date.

I, on the other hand, was not.

I was uncomfortable in my borrowed dress, self-conscious of the fact that it hugged a little too tight in certain places. Viv insisted that I looked good in it, and she wasn't one to tell me that kind of lie, so I went with it, but still... I spent the night feeling as if I might pop like a can of biscuits at any second.

If my friggin' boxes had come that Wednesday morning, like they were supposed to, this wouldn't be a problem. It was Friday *night*, and I was still without my personal things. That only added to the stress keeping me from enjoying Trent's company. And that wasn't even including the fact that Adrian had called, *again*.

Stupidly, perhaps, the thought of ignoring him made me feel guilty, so I subjected myself to ten long minutes of him promising his innocence, swearing that he would make it up to me when he was released, and... refusing to sign the divorce papers. Who knew he could do that from prison? *Not* me.

By the time we made it to my front door, I was beyond ready

for the date to be over. It had *nothing* to do with Trent's company, everything to do with my own bullshit. Trent's hand enveloped mine, and he gave it a little squeeze.

"Hey... did you have a good time?" he asked. "You seem a little... quieter than I expected."

I appreciated that there was no whine in his voice. It was just a question, and one he was completely justified in asking. He'd taken me to Ivory, a nice little upscale piano bar downtown, a few doors down from Honeybee. It was a beautiful place, decorated in black and white, with just enough romance to make it perfect for a first date... and I was zoned out for most of it.

I gave him what I hoped was a reassuring smile, then nodded. "Yes, I had a great time. I'm just..." I took a deep breath. "The circumstances that brought me back here weren't exactly ideal. I'm honestly still processing everything, because it's so fresh, and it's like the most random things just kind of... take me off into la-la-land. I am *so* sorry... it's really not fair to you, at all."

Trent shrugged, then brought my hand up to his mouth to kiss my fingers. "No worries, Beautiful. I completely understand... I'm actually divorced as well, so I know what it's like when it first happens. You're just... kind of in a daze, wondering how the hell your life changed *so* much with the signing of a document. Wondering if you're making a mistake... if it's really over. I get it."

"Thank you," I nodded, then shifted in my heels as Trent took a step closer.

"So... how about in about a week, we try this again? Grab some pizza or something... maybe something casual will be more comfortable for you."

I smiled. "Yeah... I would like that a lot."

"Good."

Gently, Trent grabbed me at the elbow, then leaned forward. My breath hitched in my chest as he pressed his lips to mine, grazing the corner of my mouth. An *almost* full-on kiss, which left behind a tiny little buzz of warmth where his lips touched. He drew me into a hug, giving me a last opportunity to breathe in his delicious-smelling cologne before he pulled away.

"Well... goodnight Charlie," he said, straightening his jacket. "We'll talk about our date for next week later."

"Sure, just... text me, or call me, and we'll set it up."

"Will do."

I pushed my key into the door, then turned to give him a little wave. "Goodnight." With a returned wave, and a parting smile, Trent headed down the stairs as I went into Viv's — *my*— apartment, kicking off my heels before I was even through the door.

The news about Trent being divorced as well was... interesting. Maybe that explained why every time I *had* paid him any attention on our date, he was rubbing at his bare left ring finger. Mental note: make sure his ass is *really* divorced.

"Daaamn!"

My head shot up, and I immediately went for the mace on my keys in response to... *Nixon.*

I blew out a heavy sigh, and propped a hand on my hip as he approached me, lip pulled between his teeth as he surveyed my body in the fitted black dress. The way he was looking at me... *have mercy.* I probably should have felt a twinge of guilt or something about the way my nipples sprang to attention under his heated gaze, considering that not even a full minute ago, *Trent* had been kissing me goodnight.

"What are you doing in here?"

I crossed my arms, more to hide my arousal than to show annoyance, even though I *was* irritated about Nixon's presence. I hadn't even had time for a glass of wine and over-analysis of my date. Yet, here *he* was.

He took a moment before he answered to circle me, getting a full view before he stopped in front of me. "You went on a date looking like *that*, and Trent got you back home this early? I'm... not shocked. Knew he wasn't about shit."

Nixon chuckled, shaking his head as his eyes swept my body with another sweat-inducing gaze.

"Well, when you're a gentleman, you get a girl home from a *first date* at a respectable time of night."

Nixon tilted his head back and laughed. "Right, right... but just yesterday, you were talking about how you might give him, uh... *a little taste* on the first date. I'm guessing that didn't happen, did it?"

Running my tongue over my teeth, I searched my mind for a response, but only came up with, "And how would *you* know?"

"Because you're back at goddamned ten o'clock." Shaking his head, Nixon moved closer. "If he'd gotten anywhere *near* that pretty little pussy of yours, he'd still be lost in it right now." He reached out to cup my chin, meeting my eyes with his sultry browns. "*I* would."

Holy shit.

Nixon was the only man I knew who could make a crude state-ment sound so... appealing. Logically, the last thing I wanted was to get myself enmeshed with him again, but... goodness, the *thought* of him wrapping me in those powerful arms, and getting — as he referred to it — *lost* inside me....

Charlie, close your damned mouth girl.

Rolling my eyes, I pressed my lips together, and squeezed my arms tighter over my chest in an effort to calm my steady-building arousal. "You're disgusting, Nix. And you *still* haven't told me why you're in— or for that matter, *how* you got in — my apartment."

"Well," Nixon said, punctuating with a chuckle before he continued, "I came to the building to holla' at Carter about some-thing. I mean... he and Viv are right next door to you, so when I was heading out, we saw that your boxes had been delivered, so he used his key for us to bring them in."

I lifted a hand. "Hold up, you expect me to believe my stuff got delivered *this* time of night?"

"You see the boxes don't you?" He gestured behind him into the kitchen, and then towards the living room, and sure enough, the boxes that were supposed to be here two days ago were waiting to be unpacked. "You'll have to take the delivery time up with the shipping company, but we were just trying to help out. I didn't even know you were gonna be back so early... I planned to get Viv's cookware and stuff put away, and have your stuff unpacked and ready for you by the time you got home. Didn't even plan to see you."

Pressing a hand to my cheek, I looked past him to see Viv's

things lined up neatly on the counter, while my open boxes peppered the floor. Now that I *really* looked at him, Nixon was actually holding my stainless steel measuring cups while we talked.

"*Oh.*"

Nixon grinned, then shook his head as he turned back to the kitchen. "Yeah, *oh*. And you're welcome," he tossed over his shoulder as he knelt to pull a set of mixing bowls from the box. "I'm gonna finish this for you, then head out... let you have your space to yourself."

"Thank you, Nix." I laid a hand on his back as I stepped over the open boxes to get into the kitchen. "Not for the leaving, for helping me with this. I appreciate it. You know you're the *only* person I would let do this for me, right?"

He chuckled. "Yeah, I do. I figured you didn't want me putting up your panties and stuff for you, so..."

"You figured correctly."

Leaning against the counter, I watched as Nix delicately handled my things, taking care not to chip my bowls, or dent my pots, or blemish my knives as he unpacked and put them away. He didn't have to look to me for guidance on where to put anything, he just... *knew*. Five years apart and ... he still knew.

I pressed my fingers to my lips, trying to keep them from spreading into a smile. When he and I first moved in together, when I joined him in the apartment over the restaurant, he rearranged the entire kitchen, for *me*. For a lot of men, that was no big sacrifice, but the kitchen was Nixon's sanctuary. *His* man cave.

That memory, of the moment I knew that Nixon really, *really* loved me — like, *real ass love*— made my eyes prick with tears.

"Um, I'm gonna go change." I cleared my throat, averting my eyes as he glanced back, in hopes that my little emotional episode would go unnoticed.

"Change for what? You look good in what you have on."

"Thank you," I said, as I carefully backed out of the kitchen. "But, this really isn't the most comfortable thing to unpack in."

"*Damn shame.*"

I shook my head, laughing at Nixon's parting complaint about my lack of desire to empty boxes in my little black dress. I stopped to pour myself enough wine for two glasses, then headed for the back of the apartment. In the bedroom, I discovered that the aptly marked containers were already there, so I opened one and pulled out a set of more work-appropriate clothes.

Tossing my change of clothes on the bed, I reached behind me to grab my zipper. *That* part wasn't a problem, but getting it down — I let out a heavy sigh — it wouldn't budge.

Probably because you have your size twelve ass squeezed into a size ten dress.

I downed my big-ass glass of wine, then sighed again as I picked up my phone to call Viv, who *of course* didn't answer. I tried everything I could think of to get out of that dress before I flopped back on the bed, out of breath from the effort.

And then I remembered — Nixon.

Sitting up, I ran a hand through my hair, not caring about the destruction of my carefully defined curls. Just the *thought* of asking him to "unzip my dress for me" felt like the beginning of a bad movie on Cinemax. Who the hell gets themselves in that kind of situation in real life?

Uh... you do.

Yeah. Apparently so.

"*Friend*," I called out, keeping my tone light. It didn't *have* to turn into something inappropriate if we didn't want it to. But... what if we wanted it to?

What if *he* wanted it to?

"What's up?"

My hand flew to my chest, clutching the front of my dress as Nixon appeared at the door.

"*Jesus*, Nixon. You scared me!"

He lifted an eyebrow. "You... *called* me... right?" He stepped into the room, bringing his mouth-watering male energy with him and my heart started to gallop.

"Oh. Um... yeah. I did."

"So... did you need something?" He cocked his head to the side, a look of confusion on his face as he took another step closer to where I was perched at the end of the bed.

Swallowing hard, I nodded. "Yeah... I... um... I need you to help me get out of this dress." I let those words spill out in a blur, in an effort to get it over. The shameless smile that spread across his mouth told me he'd understood my jumbled words, and was happy — eager, even — to help.

"Stand up."

My body reacted before my mind even processed the words. I turned around, and Nixon's hands were already at my zipper before the wave of arousal set off by the authority in his command to "stand up" settled as a throb between my legs.

Nixon took his time undoing me. He pulled the zipper down excruciatingly slow, and then instead of stepping back, he slipped a hand inside my dress. My lips parted in a gasp as his warm, strong hand glided over the soft skin of my waist until he reached my belly button, then slipped out again. His breath was warm and sweet against my neck as he pushed the dress away from my arms, down my body, and let it hit the floor.

My eyelids fluttered closed as Nixon circled me with his arms, pulling me tight against him. His thumbs skimmed the underside of my breasts making my already hard nipples ache to be touched.

Hell, *all of me* was aching to be touched.

I don't know what kind of jedi mind trick he was pulling on me, but I turned to face him, and parted my lips willingly as his mouth crashed down to mine. He brought his hands back to their previous position of *almost* touching my breasts as our tongues danced, slow and sweet. Way too soon, he pulled back, resting his forehead against mine.

"Honeybun..."

I whimpered, biting my lip at Nixon's use of a private nick-name only *he* called me. He was hard against my stomach, and even though his voice was thick with restraint, it was still edged with need.

"Yeah?" I managed to choke out, covering his hands with mine and giving them a gentle tug. I needed him to move those thumbs just a little bit further—

"We can't do this."

His reluctance was palpable as he stepped back, putting a good amount of distance between us. He turned his back to me, facing out of the bedroom door as he spoke.

"You just got home from a *date*."

I did?

Oh, crap. I *did*.

Guilt hit me like a bucket full of cold water. Here I was, naked from the waist up, in damp panties, and Trent probably hadn't even made it home yet.

"I mean... as flattered as I am that you *obviously* weren't even thinking about old boy..." — I rolled my eyes — "It would be kinda fucked up for me to... take it further than I already have."

"So... you're concerned about respecting ... *Trent*?"

"*What*?" Nixon sucked his teeth, his expression twisting into a scowl as he turned to face me again. "*Hell* no. Fuck him. I'm worried about respecting *you*. I want you, *bad*. But, I don't want something to happen between us just because you're confused, and overwhelmed with everything. I'm trying to do the right thing and give you some room to breathe."

He took a deep breath, groaning as his gaze swept over me again. "I'm gonna step out and let you get dressed."

"Get... *dressed*?" Moving on pure impulse, I closed the distance between us. "I... I'm pretty comfortable like this." Biting my lip, I grabbed the waistband of his sweats. "I think I'll skip the clothes."

Nostrils flared, Nixon inhaled another deep breath. I moved closer, his erection pressing against my stomach again, my breasts pushed against his chest as I stared up to meet his eyes. Lifting a hand, I cupped his chin.

"Nix," I whispered, sticking out my tongue to wet my lips before I continued, "It's not nice to get someone hot and bothered and then change your mind."

"Is this payback?"

Grinning, I nodded. "Yep."

Nixon chuckled, then leaned forward to speak into my ear. "Charlie... baby, stop playing. I want you bad enough right now to rip those pretty little lace panties off you and bend you over right here in this door."

Those two glasses of wine wanted me to yell *do it, do it please,* and my kitty was wet and ready for the same, but my brain and heart reeled me in. I took a step back, crossing my arms to cover my breasts.

"Is this the kinda thing you do with all of your *friends*?" Nixon teased, as I grabbed my shirt and pulled it over my head.

Giggling, I sat down on the bed to pull on my shorts. "I could ask you the same thing."

And just like that, we were back to being... whatever we were being. Long after we spent hours talking, laughing, and reminiscing as we put the kitchen in order, I lay back in my bed, freshly showered and thinking over my day. Everything up to the point of asking Nix for help with my dress made sense. The moment he showed up in the bedroom door was where things went left.

Would I have slept with him, if he hadn't had the sense to pump his brakes? Nixon was obvious about his desire to reclaim a place in my life, but in what capacity? His former role — *fiancé*— certainly wasn't available, not to him. Not *ever* again to him. But, if I slept with him... where would that lead? To *more* confusing feelings that I didn't need.

Then there was Trent. I touched the corner of my mouth, where he'd kissed me at the end of our date. That place tingled on contact, and I smiled. Now Trent... *that* was a man that I could have a future with — assuming forthcoming dates went well. He was intelligent, kind, successful, *sexy*... I just hoped the next time he kissed me would leave behind more than a tingle. Something like the hum of awakening I felt when I imagined Nixon's hands on me, skirting over my skin. Gripping and kneading my breasts. Inside of me.

Holy shit.

I shook my head.

Don't think of Nixon... or Adrian.

Shit.

Adrian.

I wished that I could just take a towel and wipe away the men of my past, to keep them from dominating my thoughts as I tried to move forward. I searched my mind, trying to imagine what that future looked like. A loving marriage, beautiful kids, and a happy home. I could *see* it, right in front of me, clear and vivid.

The only problem was... when I turned to my husband... it wasn't Trent.

Or Adrian.

You've gotta be kidding me.

chapter
six

Nixon

"YOU'RE LEAVING ME HANGING?"

It was mid-day break time at Pot Liquor, and as usual, Charlie and I were the only two people still there. We were done with the prep work, and she'd escaped to the office, which is where I found her after a quick run up to my apartment. At the sound of my voice, Charlie looked up from her task of strapping her feet into her sandals and smiled.

"Leaving you hanging, *no*. Using my free time before dinner service to go and get my haircut cleaned up, *yes*."

Shaking her head, she stood, brushing the front of her pants as she approached me at the door. She'd already taken off her chef's coat, revealing a figure-hugging tee shirt underneath.

"Damn, you're going to Fresh Cuts in *that*?"

She lifted an eyebrow, then glanced down at her V-neck top. "Is there something wrong with me wearing a tee shirt and pants, Nix?"

"I mean... I guess not." I shrugged. "You just look quite... edible."

"*Oh God*," she said, slapping me on the arm as she slipped past me in the door. "If I didn't know any better... I'd think you just don't like the idea of other men looking at me."

Damn right.

I watched her for a moment as she headed through the kitchen, my eyes magnetized to the swell of her ass and sway of her hips. Not even two weeks ago, she'd refreshed my memory of that glorious body *without* clothes, and that picture had been implanted in my mind since then.

I shrugged out of my own coat, tossing it across the desk before I jogged out of the kitchen to catch up to her at the front of the restaurant. She'd stopped to look at her phone, and the grin on her face made me wonder if she was exchanging messages with Trent. A little flash of anger rushed over me at the thought of *that* lame-ass dude.

He'd come in the restaurant the other day looking for Charlie, obviously not knowing that when she got in her zone in the kitchen, she was *in there*, and didn't respond well to interruptions. As far as *I* was concerned, his entire existence was an interruption.

He had the nerve to walk into the kitchen like he *belonged* there, and it took more restraint than I knew I had not to address him myself. But... Charlie handled him in a way that satisfied me *way* more than kicking him out would have.

Trent approached her while she was at the stove, carefully preparing the béchamel for her macaroni and cheese. He put his hand at her waist, moving to kiss her, but she leaned away, hitting him with a "who are you and what the hell do you want?" face.

I really thought he might melt right through the floor, and it was.... *damn*, it was beautiful, seeing that smug expression wiped off his face, without her even saying anything. She went right back to stirring her sauce, mumbling under her breath that she was putting somebody's face through the grill if it didn't turn out right, and he slinked back through the kitchen doors.

About an hour later, things were calmer, and I spotted the two of them in a quiet corner of the restaurant. She looked apologetic, he looked... like his little feelings were hurt and he needed a hug from mommy.

Damn.

She hugged him. Not one of those "church hugs" either, it was a *hug*. Like, a *real ass hug*, and he got a little more grabby than *I* thought was acceptable for two weeks of dating. He glanced up and caught me looking, and had the nerve to shoot me a smug grin. As if I hadn't been a panty-tug away from making Charlie forget he even existed.

But, back to today.

Charlie looked up from her phone, giving me a curious smile when she realized I was there. "What's up, Nix? You heading out too?"

"Yeah," I said, pulling the door open. "I thought I'd walk you down to the shop. I could use a little touch up myself."

"Mmhmm." She gave me a knowing look as she stepped past me out the door, then waited for me to lock up before we started down the street. "Sooo," she said, reaching up to gently tug my beard, then dodging my attempted smack of her backside in retaliation. "The beard... that's a new look for you."

I chuckled. "What, you don't like it?"

"I didn't say that. I think it looks good on you. Makes you look grown up."

"Makes me *look* grown up?"

She nodded. "Mmhm. Just *look*."

"Ohhh, you've got jokes today."

"Oh I've got jokes *every* day. What made you decide to grow a beard though?"

Shrugging, I stopped at the crosswalk in front of Urban Grind to press the button to give us the signal to walk across the street. Somebody, probably a customer, honked their horn as they passed, and I threw my hand up to wave before I turned back to Charlie.

So damned gorgeous.

It was a sunny day, borderline hot, and Charlie had propped her hand against her forehead to shield her eyes from the sun. Even with a little sweat building as she fanned herself with the other hand... she seemed so serene, although I knew she had a lot going on in her head. Just this morning, she'd shown up with red, puffy eyes that she claimed were from mishandled soap, but she wasn't fooling anybody. She'd been crying, and if I had to give it one good guess, her ex-husband was the reason for her tears.

Now though, she pulled her hand away from her head and smiled, tilting her head to the side. "Nix, are you gonna answer my question, or are you just gonna stare?"

I gave a slight shake of my head, then returned her smile. "Stare."

"Whatever," she said, wrinkling her nose at me as the traffic signal approved our trip across the street, away from the subtle coffee aroma of UG.

When we were safely on the other side, I caught her by the hand, not caring if — honestly kinda hoping that — Trent might pop up and see the implied intimacy of such a gesture.

Fuck him.

"I just got tired of shaving, really. So... I grew the beard out of laziness more than anything else. Easier maintenance."

"But you have to do something to keep it feeling that soft, right?" she asked, still allowing me to hold her hand as we continued down the street.

"Just a little beard oil. Nothing major." I chuckled a little, then turned to her with a smile. "You think my beard is soft, huh?"

She raised an eyebrow, looking a little confused. "Um... yeah... why?"

I shrugged. "No reason, really. I was just gonna ask if you wanted to test it out."

Her eyebrow drifted a little higher. "... Test it out?"

"Yeah," I nodded. "Let me know if it's a good cushion for when you sit on my fa—"

"Nix!" Charlie snatched her hand away from me, and gave me the same scolding look I used to get from my mother. A second later, I could tell she was fighting hard not to smile. "*Must you* say such inappropriate things to me?"

"I didn't do anything wrong. I'm out here trying to be a gentleman, offer you a place to rest after a long day on your feet... man, you're tripping."

She *did* laugh then, and *damn* the things this girl's laughter did for my soul... five years later, and she still had my head gone.

"*I'm* tripping?"

"Yes, *you*."

She shook her head, smiling at me as we approached the door to Fresh Cuts. "You know you need to quit, right?"

"I didn't *do* anything though, you started it."

"Uh-huh, here we go with the blame game. It's always *somebody else* that made you do it, right Nix?"

Ouch.

I didn't mean to let my reaction to that little — possibly inadvertent — jab show on my face, but before I could switch to a poker face, Charlie's eyes had already gone wide, and she was lifting her hands to rest them on my chest.

"I didn't mean it like *that*, you know that right?"

Ignoring the sudden heaviness in my chest, I grabbed her hands, bringing them up to kiss her fingers. "Yeah."

"I'm sorry."

"For *what*?" I asked, shaking my head. "You don't have anything to apologize for, baby girl. We're good."

She didn't look that sure, but instead of standing outside and dwelling on it, I reached around to pull open the door to the shop. Pressing her lips together, she tossed me a last look of uncertainty before we stepped into the cool, air-conditioned shop, surrounding ourselves with the aroma of barbacide and sandalwood.

"Pretty girl!"

Charlie's face broke into a smile at her signature greeting, delivered in unison by my Pops and his best friend — Walter and Lorenzo. They stood as she approached their reserved seats in the waiting area of the shop, and hugged both of them, blushing as they kissed her on the cheek.

"Charlene," Lorenzo said, taking her by the hand. "Girl, where is that fine ass mama of yours?"

I chuckled at that. Since I could remember, probably going all the way back to the time we were in middle school, any time Lorenzo saw Charlie around the neighborhood, he asked her the same question, and she always gave the same answer.

"I can't be sure, Lorenzo, you know she's always on the move."

From the stories I'd heard, mostly *over*heard from eavesdropping on grown folks' conversations, Lorenzo had been chasing Melissa Bennet for a *long* time, and she curved him on a regular basis — as any mindful woman would. Lorenzo was one of those old cats that always had a woman throwing a brick through his window or acting a fool at his job, and from what I could tell, it had been that way for decades. I didn't blame Melissa for always being out of dodge. I wouldn't want any of whatever the hell he was putting on those women either.

"Young blood, what's going on?"

"Not shit, Pops." I grinned at my dad as I accepted his extended hand, shaking my head when he pulled me into a hug anyway. I made sure to take a deep inhale when he got close, giving him a nod of approval when the only thing I smelled was after-shave from his recent turn in the barber's chair.

Charlie had moved on to talk to Carter, and was gesturing at her head with one hand while she showed him something on her phone with the other. She seemed excited about whatever she was saying to him, and smiled that big, pretty-ass smile as she sat down in his chair, and he draped her with a black cape.

I reluctantly tore my eyes away to respond to my dad's insistent tap on my shoulder, and obliged him as he motioned for me to take the empty seat beside him while Lorenzo took his turn getting cleaned up.

"Whassup Pops?" I asked, relaxing into the chair. "I see you're staying out of trouble these days."

He looked at me as if I'd said something crazy. "Of course. If a man doesn't have his word, he doesn't have shit."

Yeah, and you're usually shit-deficient.

"You're speaking the truth there."

"You don't have to tell *me*. But on to you... do my eyes deceive me, or do you have your lady back?"

I shook my head. "Eyes failing on you, old man. It's not like that. We're business partners, it's not a big deal for us to be around each other."

"Damn shame," he said, crossing his arms as he sat back. "You know, you never would've lost her in the first place if—"

"*Pops.* Cool it, please."

The *last* person I needed telling me what I'd done wrong with Charlie was Walter Graham.

He tossed his hands in the air. "Alright man. My bad."

I cut my eyes toward Charlie, who had her head bent, holding still while Carter held his clippers to her head.

"But I'm telling you, young blood," — I groaned — "if you'd never given that girl a ring, she'd still be yours. Shit is a curse."

Running my tongue over my teeth, I closed my eyes for a second, trying to check myself. "So that's what happened with you and mom, huh?"

"Damn right."

"Had nothing to do with you kicking it like a single man, and staying too drunk to drive yourself to work, right?"

His mouth dropped open, and he sputtered for a few seconds over his words as I stood, not waiting for him to collect himself for a response before I ambled over to where Carter was finishing Charlie's cut.

"What's up, man?" He asked, tipping up his chin in greeting as he carefully cut an intricate tribal design into the faded part of her tapered fro. "You getting trimmed up too?"

"Just the beard today, bruh. Gotta keep Charlie's seat in good condition."

Carter pulled the clippers away from Charlie's head so he could throw his head back and laugh. "Nix, you are a damn fool."

"I agree," Charlie said, giving me the stink eye as Carter cleaned the fallen hair from her neck and face, then pulled off her cape.

While he cleaned up his station, I surveyed Charlie's hair, giving her a nod of approval.

"This cut is flattering on you, baby. I like it."

"Still, with the *baby*, Nix?"

"*Always.*"

She blushed, slapping me on the shoulder and glancing around the shop to see who was looking as I sung the one line I knew of Mariah Carey's *Always Be My Baby* to her. I knew, and didn't give a shit that we had an audience. I'd tried, and *couldn't* shake her — she really would *always be my baby.*

"You gonna wait on me?" I asked, grabbing her hand again as I took a seat in Carter's chair.

She bit her lip, trying gently to tug her hand away. "I guess I can... since you were kind enough to give me a little company on my walk."

"Okay lovebirds, am I cutting hair or not?"

"Alright, Carter, damn," I said, reluctantly releasing Charlie's hand so I could sit down. Carter had moved on to his computer business, and this was his only day of the week in the shop, so I knew he probably had appointments coming in later. I didn't want to hold him up.

Charlie went to sit with my dad and Lorenzo while she waited, and I cringed thinking about what he might be saying to her. Hopefully not the same bullshit he'd fed me through my dating years, and kept in my ear the whole time she and I were together.

He *really* believed, even after me explaining countless times what actually happened, that me proposing to Charlie was part of us breaking up. Hmph. More like, his bullshit advice that I idiotically followed made me wait *too long* to give her the damned ring. But — there was that blame game that Charlie mentioned. When it really came down to it... my mistakes were just that. *Mine.*

"I think I'm gonna propose to Viv, man."

Carter's tone was quiet, and I knew he was probably eying Charlie to make sure she wasn't paying attention. She was well out of earshot, but if he was talking about proposing, it made sense to be cautious with her right in the same room.

"Do it, man. Don't wait."

Carter sucked his teeth. "Damn, Nix. That's it? Just... do it?"

"Hell yeah. Whatever the fuck you do, *do not do what I did.* You've had the ring for what, *months* now, right? Propose to that girl before she runs off and marries somebody else."

Chuckling, Carter carefully began touching up my haircut, to have a reason to keep me in the chair while we talked. "I see you're on your period today, Nix. What's up man? Charlie dating old boy got you shook, huh?"

I shot him a scowl. "Ha ha. You're the one crying about proposing as if you wouldn't throw your ass off a building if that girl left you. You're being funny, but I'm just saying... you've put that girl through enough of your emotional shit, don't you think?"

He pulled the clippers back and turned them off, then scratched his head. "Yeah... you're probably right."

"Muthafucka... *duh.* I'm telling you... lock her down."

Carter nodded, then proceeded to finish up my cut. We shook hands when we were done, and then I headed to the front to pay. Charlie was waiting for me by the door, and this time, I resisted the urge to grab her hand.

Don't wear out your welcome too soon, man.

As we started down the street, I noticed that Charlie kept looking at me — *staring* at me — out of the corner of her eyes. It wasn't until we were back on our end of the street, passing Urban Grind that I finally just asked.

"What's up, Charlene? You're looking at me like you want me or something."

She gave me "the look" again. "I've told you about calling me that, negro. And I'm *not* staring at you like I *want you*, I'm just... looking. You look good with your fresh cut."

"I didn't look good with my fresh cut last week?"

"Of *course* you did, but it's even fresher *this* week," she said, laughing as I unlocked the door to the restaurant. I let her in first, and once we were inside, she turned to me with a curious smile. "So what are you doing tonight, with your *super fresh* cut?"

I shrugged. "Same old. Probably hit up UG, drink a bit, chill... the usual. You?"

She averted her eyes, pushing her hands into the back pockets of her pants. "Dinner and a movie... with Trent."

Fuck him.

"Oh, cool. Sounds like a good time. I hope you have fun."

We both knew that was a lie, and she gave me a look that was half scolding, half amused before her expression shifted into... something else.

"What is it?" I asked, stepping in front of her as she headed toward the back.

She reached up, tugging at her earlobe for a second before she met my gaze. "Nothing really, it's just... I guess I'm surprised that you don't... have a girlfriend... or *something*."

I lifted an eyebrow. "I mean... I've dated here and there. Still do. Sometimes a little serious..."

"But not... *big* serious?"

I shook my head. "What can I say... you ruined me for other women."

Her eyebrows shot up, and her lips parted, but she quickly shuttered that expression into impassive as she dropped her eyes. When she looked up again, she gave me a little smile.

"Oh. Well... I'm gonna... go ahead and get my coat back on. Dinner service is starting soon." With a final nod, she took off, leaving me standing by the front doors as Jordan and Amina came in to start the second part of their shift.

"You alright chef?" Jordan asked, eying me with concern as he pulled his apron over his head.

"Yeah man. I'm good. Let's get to work."

chapter
seven

Charlie

"Baby... are you there?"

What would happen if I said no?

Or better yet, just remained silent.

Or hung up.

Or just... simply stopped accepting his calls?

That's what the lawyer recommended anyway, but there was still that little part of me that honestly felt bad for Adrian. Even if he was a lying, manipulating criminal, this was an adjustment for him as well. For a man used to $300 shirts, a prison uniform had to be a tough pill to swallow.

Three months ago.

That was the last time I'd laid eyes on Adrian, while visiting the prison for my first and only time, and it still felt surreal. Two days before his arrest, I'd made love to — *had sex with* —him for the last time. The only thing I gained from that was a pregnancy scare.

Even then, some part of me still hoped it was all a mistake. When I met Adrian, his energy practically screamed "good guy". Stepping into the investment firm where he worked downtown — actually not too far from Honeybee — I'd immediately gotten a good vibe. His client that left before me seemed incredibly happy with their service. Plaques for outstanding customer service and other impressive achievements lined the waiting area — Adrian's name was up there at least seven times. The firm even had great reviews online, many of them specifically mentioning Adrian. I sat there and waited for my appointment feeling *great* about potentially choosing him as my broker.

He came to the door of the waiting room to get me, and *sweet Jesus* he was fine. Extra smooth, *extra dark* brown skin, a clean-shaven face and chiseled jaw, lips that you wanted to suck on, deep onyx eyes that you wanted to dive into, and *have mercy* he was wearing the shit out of that suit. My legs were a little weak as I stood, accepting his offered hand as he led me to his office. He was saying *something*, but damned if I heard it.

By the time we made it to his office, I'd already peeped his big hands and lack of a ring, and was already wondering how likely it was that I could turn this meeting from business to pleasure.

But... business *first.*

I was fresh — like, four days fresh — off of my break up with Nixon. I didn't want to see, think about, or even hear about his ass, and the best way to do that was to *not* be in business with him. I loved Pot Liquor like it was my child, but as things sometimes go with children, mommy and daddy weren't working out. In my heartbreak-addled mind, I was horny, lonely, and desperate to be free of Nixon. I had the bright idea that investing would make my money grow faster, which meant I could buy Nix out of the restaurant sooner.

Throughout our meeting, Adrian was completely professional, so I assumed my *can't-you-tell-I'm-tryna-sit-this-ass-on-you* vibe wasn't working. I mentally checked myself, then actually tuned into what was happening. At the end of the meeting, I attempted to officially hire him as my broker, but he insisted that I take the paperwork he'd gone over with me, sleep on it for a few days, and get back to him. *That* convinced me even further that he would take good care of my money.

At his door, he took me by the hand, but instead of shaking it and showing me out, he kept it tucked in his as he ran his tongue over his lips.

"I hope I'm not misreading any signals here," he said, drawing me closer, "But... I'd like to take you to dinner... in an *un*official capacity. I'll gladly refer you to another bro—"

"Yes."

I couldn't even let the man get the request out of his mouth before I was giving him my over-eager response, but he gave me a panty-melting smile, and... things took off from there. That very night, he met me at my mother's house — where I was staying there after the break up with Nix, since we *lived* together. He thought he was picking me up for dinner, but instead, I drug him inside and took advantage of the fact that my mother was out of town.

Adrian screwed me into an orgasm-induced coma, and I went to work my shared shift with Nixon the next day, wearing a smug grin that I didn't feel. I *actually* felt like crap. I felt guilty for letting another man touch me just *four days* after I'd stopped wearing Nix's ring. I felt like I was violating some unwritten rule of post-breakup etiquette, but then I remembered what *he* had done, and I felt justified. I felt guilty about *that* too.

So, with all of that swirling around, plus the fact that I felt like my heart had been ripped out of my chest by a man that I'd loved for six years, plus the fact that I was angry, I did what was obviously the most logical course of action.

I slept with Adrian again.

And again.

And again.

We even developed a little routine. He was a busy guy, not really looking for anything serious, and I was a busy girl, actively avoiding anything serious. Our low expectations of each other worked well, and at some point, he stopped being my investment broker, who I happened to be screwing, and started being my friend — who I happened to be screwing.

Adrian and I never really connected romantically, but we certainly *looked* good together. We went to a few family dinners together, and after that, we had people on both sides pressuring us for a baby. To be fair, *my* mother wanted the baby to be Nixon's but she was content with a grandchild, period. Neither Adrian nor I was really that impressed by the pressure to procreate, but it *did* get us to thinking.

We got along well. Had great sex. Didn't have the time or

enthusiasm to look for a proper spouse. We were *perfect* for each other. So... for a second time, I took what was obviously the most logical course of action.

I married Adrian, then moved with him when he took a job at a brokerage in California.

For a while, it was great. Nixon's response to my desire to buy him out of Pot Liquor was.... unfavorable. The move to California solved my "I don't wanna see that negro's stupid ass face" problem, and I could still be part of my "child's" life. I had to forfeit a chunk of my earnings every month to pay the salary for a chef to replace me, but that was okay. I had a new business as a private chef, a new husband — yay, for *just barely* fulfilling my mother's dream that I not turn thirty without a ring— and a new life out in Cali. It was *great*.

Only... it wasn't.

I mean... I was *happy* with Adrian. As happy as you could be with somebody you didn't love *like that*, and who didn't love you *like that* either, but y'all got married anyway, so you'd better make that shit work. Somewhere along the way, I stopped being so hurt by my breakup with Nixon, — or did a better job burying it — and that cleared my mind to start thinking about what I really wanted for my future. Spoiler alert — it wasn't *this*.

But I took those vows.

And even if I didn't marry Adrian for the right — or hell, even *smart* — reasons, I still had respect for him, and I was willing to try to make the best of it. It wasn't like being with Adrian was torture. I couldn't *make* myself have romantic feelings for Adrian, but I *liked* him, I respected him, and he was undeniably attractive, so... we stuck it out, with a few adjustments. He wanted a little more "freedom" and I... wanted to fill a void in my life. So we compromised, and made logical decision number three... we started trying for a baby.

When he told me, shortly after we started trying to conceive that he was in a little trouble, I honestly didn't believe him. Or maybe it was denial. In any case, I went about my life as if nothing had changed, because to me, it hadn't.

Until my clients started "seeking other options" and "going in a new direction".

And federal agents were wanting to talk to me.

And the brokerage he'd moved to California for terminated his contract, to protect their company, and mitigate the damage to their reputation.

He assured me over, over, and over again that he hadn't done anything, he would be cleared. But then his ass got *arrested*, and call me crazy, but vows or not, being a prison wife was something I didn't sign up for.

Through all of that, he insisted on his innocence, and I *wanted* to believe him, because the accusations just didn't fit the Adrian I knew. But then, somebody decided it was local news-worthy, and the widows and retired firefighters and veterans came forward to tell their stories. Those people were *broken*, in heart and spirit as they talked about how they had been made to feel safe, and well-taken care of, but now their life savings were gone. Their retirements were gone. Their pensions were gone. And they all had one thing in common.

They'd worked with Adrian.

He wasn't even allowed to stay home, under monitoring while he waited on the endless court appearances that comprised his trial. They kept him under lock and key, and *one* visit was enough for me. I couldn't handle the news vans in my yard, microphones shoved in my face outside the gym, or accusing stares while I tried to shop for groceries. *Tried*. Because they froze the money, and not just *his* accounts. Mine too, with the money I made as a private chef, and my savings from Pot Liquor, and my private investment accounts, and... *everything*.

They took *everything*.

Once they were done tearing it all apart, I had very, *very* little left for Adrian. So, when he made these phone calls to tell me about how court had gone, or complain about the food, or whatever other random niceties he deemed worthy of the precious ten minutes a day he was allowed on the phone, I had a *very* hard time offering patience.

I really just wanted him to sign the damned divorce papers so I could move on with my life.

"Yes, Adrian. I'm here," I said finally, punctuating it with a sigh. "What is it?"

"I was asking you about these divorce papers... why do you insist on doing this? I'm telling you, Charlie... once all of this is cleared up, I'm gonna make it right."

Sitting up on the edge of the bed, I pushed my fingers into my hair, somehow resisting the urge to rip a handful out. "Adrian... there's nothing to make right. I want you to agree to the divorce, that's all. You owe me nothing else. I just want to be able to move on."

"To another man."

"I didn't say that."

"You don't *have* to. I can hear it in your voice. You're slipping away from me. I'm taking the fall for some shit I didn't even *do*, and I'm losing my wife." When I chose silence over a verbal response, Adrian cursed under his breath. "Charlie... just... give me a little time here. I'm *innocent.*"

"I hope so," I said, running my fingernails over the tiny stitches in the bedspread. "For your sake, Adrian, I truly, *truly* hope that you get vindicated, but... this situation isn't where you lost me. We were holding on to the arrangement that we made *way* past the expiration date. It's time to move on, to something that's actually sustainable for a future."

"We can do that. When this is cleared up, we can work on reconnecting, getting to know each other on a deeper level. It'll be like dating."

I threw myself back on the bed, using one hand to massage my temples. "Are you serious? You want me to keep my life on hold for you to *maybe* get out, so we can *maybe* find a romantic connection that you're suddenly concerned in building? Where was this interest, say... three or four years ago?"

"It's always been there."

"Adrian, if you don't cut the bullshit... like... I'm pretty sure you spent more time at the strip club than you spent doing things that even *bordered* on romantic for me."

"So *now* the time that I spent out with my boys is a problem?"

"*No*," I groaned, squeezing my eyes shut. "It's not a problem, it wasn't a problem, and it *never will be* a problem. My point is that you've never demonstrated that I was more than a... friend with benefits to you. I don't understand why you think I should hold out for you to start doing it now, when there hasn't been a romantic spark in *four goddamned years*."

"Okay... so I see we can't have this conversation right now. Not while you're upset."

"I'm gonna be upset for the foreseeable future, so we may as well have it now."

"You're agitated."

"Because you're agitating me."

"By trying to fight for our marriage?"

"By pretending that you *ever* thought our marriage was more than an ill-conceived decision that we just tried to make the best of. You going to prison, my business being lost, my money being kept from me, my home being taken away, my reputation trashed...this is more than I signed up for, Adrian. Again, I *really* hope that you *do* get out of this, and I hope you bounce back even better than before if that's the case. But in the meantime... I need to rebuild my life, and I want to do it with a clean slate. This is me using my out."

"Your *out*?"

"Yes. When we first decided to do this marriage thing, we agreed that if the other person decided they didn't want to do it anymore, we wouldn't hold them back. Do you remember that?"

Through the phone, I heard him push out a heavy sigh. "Yeah. I remember. But that was before I knew I loved you."

Wait.... *What*?

"Adrian, tha—"

"My time is up, Charlie, I've gotta go. I'm *not* signing these papers. I love you. Bye."

"Wait a goddamned minute, Adrian. I— Adrian? *Adrian*?!"

The only response I got was the complete silence that let me know he'd hung up, leaving me with a massive headache and a *still* unresolved divorce.

Somehow, I found the self-control to not throw my phone across the room, then finally got out of bed to handle my morning routine. I tried to block Adrian out of my head. There was no point in allowing my thoughts to dwell there, because there wasn't anything I could do about it. Unfortunately for me, he still had rights. Contesting the divorce was just... one he chose to exercise.

I dressed in shorts and a tee shirt at first, because I didn't plan to see or be seen by *anybody* today. Court TV and a pint of ice cream sounded much more appealing, but then I changed my mind. Wallowing in self-pity was just as useless as devoting brain power to trying to figure Adrian out.

Stepping into my closet, I pulled out a pretty royal blue sundress and my favorite sandals. I picked out sexy underwear, styled my hair, and put on eyeliner and lip-gloss. Fifteen minutes later, I smiled at myself in the mirror. Five minutes after that... I was propped on the couch with my ice cream and the remote.

I didn't have shit to do.

My primary focus was rebuilding a savings account, so shopping was out of the question. Carter had taken Viv on some overnight staycation getaway thing, so going to see my cousin was out. I'd been back at Pot Liquor for almost a month, so I wasn't shadowing Nixon anymore. I was on the schedule now, and today wasn't one of my days, so going there was out. The last thing I needed Nix thinking was that I was popping up to see him.

And what about Trent...

Oh.

Yeah.

Almost forgot about him... which probably wasn't a great sign. With all of the drama with Adrian, it wasn't surprising that my mind was preoccupied. Even so, things with Trent were going well. We'd gone out two more times since that near-failure first date, and I truly enjoyed his company — when he wasn't picking at that empty ring finger, or talking about his wife. But I got it. His divorce was fairly recent, only six months ago, so the pain was still fresh.

In any case... I liked him. The second date kiss was a *real* kiss, and gave me a respectable amount of tingles. The third date kiss was a lot more... vigorous — on his part — and afterwards, he kinda seemed like he was angling to be invited inside.

That would be a *no*.

First, there was the whole *still married* thing. As far I was concerned, our marriage was over, but that's not what the state of California thought. I liked Trent, but we had a *lot* further to go before I would be willing to go full-on trifling wife. Three dates certainly wasn't gonna make me into an adulteress. Besides... I saw where sleeping with a man too soon got me: Dating, while my husband was in prison.

A knock at the door drew me from my thoughts, and I stuck my ice cream back in the freezer on the way to answer.

I checked the peephole first, and the sight of Nixon at my door made my heart start to race. What did *he* want at this time of morning?

I took a deep breath before I opened the door, but as soon as Nixon was in front of me, he snatched it away.

Really shouldn't be okay to look this damned good.

He was dressed casually, in white cargo shorts, a rich blue polo, and Sperrys. He smelled yummy— friggin' *delicious* — and he *looked* scrumptious, all freshly cut and trimmed and —

"Charlie?"

"Hm?"

"I asked if you were ready to go... I see you're already dressed..."

I shook my head to clear my thoughts, then looked up to meet his eyes. "I'm sorry... ready to go? Where are we going? Why aren't you at the restaurant getting ready for breakfast service?"

Nixon lifted an eyebrow, then shifted to lean against the doorframe. "I'm not at the restaurant because we're usually pretty mellow on Thursday mornings, and we're entrusting Jordan and Amina to handle it while you and I go to the restaurant supply store to pick out the new plate ware and cutlery *you* decided we needed."

"*Ohh*," I said, nodding as the memory of that conversation came back to me. "That's... today."

Nixon scowled a little, confused. "Yeah... that's not why you're dressed? Did you make other plans?"

"What? No, I just... it slipped my mind. But I'm ready. We can go."

"You sure?"

"Yeah, just let me grab my purse."

I shook my head, leaving him at the door as I went to grab my purse and phone. After the hassle of that infuriating phone call with Adrian, spending a good part of the day with Nixon sounded like more stress, but... what the hell. At least I would get to pick out pretty new plates.

chapter
eight

Charlie

"WHAT ABOUT THESE?"

I gestured at a plate on display then ran my fingers along the polished edge of its surface. To Nixon, the plate probably looked exactly like all the other simple white plates we'd viewed, but *I* saw the difference, and had been dragging him through the aisles for the last hour.

It was kind of amazing, how from a long distance, he so easily worked my nerves, but now, back in his presence, we had such an effortless, natural... *vibe.* Even now, this quiet moment of shopping for something as mundane as *plates*, shouldn't have felt so but it just did.

It was *so* easy to forget what he'd done.

He approached me from behind, putting his hand at my waist as he leaned over me to see the plate and give me a slight tug toward him. Instead of resisting, my first reaction was to give in to his desire to have me close to him. Inexplicably, I found myself feeling a little guilty every time he wanted to touch me and I resisted, as if somewhere in me, my body still thought I belonged to him.

With him.

That was the only explanation for the feeling of *rightness* that coursed through me as I allowed him to pull me close.

"Those look good," he said, even though I could feel his eyes so intensely focused on me I knew he hadn't even looked at the plate. "Are those the ones you want?"

I glanced up, shifting slightly so that I was facing him a little more. "I really, really like these, but they're kind of over our budget."

"So?" He skimmed his thumb over my side. "Get whatever you want."

I shook my head, then started on to the next display. "Uh-uh. We have numbers to stick to, and it's not that big of a deal."

"Wait a minute now," he said, dragging me back. "I saw how your eyes lit up about those, so it *is* a big deal. Get the plates, baby."

This time, I turned so that we were face to face, and looked him in the eyes. "Nix... don't start that."

"Start what?"

"You *know* what."

He scratched his head, looking away in an attempt to hide the grin threatening to overtake his mouth. "I have no idea what you're talking about."

"Mmhmm. So you're *not* trying to spoil me?" I asked, reaching up to cup his chin and turn his face back to mine.

"Not at all."

I narrowed my eyes. "Liar."

Still, I couldn't help smiling as I slipped away from him and heading for the next display.

That was one of many good memories from our relationship. Even when we were broke, after putting all we had and some we didn't into starting Pot Liquor, Nixon always found ways to make a fuss over me. Candlelit massages, grocery store flowers, scrambled eggs and oatmeal in bed, love notes stuck to my forehead on days he was out of the door before I was out of bed... sweet little things that cost him nothing except his time and attention, but meant the world to me.

I glanced back to see him gazing at those plates, and I knew that despite my protests, he was going to buy them, even if he pulled the difference from his own pocket. I'd seen that look before, and hated that my potential disappointment still held such power over him. It would be much easier to not get wrapped up in him if he didn't care about my happiness.

"Charlie? What's on your mind?"

Shaking my head, I turned away again, pretending to be interested in the next set of plates. "Nothing."

"Didn't look like nothing."

I shrugged. "Don't know what to tell you. These plates here. I like these, and they're under budget."

Crossing his arms, Nixon cocked his head to the side and stared at me, one eyebrow lifted. "You seemed a lot more excited about the other ones."

"The other ones aren't within budget."

"I told you it didn't matter."

"Nix…"

He pushed out a heavy sigh, then unfolded his arms. "Fine." Pulling his keys from his pocket, he handed them to me, then gestured toward the front door. "I'll finalize our order, then be out in a second."

"You think I'm crazy?"

"Did I say that? Just go wait for me."

"*Nixon.*"

Nixon groaned, then turned to me, gently grabbing me by the shoulders. "Charlie… let me do this for you."

I started to speak again in protest, but the pleading in his eyes halted my words. It was pointless to argue.

Shaking my head, I reluctantly turned and headed to the car, where I cranked up the radio and air conditioner, then pulled out my phone to pass the time. When I turned on the screen, I noticed a text notification that I hadn't heard.

"Hey Beautiful. Feel like joining me for an early lunch at 11? – Trent E."

He'd sent that message at 9:42, and it was currently almost noon, so… no lunch date for me.

"Just now seeing this, sorry!"

I started to slip the phone back into my purse, but it chimed with a new message.

"No problem, it was last-minute. Busy morning? – Trent E."

"Somewhat. Ordering things for the restaurant."

"I thought you were off today? You mentioned relaxing. – Trent E."

"Had to go to the supply warehouse with Nixon."

As soon as I hit send, I regretted putting down that I was with Nixon. Not that Trent had ever given me any indications of jealousy, but I didn't want there to be *any* reason for him to think he needed to start.

Nixon hadn't exactly *bullied* Trent in high school, but after noticing his growing interest in me, Nix had threatened all manner of physical violence against him. I was *so* mad at him for that. I didn't like Trent at all, at least not in the way he liked me, but *still*. Nix scaring off potential boyfriends wasn't a trend I wanted to start, especially when he wasn't even pursuing me.

"Cool. You can just get back to me when you're done. – Trent E."

"We're done now. Do you maybe wanna have dinner tonight, since we missed the chance for lunch?"

"Already have plans. Dionne wants to talk about something. She's been trying to keep in contact a lot lately, so I guess I should see what she wants. Sorry, Beautiful. – Trent E."

Hmm. Was he making sure I knew he was going to be with his ex as a response to knowing I'd missed a meal with him because I was with Nixon?

Nah. Couldn't be.

Or at least, I hoped — for his sake — not. Because... we hadn't been dating long enough for me to honestly care that much.

"Sounds... intense."

"Sounds terrifying. Wish me luck. – Trent E."

"LOL! Good luck."

"Thanks. I need it. Talk to you later, Beautiful. – Trent E."

I slipped my phone back into my purse when Nixon opened the driver's side door and climbed in. Despite the blasting air conditioner, I could swear the temperature shot up ten degrees just from having him in such close proximity. I buckled my seatbelt and sat back as he pulled out of the parking lot, and a few minutes later, we were on the highway for the twenty-minute drive back to the city.

For a while, neither of us said anything. Nixon bobbed his head, tapping his thumbs on the steering wheel in time to the beat of the music, and I pretended to be busy on my phone until finally, I dropped it into my lap and turned to face him.

"Why did you do that?"

Nixon's eyebrow hitched upward, just slightly, but he didn't take his eyes off the road. "Do what?"

"Buy those expensive plates, even though I said the other ones were fine."

"Who said I did?"

"Really Nix?" I asked, folding my arms. "Fine. *Did you* purchase the plates that were over budget?"

He turned to me for just a moment, flashing his dimples with a smile before he looked back to the road. "Yes. I did."

"Why?"

"Why not?"

I groaned. Did we *always* have to go back and forth, instead of just giving a straight answer to a question?

"Because they were *over budget*."

"And I told you I had it."

"That's not the point."

"Then what is, Charlie? Are you really sitting here getting upset with me because I made sure we got the plates you wanted?

"No, I'm getting upset because I told you the more expensive plates weren't necessary."

"Necessity doesn't have anything to do with it."

Rolling my eyes, I bit my lip and took a deep breath, trying to reign in my quickly rising anger. "Well then," I said, pushing the words through clenched teeth. "Can you tell me what "it" *is* about?"

"Making you happy. Doing something nice for you, that's all. For the amount that we need, the difference in the order total on those plates was only a couple hundred dollars, and I paid the difference myself."

"*Why though*? Why did *those* plates even matter?"

"Because *you* matter." He glanced at me again, his face pulled into a scowl as we turned off the highway, and onto the quieter streets of our neighborhood. "You may not talk about it, not with me, but I know the last year has been crazy for you because of that shit with your husband. You may hide it well, but you're hurt, and you're angry. It's in your voice, and in your eyes, and I know that because I've seen it firsthand, because *I've caused* it before. I *hate* seeing you like that."

"So your grand plan is to fix me with *plates*, Nix?"

He shrugged. "Why not? I know how important food presentation is to you. I know that you weren't happy with the plates we've been using, and that's part of the appearance. I take you to pick out new plates, purchase the ones that make your eyes light up, even if it means I have to come out of my own pocket. Because when you put the dish that you labored over with love on a plate that you love, it'll make you feel good. It'll make you smile, and that's all I really want to do, Charlie, is make you smile."

... *Oh.*

I turned away from him to look out the window on my side as my eyes pricked with tears. It was easy to keep things cold and professional, push old feelings to the side when we were thousands of miles apart, but with Adrian acting stupid, and Trent *maybe* acting a little silly too, the sweetness of Nixon's actions and words were amplified. It was *so* like him, to have turned *plates* into an act so deeply personal, that no one else would have the knowledge or desire to do for me.

"Hey," He said, grabbing my hand once he pulled into a parking space in front of the building. "As long as I've known you, you've been funny, snarky, outgoing, and bubbly. You've always had a magnetic energy. But since you've been back, I've noticed that you've seemed kind of ... closed off. Or... maybe that's just with me. And I guess with our history I can understand that, but if that's not the case, I'm gonna keep doing whatever I can to get that fun girl that I knew back."

I shook my head, pulling my hand away from his. "You don't think I'm fun? I'm *very* fun."

"Yeah... let me walk you up to your apartment."

Nixon was out of the car before I could protest, and was already at my door before I could undo my seatbelt.

"I'll have you know," I said, accepting his hand to help me out of the car, "That I am *tons* of fun, I have a great sense of humor, and... I'm cuter than you, so there's *that*. Hmph."

I turned and started toward the building, with Nixon chuckling as he followed behind. Because I knew he was watching, I put a little extra swing in my hips as we entered the building and headed up the stairs.

"Charlie, quit playing. You keep slinging it in my face like that... don't be surprised if I take a bite."

Glancing over my shoulder at him, I winked, then continued slowly up the next flight, hanging on to the stair rail like it was the barre in a burlesque theater. If I had any hair, I would have swung it as I swayed in Nixon's face. At first, he was half a flight behind me, presumably keeping his distance, but when I looked back again, he was jogging up the steps that separated us with a grin on his face.

I laughed, turning to bound up the next flight as fast as I could, pulling my keys out of my purse on the way. I was pushing the door open when I felt Nix's arms around my waist, and before I could say anything, he'd turned me around, picked me up, kicked the door closed, and draped me over his shoulder with little to no effort.

"Didn't I tell you to stop playing?" he asked, smacking me on the butt before he sat me down on the counter in the kitchen, then stood between my legs.

"You also said I was no fun, so... I don't know what this *playing* that you speak of means."

Nixon smiled as he ran his hands up my thighs, sending pinpricks of heat racing over me as his warms hands connected with my bare flesh. "You don't, huh?"

"Uh-uh. Never heard of it."

His eyes, sparkling with amusement, traveled over my face,

down to my lips, then back up to meet my gaze. "You looked good as hell today." He bit his lip. "I mean... you *always* look good, but... this damned dress... what were you trying to do me, wearing this to go look at *plates*?" He fingered one of the thin straps, then pushed it down, leaving my shoulder bare to his touch as he ran his fingers over my collarbone, up to my neck, then back down over my shoulder.

"I... I didn't wear this for you," I managed, barely breathing as he pulled me closer to the edge of the counter, so that our bodies were pressed together.

"Yeah."

"I *didn't*." My heart was pumping so fast that I panted a little as he ran his hands up my back. "That's the—" Nixon interrupted my statement by lowering his mouth to mine with an insistent press of his warm, velvety soft lips. I kept my hands down, gripping the sides of the counter as he pulled me closer, tracing the seam of my lips with his tongue. I whimpered, then opened my mouth to his request, a little moan escaping my throat as he dipped his tongue into my mouth, massaging it against mine.

"*...truth,*" I whispered when he finally pulled away, barely giving me a chance to catch my breath before he dove in again, exploring my mouth with deep, slow licks as his hands slipped under my thighs, groping and massaging as he looped my legs around his waist. Nixon's body was firm against my skin as I pushed my hands underneath his shirt, gliding my fingers over the muscled flesh of his stomach, then around to his back. The feeling of *him*, hard against my moisture soaked panties shot my already rocketing arousal into overdrive, and I pushed myself against him, not caring what signal it sent. I would go with whatever route he took.

"*So. Damned. Sweet,*" he murmured against my lips, punctuating each word with a kiss before he pulled my lip between his, gently sucking before he nibbled it, then pushed his tongue into my mouth again. "Just like I remembered."

My eyelids fluttered shut, and I let out another moan of pleasure as he dropped his mouth down to my neck, kissing and sucking and biting and kissing a little more before he brought his lips to my ear, kissing me there before he spoke again. "I wonder if the reason I started calling you *honeybun* still applies."

I let out something between a gasp and a whimper, and a moment later, he was kneeling in front of me, kissing his way from the inside of my knee, and up my thigh, and *yes, please*—

"Knock knock!"

The sound of my mother's voice, *inside the apartment* brought me out my arousal-induced euphoria immediately. Nixon's eyes met mine, and he quickly moved to the side and flung open a cabinet, while I hopped down from the counter and pulled down my dress just in time for my mother and aunt to turn the corner into my kitchen, and... know exactly what was happening.

Or not.

But Morgan and Melissa wore identical grins as they looked between me and Nixon, who had his back turned and was rattling around in the cabinet like he was looking for something.

"Well... what have we *here*?" my mother asked, her face spreading into a full-on smile as Nixon finally turned around. "Is that my former almost-son-in-law?"

I rolled my eyes, running my tongue over my teeth as she stepped right past me to give Nixon a big hug when he stood. The way she fawned over him, one would think *he* was her child, and I was the unrelated extra whenever he was around.

"How you doin' Ms. Bennet?" he asked as they parted.

None of us said anything about his mouth — and my neck — being shiny and pink from my lipgloss.

"Oh, I am *wonderful* baby."

"Good, good. And you Mrs. Lambert?"

Aunt Morgan smiled. "*Je suis bien, merci*. Don't I get a hug too?"

Nixon's eyes flicked toward me for a second before he nodded. "Of course." He moved close to her for a hug that she extended longer than necessary, with her hands splayed across his back.

"Oh, you're *happy* to see me, huh?" She looked pointedly at Nixon's crotch, then turned to me with a knowing smirk. "Son pénis est énorme , non?"

"I have *no* idea what that means, Aunt Morgan," I said, with a tight smile that I hoped would give her the hint that the size of Nixon's dick wasn't a discussion point we would be entertaining.

"So you have forgotten your French lessons then? It means you are a lucky girl, because his—"

"Well Nixon has to be leaving now, he was just showing me the difference between a sauté pan and a sauteuse, but now I know, so he can leave, right now." I gave everyone a bright smile, then began pushing Nixon toward the door.

"You know I know French, right?" he whispered, grinning as I shoved him outside.

"Hush."

"Hey." He caught the door before I could close it, then reached out to run a finger over my shoulder, causing me a brief moment of weakness in the knees. "You know I'm not done with you, right?"

"*Hush*," I repeated, batting his hand away. "Yes you are."

That time, I closed and *locked* the door behind him, then turned and drooped against it, letting out a heavy sigh as I closed my eyes. When I opened them, the orgasm-saboteurs were standing side-by-side, arms crossed, both giving me their signature "I'm about to be nosy as hell" grins. I groaned, then shut my eyes tight, hoping beyond hope that *just maybe* they wouldn't be there when I looked again.

Damn.

"Mom... Aunt Morgan... I didn't expect to see you beautiful girls so soon."

chapter
nine

Charlie

"So are you ready to talk yet?"

With a quiet sigh, I peered over my water glass at my mother and aunt. I'd listened to them chatter about their trip while I prepared lunch for the three of us, about men while we ate, and now they both had glasses of wine in the middle of the day, and were waiting for me to spill the beans about Nixon. My mother brushed my complaints about them waltzing into my apartment without knocking off with a quick *"girl I made you, this is my apartment"*. I just shook my head. It was much easier not to argue — and lock the damned door next time.

"Talk about what?" I took a long sip from my glass, ignoring the biting stares from the sisters as I stood to take my plate to the sink. They followed shortly behind me, first my mom, then Aunt Morgan, cornering me in the kitchen.

"Young lady," my mother started, fixing me with a critical scowl, finger lifted in the air. "You tell me right now why you and Nixon Graham were wearing the same lip gloss, or I'm gonna..." She paused, her expression softening as she searched her mind for a way to threaten me. "You just tell me right now! Or... wait... am I *finally* going to get my grandbaby? Cause if so, go ahead and call him back!"

Shaking my head, I pushed past both women, wielding a soapy

washcloth to clean the table where we'd eaten. "You're on a wild grandbaby chase, my dear. There will be no babies any time soon."

"Alright. But you still haven't explained *Nixon*." She smiled when she finished the statement, then glanced to her sister as she took another gulp from her wine. When we were together — and hell, even now— my mother was Nixon's biggest fan.

From the time I was sixteen, she'd drilled into me that the crowning jewel of womanhood was becoming a wife and mother. She herself had only ever done one of those, but she insisted on wanting "better" for me. Every boyfriend was a potential husband, and she never had a problem telling me when she felt someone wasn't good enough for either role.

She always told me that anything more than a year of my time was a waste if the relationship wasn't moving toward a ring. Choose a man who's older, already established. Choose a man with money, and connections, who could give me the type of life that I "deserved". Choose a man who loved — no, *worshipped* me, who couldn't do any better than me, who couldn't see a life without me, who would *never* do anything to jeopardize the possibility of a future.

All of those "rules" went out the door for Nix, and he was so damned charming that my mother didn't even care.

Melissa and Morgan had family money, and by extension so did I. Even so, she expected me to make a living on my own — until I got that husband. Nixon and I'd always been good friends, but the trip to culinary school — a major common interest we'd shared for a while — drew us closer, to the point that I considered him my *best* friend.

We were the same age, working the same crappy line-cook jobs, trying to move our way up to better positions. No money, no connections, and the quality of life of a broke college student. But we had fun. Neither of us was thinking about each other romantically, at least not if anybody *asked*. But Nix was an appealing guy. Smart, funny, sexy, and he could cook his ass off. I was young, but I wasn't *blind*.

The shift in our relationship honestly snuck up on me. Nixon had finally snagged a job in the kind of restaurant that paid bills, so he threw a party. A *small* party, with ten or fifteen people, and we talked, and drank, and I stayed behind to help him clean up. One moment, I was stuffing pizza boxes in a garbage bag while I told him how proud I was, and the next, he'd hauled me into his arms and kissed me like it was the last time he would ever see me again.

I've been wanting to do that since I first saw you in Algebra class. That's what he afterwards, and that was the end of my control over my own heart. You know how people say they "fell" in love? Nixon and I didn't fall, we *plummeted.* Every moment we had outside of work, we were together. Making love and plans for the future. We didn't want to always work in someone else's kitchen, at the mercy of short-tempered executive chefs who saw our younger generation's outlook on modernizing everything from to food itself to the plating as degradation of the craft.

Eventually, Nixon gained all of the qualities my mother recommended in a husband. He loved me, provided, and swore he couldn't be without me, but truthfully, I would have married him in a heartbeat back when we were broke. He treated me as if he thought other mortals should bow at my feet. But... he shut down at even the *mention* of a ring. And when he *did* finally give me one... it was all just a disaster.

"The answer isn't gonna be what you seem to want to hear," I said finally, pulling myself out of my musing. "You're not about to be a grandmother *or* a mother-in-law. Nixon and I *will not* be getting back together."

Aunt Morgan lifted an eyebrow at me as I passed her on the way into the kitchen to put down my towel. "Not what it looked like to me."

"I can't tell you what to think." I shrugged, then left the kitchen again. "But Nixon and I are *not* a thing. I'm actually dating someone else."

"Does he know Nixon was in your kitchen about to *examine your pipes*?" Melissa asked, sharing a wink with her sister.

"*Mom!*"

"*What?* I can't imagine that any man would take kindly to a man like Nixon lurking around, but go ahead, tell me about him. What's his name?"

"Trent Ellis," I said, taking a seat on the couch. The other women followed suit, my mom taking a seat on the couch beside me while Aunt Morgan chose the armchair.

"You're talking about that little nerdy boy who used to follow you home from school?" My mother sat back, her expression tinged with disgust as she took another sip of wine.

"He's *not* a nerdy little boy anymore. He's tall, and handsome, and successful, and—"

"Sounds positively *boring*," Morgan chimed in, her lips twisted as if she'd swallowed a spoonful of castor oil. "I bet he's a perfect gentleman too. Never an inappropriate word, or grope in public, or anything *fun*."

I lifted an eyebrow. "And what makes you say *that*?"

"Because you describe the man like you're placing an ad in the classifieds. Even your adjectives are boring. Tall. Handsome. Successful. *Merde.*"

"Seriously, Aunt Morgan?"

"*Yes*, my dear. Do me a favor, close your eyes and describe Nixon to me."

"What?"

She lifted a hand. "Please, just indulge me."

Rolling my eyes, I let out a heavy sigh, then leaned back into the cushions of the couch. I closed my eyes, and began to speak. "Nixon is... magnetic. And... stimulating, and passionate, and *manly* —"

"He makes your heart, among other things flutter, *non*?"

I opened my eyes, slowly nodding as I sat up.

Aunt Morgan smiled, then took another sip from her mid-day wine. "Do you see the difference, chérie? I do not understand what is wrong with you young girls these days." She sighed, then turned to her sister. "Melissa, I think we may have cursed our children. They *both* seem to think the "safe" man, who looks good in a suit, but does nothing for your heart is the way to go. Charlene, with Adrian — we see where *that* got her — and now this Trent character. Vivienne with that disgusting *Darren. Mon Dieu*." Shaking her head, Aunt Morgan shifted her attention back to me, with admonition in her eyes. "You and your cousin should consider yourselves very lucky that this is not thirty years ago, because your aunt and I are the type of women that would make a *Carter* and a *Nixon* forget that a *Frenchy* and a *Charlie* ever existed."

"Morgan is absolutely right, sweetheart," my mother said, reaching forward to place a hand on my knee. "I wanted you married, not bored to death halfway across the country. And with a *criminal*."

"You *liked* Adrian."

She shook her head, holding up a finger in correction. "I liked that you seemed to be happy. You did a good job fooling your mama before, but I've got my eyes on you this time, and when you described Trent, girl you looked about as excited as somebody going to work the Monday after vacation. When you described *Nixon* though —"

"She looked like she would orgasm on the spot, non?"

Both women broke into a laugh as I rolled my eyes. So *maybe* they had a legitimate point, about choosing a "safe" guy, but what made Nixon the Holy Grail? Listing his positive qualities against the negative, the positives won by a landslide, but what did that matter when he broke my heart?

I shook my head, thinking of the moment my aunt and mother had interrupted. The mistake they'd kept me from making. Because... no matter how charming, how sweet, how much he *loved* me, even now... the fact remained that *he* was the one who destroyed our love.

How the hell was I supposed to forget that?

Morgan and Melissa were still laughing at my expense, so I reached forward with my foot, nudging my mother's leg. "Hey, mom."

"Yes sweetheart?" she asked, giggling as she took a sip from her glass.

"Lorenzo asked about you."

I offered nothing except a satisfied smirk as she choked on her wine. *That* always shut her up.

"Well, Morgan dear, time to go."

Melissa wouldn't even *look* at me as she hurried up from her seat. Morgan was slow to join her, wearing an amused smirk as she finished her wine before she stood.

"Mom, why do you always clam up about Lorenzo? You know that *makes* you look guilty, right?"

She cocked one perfectly groomed eyebrow, propping a hand on her hip. "Little girl, guilty about *what*? My business is mine — and *your* business is mine too, before you come back with a smart remark. I have no interest in that... casanova. That's that."

"I guess she *told* you," Morgan quipped, snapping her fingers as she laughed.

"She *did*, didn't she?" I giggled with my aunt, earning us both an eye roll as my mother headed for the door. We said our good-byes, and just before I closed the door behind them, Aunt Morgan peeked her head in one last time.

"My dear Charlene," she said, grabbing my hand. "Please call that young man back. When he hugged me... my goodness... that is a *lot* of man. It would be such a shame to—"

"Bye Aunt Morgan."

I could hear them laughing on the other side as I shut the door, locking it behind them. Now that they were gone, I took a long, hot shower. After dealing with Adrian, then Nixon, and *then* the wonder-twins, I was mentally and emotionally fatigued in a way that few things would fix. Sleep, shower, sex, social drinking, or sisters. Sex was out, so the other four would have to make do.

When I stepped out of the shower, my buzzing phone notified me that I'd received a text. When I picked it up... I couldn't decide if I was surprised or not that it was from Nixon.

"What time should I swing by again? – *This* **mutha-fucker ...#1"**

Oh, I should probably change his name since we called a truce and said we were friends.

"Try NEVER."

"It's like that, baby? - *This* **muthafucker ...#1"**

"Yes, Nix. You and I both know that what almost happened earlier would have only been an unnecessary complication to our friendship and working relationship."

I gave myself a mental pat on the back, proud of my polite,

professional response as I sat down on the edge of the bed, going into my contact settings to change Nix's name to something a little less... petty.

"Speak for yourself, honeybun. I'm trying to see if you've still got it or not. Amongst other things. – Friend."

"What does that even mean?"

"It means I wanna taste you. I want that sweetness of yours on my face. Like icing. Remember? - Friend."

Have mercy.

My thighs clenched involuntarily as I read that message a few more time, with his voice in my head.

"You know you want that too. - Friend."

"You want me to kiss it. - Friend."

"Lick it. - Friend."

"Devour you. - Friend."

"Make you squirm. - Friend."

"Make you scream. - Friend."

"Make you pass out. - Friend."

"Do you remember that time? - Friend."

" *correction. Couple of times... a week. - Friend."

"Nixon..."

"Yes, baby? - Friend."

"I'm... damnit, you know I'm seeing someone."

"Fuck him. - Friend."

I scowled at the screen, then tapped out a new message, sent it, and sat back with a smirk.

"Is that a demand?"

"Charlie.... - Friend."

"Don't get that dude punched in his mouth. - Friend."

"He's lucky I haven't already done it. - Friend."

"I promised that shit to him years ago, guess he forgot. - Friend."

"Nix..."

"Yes, baby? - Friend."

"You realize that was like... fifteen years ago, right?

"A promise is a promise. - Friend."

"NIX!"

"I'm playing. I'm not gonna do anything to your lil boyfriend. Yet. - Friend."

"Thank you."

"Fuck him. - Friend."

Shaking my head, I sat the phone aside long enough to put on a tank top, a tee shirt, and yoga pants. When I was dressed, I sat down on the edge of the bed again.

"Aren't you supposed to be back at the restaurant right now?"

"I am. Snuck away from the line. The only reason I didn't come back to your place in the break before dinner service is because I figured your mom and aunt were still there. I see you survived that. - Friend."

"With only a mildly bruised ego this time. And no, I don't wanna talk about it."

"Ok. You know you can if you need to though, right? - Friend."

I smiled at his message as I tapped out a response.

"Yes. I do."

"Good. Well... I'm gonna let you go... for now. – Friend."

A few seconds later, an audio file popped up on my phone. I tapped the play button, and the panty-wetting sound of Nixon singing to me came through the speaker.

"They say if you love something let it go, and if it comes back then that's how you know..."

I pushed out a heavy sigh, knowing without needing to ask that it was a line from Marques Houston's *Circle*. I also knew *exactly* what he was getting at. My phone chimed again, and I closed the audio file to read the new message.

"We've already established that I summoned you back with my bomb-ass singing ability, and general hot-shitness, right? – Friend."

I bit my lip to keep from smiling, but before I could respond, he'd already sent another message.

"I'm a patient man, baby. What's meant to be, will be. – Friend."

Tossing myself back onto the bed, I scrolled back through

our conversation. It amazed me that we'd easily slipped back into the easy communication we shared before our relationship became romantic. *Then* it occurred to me that over the years since our breakup, even when I was upset with him, even when I thought he was the scourge of the earth, he'd *always* been able to pull me into an enjoyable banter. Even if what *I* was enjoying was calling him everything except a child of God.

Voodoo dick, I swear.

I opted not to respond to his last message, instead rolling out of the bed and shoving my feet into my soft moccasins. I grabbed my phone, keys, and a bottle of wine, then left to knock on Carter's door. It was a little early to drink, but hey, if Morgan and Melissa could do it, so could we.

I smiled as the door swung open, expecting to see my cousin, but instead, tall and sexy and loc'ed smiled at me.

"Charlie... girl, goddamn, how are you fine as hell even in bum wear?"

Shaking my head, I reached out my arms for a hug. "Hello, nice to see you again too Eddie."

"Yeah, yeah. Get your fine, thick ass in here. Viv was just about to call you, but she was hiding out from "the moms" as she calls them."

If *ever* I was in need of a sincere, borderline inappropriate compliment, I could count on getting one from Eddie. We first met when Nixon and I went into his tattoo shop, DistInk'd. Eddie was the one who'd tattooed tiny macaroni shells, in the shape of an infinity sign, onto my hip. Since then, he'd always been openly appreciative of my "thickness".

"You're welcome bitch," I called out to Viv as I stepped inside. "You're in here hiding, so *I* had to deal with Thing 1 and Thing 2. We're drinking *your* wine... first." The sight of Viv with a red nose and glossy, pink-rimmed eyes made a lump rise to my throat. "Viv, what's *wrong?*"

I took the empty seat beside her at the bar, pulling her into hug. On the other side of the counter, Eddie poured us wine, then mixed himself a drink. "She's just having a moment," he explained, before taking a swig from his glass. "Crazy ass thinks that boy isn't gonna marry her."

In response to that, Viv sat up, shooting him a scowl as she reached for a tissue to dry her face. I lifted an eyebrow at her, nudging her with my knee when she still didn't say anything.

"Fine," she muttered. "It's not exactly *that*. I am in no hurry to get married, but it just... *concerns* me that Carter was pressuring me to talk about it, pressuring me about a baby, and now all of a sudden, he's just... stopped."

I lifted an eyebrow. "Stopped?"

"Yes, *stopped*," she nodded. "And now, I feel like a crazy person, because I am wondering if he is having doubts about us... doubts about me... doubts about *himself*."

"So... why don't you just... talk to him?"

"*Same thing I said*," Eddie coughed.

Viv sighed, then picked up her wine glass, draining it in one gulp. "Because I do not know what to *say*. I do not know what I want from him. I like our life just fine the way it is for now, but... a little part of me *wants* to go ahead and get married before he has a chance to panic like he did before."

"So you want to propose to him?"

"No," she scoffed. "I want to *tell* him, we are getting married, it is not up for debate."

"*Hell no.*"

Eddie and I barked out that word in unison, his deeper voice blending with mine to create a chord that made Viv recoil before she glanced between us, confused.

I grabbed her by the shoulders, turning her to face me.

"Listen to me. *Don't you dare* pressure that man about a ring. Do you hear me? When and if he is ready to lock you down, *he* will do it."

Viv tipped her head to the side. "And just what is wrong with wanting clear expectations for our future, and wanting to set a timeline? Am I unreasonable for not wanting to wait around for years wondering?"

"You mean like me?" I gave her a pointed look, and Viv's mouth dropped open as she brought her hands up to grip mine.

"Charlie, I did not—"

"It's fine, really. You have a great point. I waited six years for Nixon to decide I was worth a ring, and I don't think that's okay, but it's *barely* been a year for you and Carter. Don't be like me, pressuring the man to marry you, and end up pushing him away."

Eddie gave a dry laugh, shaking his head before draining the last of his drink. "Viv... sweet, beautiful girl. *Please listen this time.* Last time the super friends warned your ass about something and you didn't listen, you got your feelings hurt. Your cousin is telling you the truth. No man likes an ultimatum— at least not when one of the choices is a lifetime commitment. I'd dropkick your ass to the curb if you brought that shit to me. No offense, Charlie."

I took a long swig of my wine. "None taken."

And why should it be? It was the damned truth, and something I wish the "super friends" had been around to tell me back when it mattered.

Before any of us could say anything else, we heard the sound of keys in the door, and a few seconds later, Carter was rounding the corner into the kitchen. At first, he smiled, starting to tip his head up in greeting, but his grin dropped quickly into a mask of concern when he saw Viv.

"Baby, what's wrong?" he asked, rushing up to her and cupping her face in his hands. "Did something happen?"

He looked between Eddie and me but we both shook our heads, then Eddie signaled to me that it was time for us to go.

As I stood, I kissed Viv's head, discreetly whispering, "Do *not* be like me." to her before I patted Carter's arm, and headed for the door, with Eddie close behind me.

"I think they're gonna be okay," I said, when we were out of their apartment, and out of earshot.

Eddie nodded. "Man, I hope so. I would hate to have to choke ole boy for hurting her again."

I laughed, then exchanged another hug with Eddie, which he took as an opportunity to dip his hand a little lower on my back than it belonged.

"Alright now, Eddie," I scolded, swatting his hand away. "Don't start nothing!"

"But it's so *soft*. One more feel, come on."

I sucked my teeth. "What would the guy I'm dating think?"

"That I might take his girl from him," Eddie said, smiling as he stepped back to head for the stairs. "Tell him he'd better watch out. Between me and Nix, ole boy had better step his game up!"

Laughing, I returned the "deuces" gesture he gave me as he went down the steps, then turned to go back into my own temporary apartment, which suddenly seemed even lonelier than it had before I left.

Only one of my five S's — Sleep, shower, sex, social drinking, sisters— was left to try.

Sleep.

With my phone, kindle, and a glass of wine, I climbed into bed. I was the entire way through the wine, and only halfway through the first chapter of my book before I drifted into sleep.

chapter
ten

Nixon

CHARLIE MUST NOT HAVE GIVEN TRENT THE MESSAGE.

Admittedly, one too many crown and cokes may have had something to do with my rapidly declining desire *not* to punch his ass in the face, but it was mostly due to the fact he wouldn't keep his damned hands to himself. Every time I looked up, he had a handful of *her*, and it wasn't helping that she wasn't smacking his hands away.

I've gotta get the hell outta here.

It was Roman and Simone's first night back for open mic at Urban Grind, and it had turned into an impromptu "welcome back" party from their honeymoon. What started as a great night, surrounded by people I vibed with, laughing, drinking, getting plenty of face time from Charlie went irrecoverably south as soon as *that* muthafucka showed up at our table.

Charlie seemed surprised to see him, and from the wary look he gave the group as we all — reluctantly, or maybe that was just me — greeted him, I got the distinct impression that she hadn't invited him. It probably went something like: "**Hey, where you at?** *Oh, I'm chilling with people I actually like, having a blast, don't need you, why?* **Oh, word? Where at?** *You wouldn't know it, it's in the old neighborhood that you're too bougie for now, an excellent place, Urban Grind.* **Ok, see you soon.** *Wait, what?*"

Once he was settled in, all up under Charlie like he thought she was gonna disappear, *then* he wanted to hold a conversation, with her hands tucked in his like they were newlyweds.

Fuck him.

As soon as the music started, I swooped Charlie from the table to dance. Ignoring the slighted look on his face, I kept her close, where she *should be*, laughing and dancing until a slow song came on. Then, she looked up at me with pleading eyes, and I knew what she was about to say before she said it. *I shouldn't, not with Trent right there.*

I shrugged, and let her go back while I posted up at the bar. I shook my head in disgust as I watched her take the empty seat beside him, smiling in what seemed to be an attempt to wipe the sour look from his face. A *real* man would have just come and taken his girl back if there was a problem, instead of sitting there looking bothered.

It annoyed the shit out of me to watch Charlie bump shoulders with him, laugh, and joke, trying to get him *not* to look like he was sitting there under duress. He leaned to speak into her ear, saying something that made her face crumple into a scowl just before she shook her head, then got up to make her way to the bar.

Per usual, Charlie was looking good as hell, in platform-heeled sandals, skinny jeans, and some kind of top that was silky, and soft, and showed a lot of cleavage. So... perfect. When she reached the bar, she made sure to skip a seat between us before she sat down and ordered herself a drink.

"Trouble in paradise?" I asked, earning myself a stern look as she accepted her cocktail, and downed it in one gulp.

I started to move to the seat beside her, but she shook her head, glancing back toward where Trent was still *sitting*, instead of, I don't know, *having a good time*. It didn't even seem like she was feeling him, and I wanted to ask, but I already knew what she was gonna say. *Nix... negro, mind your business.*

So I did.

About twenty minutes and two drinks later, I was glad I did, because apparently she and Trent had gotten past whatever issue they had, and were cuddled into a booth, with his hands all over her.

Shaking my head, I stood up from my seat at the bar, intending to head home. There was no point in sitting here watching Charlie get felt up. I really didn't even wanna be in the same room as that shit. It exponentially increased the likelihood that I might *actually* punch ole boy's lights out.

Before I could get out the door, I bumped into Roman.

"You heading out man?" He asked, extending his fist.

I returned his gesture as I nodded. "Yeah, man. Gotta go sleep off this liquor, then start looking over the books for this quarter. Gotta stay on top of it."

Sucking air between his teeth, Roman shook his head. "Who you telling, bruh? I'm gonna be on the same thing here soon. Hey, I'm gonna hit you up at some point this week to talk about those renovations man. We've gotta get the rest of the block on board so we can get this done before something stupid happens."

"I'm ready when you are, Rome. It's these other knuckleheads..."

"I know. We'll work it out though. I'll catch you later man."

"Aiight. See you."

Urban Grind was right next to Pot Liquor, so it took me no time to get to my apartment over the restaurant. Even once I'd showered and climbed into bed, I still couldn't sleep. I'd invested a good amount into soundproofing so I wouldn't be bothered by noise pollution, but the dull, thumping beat from UG — which didn't usually trouble me — made relaxation impossible tonight.

Or maybe it was the image of Trent with a handful of Charlie's ass playing in my head.

In any case, sleep eluded me, so I threw on some clothes and headed downstairs, using my private entrance to get into the restaurant. In my office, I went to work, pulling up expense reports, invoices, and inventory, intending to spend an hour knocking out as much of our quarterly report as I could. This shit was guaranteed to make me want to close my eyes and pass out.

I was nearing the end of my hour when I heard something coming from the kitchen. I knew the doors were still locked tight from earlier, and I hadn't used the front entrance, so... what the hell? I got up from the desk and stepped out of the office, looking around to see where the noise was coming from.

If it was robbers, unless they were into commercial kitchen supplies, groceries, or dining chairs, there wasn't anything of value in Pot Liquor for them to steal. Vandals weren't usually a problem in the neighborhood, but they could certainly get their asses kicked toni—

"Charlie?"

As I turned the corner into the prep area, she looked up at me with red-rimmed eyes. She averted her gaze, then went back to her task of... chopping vegetables. I approached her slowly — because she was kinda obviously tipsy, with a big knife in her hand — placing a hand on her back as I moved to stand beside her. She'd put on a chef's coat over her clothes, and once I was at the counter with her, I realized that she was chopping ingredients for the veggie omelet I'd watched her make hundreds of times.

"Hungry?" I asked, turning opposite to her as I leaned against the metal counter, so I could see her face.

She nodded, but didn't look up. "And tired, and pissed, and... stupid."

I lifted an eyebrow, then reached forward to cup her chin, turning her to face me. "Explain."

Shaking her head, she pulled away from my hand and went back to cutting up peppers. "I... was watching Viv and Carter together tonight, and they were so happy and in love. And I was watching Roman and Simone together, and *they* were so happy and in love. And then I look at myself, and Trent is groping me, and I'm telling myself that it's fine, that I'm supposed to like it, because we're dating, and touching is *supposed* to happen, but I'd really rather just have a glass of water instead. You know? It's like... I don't understand why I can't have that too, you know? I mean... you and I had that for a while, and then we fucked it all up. And now I'm thirty-three years old, broke, with a "boyfriend" that annoys the shit out of me, and a failed marriage. To a criminal. I am *losing* at this whole "love" thing, I tell you. And now I'm old, and a failure, and getting fat, and I can't even seem to have a..."

Charlie tossed the knife down onto the cutting board as her

voice broke, and she stepped away from the counter. She tried, unsuccessfully to stem her tears with the backs of her hands. "I'm sorry," she said, sniffling as she finally looked my way again. "I'm a mess. Ranting, and crying... I probably look like a crazy person."

I chuckled, stepping away from the counter myself to wrap her into an embrace. "It's not the ranting and crying that makes you look crazy, baby. The tipsy, midnight vegetable chopping in heels does that."

She broke into laughter, snuggling her face into my chest as I pulled her tighter. I didn't care that she was getting my shirt all snotty.

"Hey," I said, drawing back so I could see her face. She looked up at me with glossy eyes... *fucking gorgeous*, even when she was crying. "You're not stupid. And you're not a failure. And you're not old. And you're for *damn* sure not fat. Stop beating yourself up like this. Maybe your life isn't the way you want it right now, but so what? That doesn't mean it never will be. I mean... *my* life isn't the way I want it, but you don't see me crying about it."

Charlie scoffed, her eyebrows lifted in disbelief as she gently pushed her way out of my arms. "Oh, please Nix. You're a *man* who's attractive, successful, and single."

"I could say the same for you, attractive, successful single woman."

"It's not the same."

"How so?"

She sighed, crossing her arms over her chest. "Nobody really expects *you* to be settled by now. You have a good seven years, until you're forty. *Then* people start looking at you sideways. You're not...missing anything, I am."

"Who says I'm not missing anything?"

Sucking her teeth, Charlie gave me a derisive grin. "Oh *please*. Tell me Nix, what are you missing?"

"You."

Her eyes went wide, lips parted as I held her gaze. She just... stayed there, as if she was stuck, until her chest heaved a little and a fresh round of tears filled her eyes. Finally, she tore her gaze away, not turning her face, but shifting her eyes, with a suddenly renewed interest in the chopped vegetables on the table.

"Yeah right."

My eyebrows shot up. Had I heard that correctly? Was she *still* doubting that?

"*Yeah*," I said, taking a step toward her. "*Right*."

She backed away from me until she couldn't anymore, held in place by the cold metal edge of the counter. "Charlie... you say that you want the kind of love you see in Viv and Carter, in Roman and Simone... baby, it's right in front of you." She started to shake her head, but I held up a hand. "I know. I *know*. I fucked up back then. *I know*. But I'm telling you... I learned so much from that mistake. *Those* mistakes. You meant *everything* to me, and you... *still*. You still do."

I leaned down to rest my forehead against hers as a few tears escaped her eyes. She met my gaze again, with a somber smile. "Nix... you've been drinking."

"So? I'm not drunk. Well... I'm maybe a *little* drunk."

"Me too," she giggled, finally breaking into a smile.

I raised my hands to wipe her tears away with my thumbs. "I want you *so* badly right now."

She bit her lip, flicking her eyes away again for a second before she brought them back. "Me too."

So I kissed her.

She responded immediately, wrapping her arms around my neck as I pulled her closer, tasting and savoring the sweetness of her lips. She parted them, inviting me to explore her further, to deepen the kiss, to lose myself right there, letting her essence cloud my senses.

But I wasn't lost.

I was right there in the moment with her, nourishing myself with her energy. A week had passed since that kiss in her apartment, and I felt like I'd been starving since then, just waiting for another chance to indulge in her.

One by one, I undid the buttons of her chef coat, then slipped my hands inside and under her blouse. I groaned against her mouth, deepening the kiss as the feeling of her warm, soft skin made my appetite for her even worse. She whimpered as my fingers skimmed the soft lace of her bra, and that sexy little sound was my tipping point. I pulled away, and looked her right in the eyes.

"Come upstairs with me."

She swallowed hard, looking slightly dazed as she considered my request.

Don't say no. Don't say no. Don't say no.

"... Yes."

***

CHARLIE HAD ON TOO MANY CLOTHES.

That was my first thought, once I got her beyond the door to the apartment, and into the bedroom. I had pulled her in there with me, dimming the lights and putting something slow and sexy on in the background before I sat down on the edge of the bed, motioning for her to stand between my legs. She kicked off her shoes, slowly stripped out of her clothes while I watched, and stayed where she was, not saying anything, but still somehow begging to be touched.

But I didn't.

I *wouldn't*, not until I'd studied every inch of her magnificently curvy body in the lowered light, taking my visual fill before I ventured toward a psychical touch.

"Nixon..." she whispered, biting her lip as she shifted on her feet. "What are you doing?"

Meeting her eyes, I noticed that they were glossy again, like she was just on the verge of tears. "I'm just... *looking* at you."

"Why?"

"Because you're beautiful. Because you're sexy."

"... Oh."

I smiled. This was the Charlie I remembered. Full of confidence, but so devoid of conceit that she forgot the affect she could have on a man. Especially like this, bare faced, natural curls, stripped down to nothing... exquisitely sensual, without even *trying*.

"Come here."

This time, she obliged, but she did it unhurriedly, taking her sweet, sexy time to come to me. When she stepped between my legs, I moved my hands, running them up the backs of her thighs to reach her ass. I squeezed her there, then continued my exploration, skimming my fingers over the soft, flat plane of her stomach, then ran my thumbs underneath her breasts.

She lowered her mouth, and I gave her what she wanted, fingering the soft curls at the nape of her neck while I kissed her — a slow, hungry kiss, full of the passion I'd been saving up for five long years. The kind of kiss I could only give *her*.

I looked up at her, observing the expression on her face as she watched my fingers trace her areolas, noting her sharp intake of breath as she waited for me to touch her pretty, dark-copper nipples.

She whimpered as I tipped my head forward, pressing soft kisses under her breasts, on them, beside them, between them, everywhere except those hardened peaks as they strained and hardened, begging for attention. She cupped the back of my head, trying to guide me where she wanted me, and letting out a frustrated groan when I wouldn't let her have control.

"Nix, *please*," she said, a breathless plea that I couldn't have ignored if I wanted to.

The gasp she let out when my tongue touched the outside edge of her nipple sent a fresh wave of blood rocketing to my groin, making me harder than I already was. She pressed herself forward as I covered the peak with my mouth, lapping it with my tongue before I focused my attention on the other side.

"Like this?" I asked, even though I already knew the answer before giving her a gentle suck. "Or like *this*?" That time, I sucked harder, and she crawled into my lap, pressing her hands against my head to keep me in place.

Guess that's my answer.

So I did *that* again, moving back and forth, until the soft, sexy sounds she was making weren't enough. I needed *more*.

I cupped the nape of her neck, pulling her down into a kiss as I slipped my hand between her legs. As soon as my fingers made contact with her slickened flesh, I groaned into her ear. "Why are you so perfect?" I asked, sliding and exploring her as I gently tugged her earlobe between my teeth. "Always *so* fucking wet."

Her only response was a moan of pleasure as I pushed inside of her, using my thumb to tease her clit as I plunged further, searching for a spot that I remembered well. She arched her back, rolling and moving her hips, lips parted in a soundless cry of bliss as I found the spot and concentrated there. I teased and massaged, pushing her further and further toward the edge until her body tensed, and she buried her face in my neck as she came.

We stayed like that for a few moments, until the decline in her heart rate told me she'd caught her breath. I pulled my hand from between her legs, taking a moment to lick her honeyed juices from my fingers, which she watched through sex-heavied eyelids.

"Still as sweet as I remember," I told her, just before I kissed her again, then flipped her on her back and spread her legs.

Have mercy.

Seeing her like this, wet, and ready, with her already kiss-swollen lips begging to be kissed again, was a picture so erotic I had to close my eyes for a second and pull myself together. I toed off my shoes and socks, pulled my tee shirt over my head, and yanked off my sweats and boxers in one swipe. Moving her up, I positioned myself between her legs, then leaned in to take her mouth again.

We were long past the exploratory kisses of new lovers. Now, it was about fulfilling a need, and I needed Charlie like I needed water and air. The next few kisses were wild, ravenous, clumsy ones, before I moved away to place those same kinds of kisses on her neck.

I plunged my fingers into her again, stroking her until her legs began to tremble before I lowered my head between her supple thighs. I inhaled deep, breathing in the intoxicatingly sweet scent of her sex, then finally covered her with my mouth.

Charlie's hands slipped over my head, dragging handfuls of my hair between her fingers and I kissed and licked her lips down there, flicking my tongue over the sensitive flesh of her clit before I gently pulled it into my mouth. I stayed down there, with her thighs locked around my neck, until I got my wish of her squirming, screaming my name, and coming hard as her body quaked, covering my face in what I referred to affectionately as her icing.

"Nix," she said, pushing out my name in a shaky breath.

"Yeah baby?" I asked, positioning myself over her.

"*Now.*"

Who was I to argue with that?

I buried myself inside of her, releasing a harsh groan as she surrounded me in wetness and warmth. I gripped her thighs, pulling her closer so I could plunge deeper as she pushed her hips upward, meeting my strokes with eager movements of her own.

Goddamn.

This was... heaven.

This was *home.*

It was almost... surreal, having her here with me again, when the last night we'd spent here together was five years ago. But she was back.

Like the songs — and the old folks said — I loved her, so I let her go, and she was *back.*

She pulsed around me, getting hotter and wetter with every stroke, every kiss on her neck, every caress of her breasts, every grope of her ass. Her whimpers, moans, coos, and purrs made me drive deeper, and harder, letting her know that she was *mine*, and this time, I wasn't letting her go.

Cause *she came back.*

Myth or not, I was holding on to that as my sign that it was meant to be.

I lowered my mouth to her neck as she hooked her legs around my back, kissing, licking, and then finally sucking the spot that I knew from experience would take her into an orgasm that was on a whole other, unearthly plane. She gasped, gripping my head to hold me there as her body began to shake.

"*Nix, Nix, Nix,*" she whimpered repeatedly, her mouth pressed against my ear. "I... I..." she pulled back, looking me right in the eyes as she tensed, "*I love you,*" she said, her voice raspy with pleasure as she came, squeezing her eyes tight as her body milked me into an explosion of my own.

We collapsed together, out of breath and out of energy. I

summoned just enough to pull her against my chest and cover us up, wrapping her in my arms before I lowered my mouth to her ear to tell her the words I'd been waiting five years to say again. Not just *I love you*, but...

"I love you too, Beautiful."

chapter
eleven

Charlie

MACARONI AND CHEESE.

I smiled a little as I traced the tiny, infinity shaped cheese just above Nixon's hip. It was in the same spot that the infinity-shaped macaroni shells were on me. That was a crazy, silly night. I couldn't even blame it on being drunk, but we were *certainly* high. Off each other, off love, off life...off the lease we'd signed earlier in the day, for the building that housed our baby.

We were two years into our relationship by then, and "mac & cheese forever" just... made perfect, stupid sense to us. We spent the year after that working and sleeping, getting the restaurant opened. The next two years were beautiful. Still a lot of working, but a little less sleep, so we could be sure to make time for each other.

The year after *that* was the one that broke us.

The memory made me pull my hand away from him.

I was laying here in Nix's bed reminiscing, as if last night hadn't been full of the exact mistakes I didn't want to make. As if I hadn't just burdened myself with a heap of new complications.

Like telling Nixon that I loved him.

It's not as if it wasn't true. I was past the point of denying those feelings, because truthfully, I don't know that I ever stopped. But what point did it serve for him to know such a thing when I had no plans of going back *there* with him again? *Ever.* At least not while I could remember what it felt like to pull that engagement ring off my finger and give it back.

I felt like shit.

Or maybe something worse than that.

Nixon was sleeping just like I remembered, sprawled out, lips parted, looking completely at peace. After the first time, we'd wordlessly made love again, then got in the shower and made love there too. I could only wonder at what was happening in his mid, but I was sure it was something like "mac + cheese, together again". And why *wouldn't* it be, after my dramatic-assed, breathless, mid-orgasm declaration of love?

He didn't respond immediately, and I almost hoped that I'd only said it in my head. I was aware, but still tipsy from overindulging at the bar in UG, so maybe it was just a trick of the mind. But then he spoke the words that I didn't know I wanted to hear until he said it.

"I love you too, Beautiful."

It wasn't as if it was breaking news. Even if I hadn't known it before last night, from the way he kissed me in the kitchen, to the way he easily slowed me down and took his time with me once we were in his apartment, he'd already communicated that sentiment before he said it. He was waiting on me to give him a green light, and in my alcohol soaked, emotionally fraught state, I'd given him exactly that, even though I was far from ready.

I wouldn't *ever* be ready, not for that.

I rolled over onto my other side, retrieving my phone from the bedside table. Turning it on, the first thing I saw was seven missed calls. Two from Viv, four from Trent, and one from Adrian. My text message inbox looked about the same.

"Cousin, you're worrying me. Let me know you're safe. – Viv"

I smiled at the screen, then responded. *"I'm okay... stayed with Nix. Talk about it later."*

"!!!!!!!! SERIOUSLY?! WHAT HAPPENED?!?!!!!! – Viv"

"Talk. About. It. Later."

"You're such a tease. Okay. – Viv."

"Oh, and Trent is looking for you. – Viv."

Rolling my eyes, I backed out of the message exchange with Viv, and tapped on Trent's name. I blew out a heavy sigh when I saw that he'd sent at least five texts in addition to the four missed phone calls.

"Charlie... You've been gone for almost twenty minutes. That's a mighty long trip to the bathroom. Are you okay? – Trent."

"Charlie, are you still in the coffee shop? I've been looking for you, and the woman I just asked says there's no one in the bathroom. – Trent."

"Okay, so I guess you left. If you're upset, fine, but you could have said that instead of leaving without saying anything. I'm going home. – Trent."

"Baby, I'm sorry about last night. I didn't mean to ruin your night with your friends. I was in the meeting from hell with Dionne before I stopped by, and seeing your ex all over you just put me in an ever worse mood. – Trent."

"Is this because of me touching you? Because you didn't seem to mind it from Nixon, so I don't get why it's a problem for me to touch you. We're dating. Touching happens. – Trent."

"Okay, I'm starting to get worried. Will you answer your door, please? I already know you've got your cousin covering for you, so... - Trent."

Ugh.

As if I wasn't already turned off enough about the "touching" he referred to, which was more like trying to make a soft porn in the middle of a crowded coffee shop, this long string of text messages, none of which I answered — or *planned* to answer — made his attractiveness plummet. If I wanted to deal with *this* kind of emotional reaction, I would get a damned girlfriend.

I backed out of the text messages, and cleared all of the notifications. I pushed the phone back onto the bedside table and closed my eyes, suddenly feeling tired.

Trent, Nixon, Adrian. Nixon, Adrian, Trent. Adrian, Trent, Nixon.

Shit.

This entire mess was honestly more than I felt like dealing with, especially when the only one of these men I felt an emotional attachment to was Nixon. I found my mind drifting into memories of the night before, hearing him tell me that the loved I wanted was right in front of me waiting. Wishing that I could fully believe that was true. Wondering if I could ever forget he'd looked me right in the face and told me he loved me, then slipped a ring — *the* ring I'd been yearning to receive — on my finger, knowing what he'd done. *Knowing* that it would hurt me.

Last night I didn't care.

I was feeling the full weight of all the bullshit from Adrian, the emptiness of my life, the loneliness of my heart, and Nixon kissed me and took all of that away. I just wanted to escape, even if it was in the arms of the one person who'd scarred me more than anyone else.

Because if nothing else, I knew he loved me. Only problem was, I loved him too, and... what would he be expecting, now that I'd said it?

Macaroni and cheese, probably.

My eyelids grew even heavier, and I reached for my phone again to check the time. It was only three in the morning, simultaneously too late and too early to continue letting this plague my mind. I let my eyes close again, and drifted to sleep.

***

I WOKE UP TO KISSES ON MY NECK.

At first, they were soft, sweet pecks, delivered between quiet requests of *wake up, Beautiful.* I said nothing, and kept my eyes closed, but as soon as I *was* awake, they turned into something else. Wet, erotic, open-mouthed kisses, punctuated with a bite here, a suck there, and an occasional lick were Nixon's way of marking me as his.

As if I'd ever belonged to anybody else.

He was behind me, with his arm tight around my waist and his erection hard against my back as he moved his tongue in slow, lazy circles at the top of my spine. I bit my lip, trying to suppress a moan.

We shouldn't be doing this. Not again.

But then his hand moved to cup my breast, and both nipples peaked in response to his touch, and it felt so good that I didn't want him to stop. His fingers were gentle, hot, and well-practiced, and his attention set off a throbbing at my core that overpowered common sense. He kissed his way across my shoulder, then back to my spine, then around to my neck as his fingers left my breasts to make the slow journey down my stomach, past my bellybutton, between my thighs.

"*Nix, wait...*"

My heart was racing, and my eyes welled with tears as he moved away from me, but a moment later he was balanced over me, his eyes filled with resignation.

He already knew what I was going to say.

"I'm sorry," I choked out, running my fingers through the thick, soft hairs of his beard as I reached up to cup his face.

Nixon shook his head. "Don't be. I get it." He gave me a little smile that was more sad than anything, but he flashed those dimples at me anyway. Then he lowered his forehead to touch mine, and before I could say or think anything, he was kissing me.

And I was kissing him back.

Now that I was sober, I could think clearly enough to know that this was a bad idea, but my body and my heart didn't seem to give a shit about that. Five years of suppressed desire, and passion, and *love* for him broke free, and I threw my arms around his neck and pulled him close.

He was heavy, but it felt good, having nothing between us as we kissed. Just his skin against mine, his hardness pressed against my stomach, our legs tangled together as teeth clicked, tongues mated, lips crashed in a kiss that was all hunger, no restraint.

Finally, when we were out of breath, he pulled back, and moved away from me. I felt a sob building in my throat as he backed off the bed. The simultaneous anguish and adoration in his

eyes was more than I could take, and I suddenly couldn't understand or justify hurting him like this.

"Nixon, I—"

"Shh."

I shivered as he placed his hand on the back of my calf, then
raised my leg, bringing my foot up to his mouth. One by one, he
kissed my toes, then the bottom of my foot, then the top. A shud-
dering breath left my chest as he kissed his way from my ankle to
my knee, then repeated the same tease on the other leg. When he
gently nudged my knee, a directive for me to open my thighs, there
was no hesitation. I spread them eagerly, trembling with anticipa-
tion, and he licked, kissed, and sucked a path all the way up to the
apex of my thighs.

He kissed me there, with the same quiver-inducing passion,
hunger, and intensity that he'd kissed my lips. He pushed his
fingers inside to stroke me while he covered me with his mouth,
flicking his tongue, and sucking, and nibbling, and licking, until
a pleasant buzz of static began to fill my ears. He dipped his
tongue inside me, moving in conjunction with his fingers for a
moment until he dragged it slowly upward to cover me, igniting
tingles of electricity all over my skin as he went. With one hand,
he stroked me, while the other hand lovingly groped and kneaded
my ass.

I had his head cupped in my hands, keeping them there while I
shameless rocked my hips upward against his face, keeping the
rhythm he'd set as I rode his fingers.

"*Nix*," I moaned, threading my fingers through his hair.
"*You're.... you're... oh my God...*"

"Is this good for you?" He stopped devouring me just long
enough to ask, then his mouth was on me again, hot, and wet, and
hell yes, good.

"*Y-yeah,*" I managed to breathe, biting my lip as he plunged his
fingers further.

"What about that?"

"*Yes.*"

He pulled back a little, moving his tongue in deliberately slow
circles and zigzags, sending my already stimulated flesh into such a

frenzy that I propped myself on my elbows, panting as I watched. "That feels good?"

"*Yes.*"

A little smile spread over his face, and then he plunged his fingers deep as he covered my clit with his mouth and sucked hard, lapping the sensitive nub with his tongue. I... saw stars. A sound I didn't even know I could make escaped my throat as my whole body tensed, and held, and then *released*. A feeling of unadulterated bliss swept over me as time slowed down, rippling around me as I rode the prolonged wave of ecstasy. My ears were still ringing by the time I felt in control of my body, and when I opened my eyes, Nixon was looking at me, with something like amazement in his gaze.

"I take it you liked that?" he asked, in a low voice that sent shivers up my spine. Still panting, I nodded, but Nixon shook his head. "Speak up for me baby, I wanna hear you. Did. You. Like. That?"

My chest began to heave, and I swallowed hard, wetting my suddenly dry throat so I could answer. "Yes."

"Yes?"

"Yes."

"Good."

Nixon sat up on his knees, catching me by the ankles and opening me wide to prop my legs on his shoulders. He looked me right in the eyes, watching my reaction as he entered me, slowly, pushing deeper until he was as far as the position allowed.

And then he started to move.

A slow, steady, *deep* stroke that made me bite my lip as he pushed in, and exhale as he pushed out. He felt *incredible*, thick, and wide, and heavy inside me, pulling whimpers, coos, and moans from my throat as he worked. One hand teased my nipples, while he brought the other up to push the fingers that had been inside me into my mouth.

"See how good you taste, baby?"

He smiled when I licked them clean, then teasingly sucked and licked as if it were *him* in my mouth. A moment later, he moved my legs from his shoulders, draping them around his waist so we could be closer. I cupped his face in my hands as he pushed harder, and *hell yes*, faster, in breathtaking, intoxicatingly deep strokes that made my heart flutter.

"You feel... fucking *amazing*," he growled into my ear, hooking his arm under my knee so he could push even deeper. "Is this good for you?"

"Yes," I moaned, digging my nails into his back as pressure began to mount at my core.

He pressed his mouth to my neck, pounding faster. "What about now?"

"*Hell yes.*"

"Tell me again."

"*Hell yes.*"

Nixon sat up, grabbing my ankles and pushing them up by my ears as he buried himself in me over and over, skin slapping skin, both of us sweating, and cursing, and praising the lord, and rocketing closer and closer to release.

"*Nixon,*" I whimpered, dragging my hands down to grip his ass. "*Please* don't stop."

"Don't stop?"

"*Please.*"

He chuckled, then groaned a little as I rocked my hips into his. "Don't stop until when?"

"*Never.*"

"Never?"

"*Never.* Don't. *Ever.* Stop," I breathed, looking up to meet his eyes.

Smiling, he lowered his mouth to mine, sucking my bottom lip between his. "Whatever you want, baby."

For some reason, that made me wetter, and somehow he slipped deeper, making me cry out in pleasure.

"Goddamnit Nix," I said through clenched teeth, grinding my head into the bed as my legs began to jerk and tremble. I repeated his name as pressure built, and it seemed to spur him on.

"Whose pussy is this?" he asked, looking me right in the eyes as he kept stroking, not breaking rhythm, just pushing me closer, and closer, and...

"It's yours."

"Tell me again."

"*It's yours.*"

And then I was falling, falling, falling into an orgasm so intense that I lurched away from the bed, wrapping my arms around Nix's neck as I came. He freed my legs, but kept pounding until he came with a guttural groan in my ear, while I still pulsed around him.

It took a minute for me to see straight or feel anything, and when I became fully aware again, Nix still had me wrapped in his arms. We were sitting up now, somehow, with me in his lap, still full of him as I relaxed into his embrace. I don't know how long we stayed like that, but the light in the room changed from dusky to bright before he finally let me go, and pulled back to see my face.

I didn't feel like it was fair to him, for me to shed the tears when I was the one rejecting his offer. Still, I couldn't help the tears that escaped, dripping onto my cheeks before he reached up to wipe them away.

"Don't," he murmured, cupping my chin in his hands. "This... this is my own doing. I fucked up... I know." He gave me a wry smile, then wiped away a fresh wave of tears as they trickled down my face. "I just wish you could forgive me."

I licked my lips, sniffling before I looked up to meet his gaze. "So do I."

***

THANK GOD FOR BREAK ROOM LOCKERS.

I'd just finished using Nixon's bathroom to take a shower, and when I stepped out, there was a change of clothes waiting for me. He'd gone downstairs to retrieve one of the several sets I kept in my locker — never knew what might happen in the kitchen — and I was grateful that my exit from his apartment didn't have to be a walk of shame in my partying clothes from the night before.

I dressed quickly, not wanting to prolong the awkwardness of me being there, knowing that both of our emotions were raw. When I exited the bathroom, Nix was standing at the window, holding a cup of coffee in his hands as he stared out over the street.

This was a ritual of his, a moment of quiet reflection while he finished his first morning dose of caffeine. He hadn't dressed yet, but had put on boxers, and the picture he made, a picture I'd woken up to many, *many* mornings was easily a photographer's dream.

As if he felt my eyes on him, he inclined his head, glancing over his shoulder. When he saw me standing there, he turned around, and the set of his jaw told me something had shifted.

"You want some coffee?" he asked casually, contradicting the tension in his shoulders and frustration in his eyes.

I shook my head, then headed for the bedside table to retrieve my purse and phone.

"Trent called."

My hands stilled a few inches over the phone, and my heart slammed to the front of my chest. "Nixon, you—"

"Don't worry. I didn't answer it. It started ringing, I glanced at the screen and saw his name. That's all."

Relief swept over me. The *last* thing I needed, on top of everything, was the reoccurrence a high school feud. "Thanks for letting me know."

"You're welcome," Nixon said, putting his coffee down on the desk as he ambled toward me. "So I guess you're gonna run back to him now?"

I lifted an eyebrow as I pushed my phone into my purse and closed it. "Is that a problem?"

"Charlie..." Nix paused, chuckling as he crossed his arms over his chest. "Yeah, Charlie. It's a fucking problem."

"And why is that?"

"Because you said you loved *me*. I'm supposed to be okay with *that* muthafucka getting to have you, after what happened between us last night and this morning?"

"You said you understood," I said, struggling to keep my voice from creeping into a scream. "Not even two hours ago, you told me you "got" it!"

"Well I *lied*, okay? Because no, I *don't* get why you can entertain ole boy who you don't even really give a shit about, while I'm right fucking here, trying to love you, and you reject it! No, Charlie, I don't understand that."

I shook my head, breathing out a heavy sigh. "Am I in the goddamned twilight zone right now? You don't understand why I'm not falling all over myself to be back with you?"

"*No*, that's not what I'm saying. I don't understand why you won't even give me another freaking *chance*. How long am I gonna have to atone for that one mistake?"

"I'm not asking you to "atone" for *anything*, Nixon. I am well within my rights to choose what I will and won't accept, and I decided not to accept the bullshit that *you* did — *not me*."

He scoffed, tilting his head back toward the ceiling as he laughed. "So you were little miss perfect in the situation, huh Charlie? Your actions didn't set anything in motion? The bullshit *you* did had nothing to do with any of it?"

"Don't you *fucking dare*." Before I could think twice about it, I was in Nixon's face, nostrils flared, face pulled into a scowl that probably matched his. "Yeah, Nixon. Okay. I shouldn't have pushed you. Shouldn't have made you choose. Okay, I'll accept that. But what you *won't goddamned do*, is act like I made your grown ass do *anything*. We could have recovered from *my* bullshit. *Did* recover from it, remember? So while you're passing out blame, trying to act like I'm not justified in my unwillingness to jump back into your arms... remember that *you're* the reason we aren't together in the first place."

I didn't wait for a response.

Didn't *need* his response.

I snatched my arm away when he tried to get me to wait, ignored his frustrated pleas to "talk about it". There was nothing else to say, as far as I was concerned.

I slammed my way out of his apartment and out the front door of the restaurant, not bothering to lock it when I saw Jordan and Amina walking together, heading up the street toward me. I managed a quick smile and a head nod, then hurried past them, only making it to Viv's shop, before tears started flowing down my face. I knocked on the locked front door, then paced in front of it, hoping that she was there. My knees went weak with relief when I saw her face peek through the window, then crease with alarm when she saw my emotional state.

She hurriedly unlocked the doors, then ushered me inside where she pulled me into a hug. "Charlie, tell me what is wrong!"

"*Everything*," I sobbed, sniffling as I scrubbed a hand over my face. "Everything is just....all screwed up."

chapter
twelve

Nixon

back in the day...

"I'M... SORRY. CAN YOU SAY THAT AGAIN?"

Charlie didn't look up from her plate. Instead, she remained focused on sliding her fork around, making patterns in the marinara sauce left from dinner.

"You heard what I said, Nix. I think we should get married, or consider the possibility that maybe this just isn't working anymore. I mean... it's been six years."

I lifted an eyebrow. "And? I love you. You love me. We're together. We have the restaurant. Everything is good, so what's the problem?"

"The problem is that I want more," she said, finally looking up. "I think over the years I've proven myself to be a more than worthy spouse. I work, I cook, I clean, I keep my appearance in order, we have plenty of sex, I've never embarrassed you, I—"

I tuned that shit out. Why was she sitting here listing her qualities like she had to sell herself to me? Like I wasn't already wrapped tight around her little finger? Like I wouldn't do damn near anything for her.

Except... that.

Yeah. I shook my head. Except that.

I couldn't understand why she was stuck on this whole "let's get *married" thing, as if it were anything more than a piece of paper. I was* here *with her, I was committed. Everything I did, every decision that I made, was done with* her *in mind. Because I wasn't interested in anything involving rings, she wanted to "consider the possibility that it wasn't working anymore?"*

What the hell?

"Nixon, are you even listening right now?"

"No."

Charlie sighed, tossing her fork onto her plate with a clatter as she sat back, folding her arms. "So this is funny to you? Or does it just not matter at all?"

"Both." I propped my elbows on the table, chin resting on my hands as I looked at her. "Ever since we lost the—"

"Don't," she muttered through clenched teeth, a flash of hurt and anger crossing her face as she sat forward. "Don't you talk about that."

"You never *wanna talk about it, Charlie. As if* that *didn't matter. As if our* ba*—"*

"Nix, please." Her voice shook when she said that, as if she were barely holding herself together, and I knew tears would come soon. Her eyes were already glossy.

I raised my hands in concession. "Fine. Since that *happened, you've been on me about a ring, as if it's gonna bring about some magical change. It's* not. *It's gonna bring about* bullshit."

And that *I knew for a fact, after growing up in the constant warzone of my parent's home. They were living together, but not married when they had me, and didn't take vows until I was sixteen years old. Once they did, it was like somebody flipped the switch that would set off a nuclear bomb of fights, and arguing, and cursing, and yelling, and name calling in our household. My mother was hyper-conscious of fighting in front of me — as if I couldn't hear it through the wall — and wouldn't speak about it. Everything I heard from my dad was* son, don't ever do this to yourself or the woman you love. Don't fall for this bullshit.

As soon as I turned eighteen and graduated high school, I got the hell out of there, and they finally divorced shortly after. They got along reasonably well now, but for me, I saw *the clear dividing line.*

Happy cohabitation = peace. Marriage = war. Why the hell would I blow up the beautiful *relationship Charlie and I had, just for the sake of having another official document to stuff in a safe and forget about?*

"Your parents' marriage doesn't have to be ours. We have a chance to create a new *legacy here, don't you see that?"*

"The only thing I see is you trying to force an issue that I don't want to talk about."

"If you loved me like you claim to, you would consider it."

A heavy sense of coldness settled over my chest as I tilted my head to the side. "If?"

"Yes, if." She nodded. "I don't see how you can claim to love me, but not even consider marriage as an option after I've given you six years of my life."

"So this is what you're hinging it on? "If" I loved you, I would marry you, never mind that I fucking live *for you, Charlie?"*

She dropped her eyes, and her shoulders sagged as she brought her gaze back up to meet mine. "It's important to me, Nix. I'm telling you, this *is important to me. If you* live *for me, like you say... why won't you marry me?"*

"Because I don't think it's worth it."

"So you don't think I'm *worth it."*

I shook my head, pulling my face into a frown. "That's not what I said, Charlie. Don't twist my words. I love you, but... we're not getting married. That's it."

"That's it?"

"That's it." I picked up my fork and started eating again, but the pasta felt plastic, tasteless now.

"No."

When I looked up at Charlie, she had her hands pulled into fists, nostrils flared, and those tears I'd expected were now dripping from her eyes.

"We will *get married," she said, her voice choked. "We'll talk to somebody, work out your issues so we can move forward, but I won't continue like this, Nix. We're getting married."*

I threw my head back and laughed. "The hell *we are, Charlie.*

I'm a grown goddamned man, you're not *gonna tell me what I will and won't do."*

"You're gonna be a grown goddamned single *man if we don't do this."*

"So what exactly are you saying?"

"I'm saying that we can get married, or we can move on, Nixon. Those are the options. Again... it's been six years. I'm not going to keep waiting while you do everything except *what I'm telling you is important to me."*

Lifting my shoulders, I sat back in my seat. "I'm guessing that my *feelings about marriage are invalid then?"*

"Not invalid, but certainly misguided. You can't look at your parent's marriage and extrapolate it to the entire institution!"

"Okay, but what about the other hundreds of thousands of failed marriages? Are we gonna ignore that?"

"Or, we can look at the hundreds of thousands that didn't *fail. Stop deflecting, Nix. You can come up with all the excuses you want, but when it comes down to it... you're either in or you're out."*

I just stared at her, amazed that she was actually making me choose between two options that both *meant the end of the relationship to me. Get married, and watch our relationship slowly decline to the point that we hated each other, and couldn't wait to be apart, or... end it now, and save ourselves the trouble.*

Pushing my chair back from the table, I stood to take my plate to the kitchen, then grabbed my phone, wallet, and keys. With one hand on the front door, I turned to look at the woman I loved more than anything in this world.

"I guess... we can talk later about which one of us is gonna move out."

And then I was gone, leaving her there at the table with tears dripping into her plate.

I ended up at a bar, an hour away from my neighborhood because I was looking for my dad. Somebody *who would understand where I was coming from.*

I ended up with a first, then second, then third drink in my hand because he wasn't there, and I was looking for relief. Something *that would numb the pain of knowing that after working as hard as I could for six damned years to make Charlie happy, just being together, living together, loving together wasn't enough.*

I turned down the first two girls, but I was four drinks in by the time the third came along. I ended up in her bed, because I was looking for an outlet... and acceptance. Somewhere *to go where I didn't have to think about what a breakup meant for our future. For the business, home, and life we'd built together. But what did it matter anyway? The relationship was over... six years down the drain, because everything I did wasn't enough.*

I wasn't enough for her.

***

"Nixon?"

I nearly jumped out of my skin at the feeling of Charlie's hand on my shoulder.

I'd been relaxing, with the big window open in the bedroom and a chair pulled up to it, breathing in the air and light and energy of the city. More accurately, I was trying *to relax.*

Three days had passed since my breakup with Charlie, and I hadn't seen her since then. She was still on medical leave, so I was handling all of the restaurant shifts, but she hadn't been home to our apartment either. At least not while I *was there. It only took a little asking around to know that she was staying with her mother.*

"You scared the shit out me," *I said, sitting up from my inclined position so that I could stand up.*

She gave me a little smile. "Sorry. You had the..." *she pointed to my head, and I remembered just then that I was wearing headphones.*

With a dry laugh, I pulled them off and tossed them onto the chair along with my phone, then pushed my hands into my pockets. "So... What's up? How have you been?"

"I..." *she shook her head, and when she turned her gaze back to me, her eyes were glossy with tears — a look that had become painfully familiar over the last few months. "Not good."*

"What's wrong?"

Charlie scoffed, then shot me another one of those half-smiles. "Do you really have to ask, Nix?"

I didn't. It was all over her face, in her puffy eyes, and conspicuously missing glow. She missed us *just as much as I did.*

"I don't want us to break up because of this, Nix," she said, meeting my gaze. "Marriage or not, I... I don't wanna be without you. I'm sorry for making you choose, but—" Her voice broke, and I wrapped her in my arms, pulling her against my chest. I had to, couldn't just stand there watching her break down and not doing anything. She sniffled against my chest. "After we lost the baby, when I was so far along, it's like... we were so close. *So close to having our little boy, just three more months, and then he was just* gone. *And I started thinking about how you and I have come* so far. *I was scared that if we waited any more, if we didn't go on and do it... you would be gone too."*

I squeezed her tighter, burying my face in her curls so I could kiss the top of her head, and then I pulled back, tipping up her chin so I could look her in the eyes. "Charlie... I wasn't going anywhere. I'm not *going anywhere."*

"How was I supposed to know that?"

"Because you know me. You know I would do anything for you."

She chuckled a little, then shook her head. "Except marry me."

I gave a heavy sigh, then pulled away completely, walking over to the closet. I opened it and stepped in, rummaging through boxes until I found what I was looking for, then came to stand in front of her again.

I put the tiny black box in her hands, then opened it for her to see princess cut diamond solitaire inside. She gazed at the ring for a moment, then looked up at me, confused.

"I bought this ring almost a year ago, a few months before you got pregnant. I've ... struggled over it. I knew you wanted to get married, Charlie, and I wanted to give that to you, but you've gotta understand... I've seen plenty of great relationships, but I've never seen a happy marriage. Even so... if this ring is what you need in

order for there to be no doubt in your mind that I love, and cherish, and adore you, baby... I will get married today."

Charlie covered her mouth with her hand, attempting to choke back a sob. It took her a moment to collect herself, but then she shook her head. *"I get it, Nix. You don't have to do this."*

"Yes I do," I said. *"I do. You're worth it. So... are you gonna marry me or not, woman? Don't just stand there and cry."*

She laughed, then looked down at the ring again and slowly nodded. *"Yeah. I will."*

Charlie sobbed and sniffled while I pushed the ring on her finger, then threw her arms around my neck and kissed me, slow and deep. *"If I wasn't still in recovery, Mr. Graham, I would be all over you right now."*

I chuckled. *"Post break-up slash engagement sex?"*

"Post break up? Those couple of miserable days? That wasn't a breakup, more like a... commercial interruption. We just... had a fight. Said some stupid things. And now... we're back. And I love you. And it's not because I'm finally wearing a ring... but because you wanted to give it to me."

I ignored the uneasy feeling in the pit of my stomach as I smiled. *"I love you. I'm scared as hell, but I love you."*

Charlie kissed me again, then gave me a tearful grin. *"Perhaps a long engagement, to help ease your fears?"*

"How long?"

"As long as you want."

"Maybe.... Forever?"

"Nixon!"

"What? You said as long as I want!"

***

I couldn't do this.

Every time I saw her glance down at her ring, then glance up at me and smile, it drove the knife of guilt even deeper.

But she was so damned happy.

I tried to tell myself that I would only be appeasing my own guilt by telling her I'd slept with someone else that night. Tried to convince myself that it was because I was drunk, and emotional, and stupid, so it didn't really matter. Tried to tell myself that we were broken up, so it wasn't really cheating. But I knew Charlie didn't see it like that. It was a cop out. What was the point of doing this marriage thing, even trying, if I was going to let it start with a secret?

A week hadn't even passed since I'd given her the ring. For Charlie, everything seemed new, and fresh, and happy, and wonderful again, in a way it hadn't since before the horrible appointment where we found out the baby had passed. God knows I really didn't want to tell her this, but I also didn't want it as a burden going into a marriage.

"Charlie..."

I found her in the test area of the kitchen at Pot Liquor, developing a new recipe, cooking with her ring on, which was a hazard. She knew it, and still wouldn't take that damned ring off.

"Yeah baby? What's up?"

She turned to me with a smile, spatula in hand.

"Turn the stove off, Beautiful."

She lifted an eyebrow, but must have noted the gravity in my expression, because she did exactly that, pulling a skillet full of caramelizing onions from the heat and placing it on the counter.

I took a deep breath, and then I told her. About looking for dad, about getting drunk... and then about going home with another woman.

The look on her face shifted slowly, from concern, to confusion, and finally, to anger.

"Nixon," she said, her voice dangerously low. She took a deep breath, then ran her tongue over her lips. "Are you telling me that while I was at our apartment... crying my eyes out over you, and our baby, and our love... you were out fucking somebody?"

"Baby—"

"Don't you baby me!" Her bottom lip trembled as she backed into the counter, shaking her head. "I really... I can't believe you, Nix. The same night. Already?"

"It wasn't like that, I wasn't — "

"You weren't what, Nix? Thinking? No. You couldn't have been."

She looked away from me, and the ring caught her attention. When she looked at me again, there was cold anger in her eyes.

"Is that why you gave me this?" she asked, holding up her hand. "What, you thought giving me the ring was gonna make me accept this bullshit. You thought this ring would give you a pass for cheating on me? Fuck you, Nixon."

I didn't see her grab it, but the next thing I knew, that hot skillet was coming my way, bottom first, and I threw my arm up to deflect it. It hit my forearm, then clattered to the ground, and the next second Charlie was wrenching the ring from her finger. She threw that too, then shoved past me to leave.

Grabbing her arm, I pulled her around to face me.

"Charlie, no. I gave you that ring because I love you. I know I fucked up, but I'm not trying to bury it. I'm standing here owning up to my mistake, so that we can have a successful marriage. When I went to that bar, it was with the impression that we were done. It wouldn't have happened otherwise."

"Justify it however you want, Nix. The fact remains that a few hours after an argument, without even talking to me, you were screwing someone else. All these ways you claim to love me, yet you couldn't keep your dick in your pants. I practically had to beg to get you to marry me. But you love me." She laughed, then yanked her way out my hold. "Imagine that."

What else could I say, if she was already convinced? I let her go, saying nothing else as she stomped her way out of the kitchen... and out of my life.

— present —

"You know Charlie called to wish me a happy birthday this morning?"

I gave my mother a sober smile as she sat back, taking a sip from her mimosa. "Is that right?"

She nodded. "Mmhmm. Every year, she calls, even though I'm just her *almost* mama in law. Such a sweet girl."

I snorted, then stuffed my mouth full of bacon.

Every year, on her birthday, I made the two hour drive to the coast, where my mother lived, to take her to brunch. She often told me it was her favorite part of the day, even though I'm sure whatever lavish thing her husband had planned for her easily topped it.

That was *my* favorite part of her birthday, knowing that even though my own father had been a shitty husband, she was being pampered by someone who appreciated her.

As a kid, and even into adulthood, my view of my parent's marriage was skewed by the way my dad was quick to blame the problems of their relationship on the fact that they'd taken vows. It wasn't until my mom smacked me upside the head after she learned the details of my breakup with Charlie, and sat me down to tell me the *real* deal that I understood what was really happening.

My dad was a damned drunk.

It started shortly after their wedding, when he was hurt in an accident on his job. He didn't believe in taking prescription pain management, so he *drank* his way into numbness instead. He was what they call a "functioning" alcoholic, but of course his personality, priorities, and whole demeanor changed. He would pick fights with my mother as an excuse to hit the bar, wouldn't keep a job, wouldn't help at home. If they hadn't gotten married the weekend they did, he wouldn't have been working overtime to catch up, and therefore wouldn't have gotten hurt.

I don't think I closed my mouth for a full minute after my mother revealed *that* as his twisted ass logic. *Marriage* made him a trash-ass husband and provider.

Right.

It was hard not to resent him for that, especially when he was a large part of why I had the views I did on marriage. If I hadn't been listening to him, I would have married Charlie probably a *year* in, fancy ring be damned, and could be happily wed *right now*. But... that was twisted logic too. I was a grown assed man, and when it came down to it, I was the one who had to be accountable for my own decisions.

"I wish you hadn't let that crazy daddy of yours mess up your head. I could have had two or three little pretty grandbabies by now. She told me she's back in town... back at the restaurant with you. You weren't gonna say anything about that?"

I shrugged. "What is there to say? Charlie is back, and she's not trying to have anything to do with me."

"Oh, baby," my mother waved her hand in the air, brushing away my words. "The girl just needs time."

"It's been five years."

"Has she even been back in the city five *weeks*, Nixon?!"

"She's *dating* somebody."

"Rebound guy."

"She *married* somebody."

My mother laughed. "That was a rebound guy too, just lasted a little bit longer. Listen to me, son. I heard the hitch in her voice when I asked her about you. I've been hearing it once a year, every year, for *five long years*. Give the girl some time."

I sighed, draining my orange juice before I sat back. "How *much* time?"

Her expression shifted into the "look" only my momma — and *Charlie*— could give me, that would make me immediately sit up in my seat. She looked me over, then raised an eyebrow.

"You made the girl wait for six years, son. You give my sweet Charlie as much time as she needs."

".... Yes ma'am."

chapter
thirteen

Charlie

ADRIAN WAS CALLING.

It was only a little after ten in the morning, and already the third time my cell phone had lit up, flashing the number he usually called from across my screen. I didn't know what he was doing, whose palm he was greasing to get these kinds of phone privileges, but I really wished he would find somebody else to call. His momma, his sister, his little piece-on-the-side that he didn't think I knew about, *anybody*. Just leave me the hell alone.

Damn.

Maybe he heard my thoughts, because the phone stopped ringing, and I turned over again in the bed, burying my face in my pillow. Two days had passed since the thing with Nix, and things were still..., weird. Yesterday, I'd spent the whole day at Pot Liquor, filling in for him while he celebrated with his mom for her birthday. Today, the responsibilities of the restaurant fell to him.

Because I was busy, I'd been mostly able to avoid talking with Trent, and hadn't yet apologized for ignoring him. Or leaving the coffee shop that night without telling him. Or having sex with my ex-fiancé while he and I were dating. Not *intimate*, but still dating.

I dragged myself from the bed and took a shower, then dressed in jeans, a fitted tee shirt, and a cute blazer — perfect "sorry I told you I was going to the bathroom when really what had happened was, I was somewhere getting my back blown out" attire. Trent had asked me to meet for lunch, so I was prepared for some heavy explaining. No lies, just... explaining.

When I was ready, I caught a cab, and twenty minutes later, I was sitting down across from Trent at one of the high-end restaurants he favored. As usual, he looked incredibly handsome, but something in his expression was a little different than normal. He looked so... *happy*. Not that he usually seemed sad, just laid back. Today, the man was damn near glowing.

"You look good," he said, smiling at me across the table. "But then again, you always do."

"Thank you." I smiled up at the server as she delivered our waters, then turned back to Trent. "You're looking a little different yourself. What's going on, you get your name on the wall at the firm or something?"

Trent grinned a little, then shrugged, licking his lips as he leaned back in his seat. "Um... that's actually what I wanted to talk to you about."

"You *did* get your name on wall!?"

"No," he laughed, holding up a hand. "I wish, but no. Something else happened."

"Oh. Okay. What's going on?" I took a sip from my glass, then sat back, something about his expression making me suddenly feel a little uneasy about this conversation.

"You know the other night, when you left me waiting on you at the coffee shop, then ignored all of my calls and texts looking for you?"

I shifted uncomfortably in my seat, then nodded.

"Well, aside from the fact that leaving without telling me was *wildly* disrespectful, it really just confirmed something that I was ignoring — you're just not that into me. And *that's okay*. Because if I'm completely honest with myself, I was forcing it with you too."

I lifted an eyebrow, then looked around to motion for the server. *This* shit was going to require something a little stronger than water with lemon. "Is *that* right?"

"That's right. You're a beautiful woman Charlie. Funny, interesting, sexy, but truth is... I'm still in love with my wife."

Where the hell is that server?

"The wife you've characterized as not that nice? Does she still want you?"

Trent let out a sigh. "That was... childish of me. I was angry, and we let things get a little too far. But then I went with her to the first prenatal appointment yesterday, and—"

"Whoa whoa whoa... *prenatal* appointment?"

I fixed my shocked expression as the server approached with a smile plastered on her face. I ordered a glass of wine, then turned back to Trent.

"What the hell do you mean, prenatal appointment?"

Trent licked his lips, then shifted back to a serious expression. "I mean that my ex-wife is pregnant."

"*How* pregnant?" I picked up my water to take a big gulp.

"Two months."

I nearly choked on my water as I pulled the water from my lips. "Two months? So... you were still sleeping with her right before you started dating me? And I thought you told me you two have been divorced for like six months?"

"We have, but... stuff happens. Dating you was my attempt to go ahead and get over her, move forward with something new, but... Charlie... seeing the way you and Nixon interact with each other just highlights a chemistry that *you and I* don't share. But I have it with Dionne. You have it with Nixon. You and he are still as in love as my wife and I are, and it's obvious. So why are we doing this?"

The server came to deliver my glass of wine and left, but I didn't pick it up. I just stared at it as I searched my mind for an answer. Why *was* I doing this?

"Listen... Charlie," Trent said, reaching forward to place his hand over mine. "No hard feelings, okay? This brief time we've had together was nice, but that mess the other night made me take a hard look at what I was missing with my wife. We talked about it yesterday, and we're going to give it another shot. Hell, when you disappeared the other, my first thought was that you'd gone back to Nix. Ole boy has been in love with you since high school, so it made perfect sense when you guys got together."

I scoffed. "Boy, *what*? Nixon wasn't thinking about me like that back then."

"Yeah, Okay." Trent chuckled, then sat back in his chair again. "In any case, I wish you the best of luck. I really do think you're a great girl, Charlie. What you pulled the other night was messed up, but *still*... I get it. I think you deserve to be with someone who makes you happy."

Finally I picked up that glass of wine, knocking most of it back in one gulp. "So... can I ask you a question?"

"Go for it," Trent said, taking a drink.

Leaning forward, I propped my arms on the table. "If you two can get back together, just like that... what the hell did you get divorced for?"

"Oh man." Trent ran a hand over his hair, shaking his head. "She gave me an ultimatum."

I drained the rest of my wine, then motioned for a refill. "*Oh no.*"

"Yeah. It was *wild*. One minute we're on the same page about not having kids, then it was like somebody flipped a switch, and all of a sudden she was worried about biological clocks and birth defects. We just *had* to have a baby right then. But I wasn't down with it. We said 35, so I was hell-bent on *sticking* to 35. We had money to do what we wanted, freedom to come and go as we pleased, a *quiet* house. I wasn't ready to let go of that childfree lifestyle, you know? She told me, we can have this baby now, or we could move on. I could be childless, and she could be free to have her baby. So I called her bluff."

The waitress came by to refill my glass, and I had it up to my lips again before she'd completely pulled the bottle away. "*Wow.*"

"Yeah, *wow*. We both just got mad after that, and things snowballed, and it all got bigger and bigger, until... we ended up divorced. It really took me losing her, and being without her for this time to realize what I was missing. We couldn't even stay away from each other, which is how she ended up pregnant. Man... hearing the baby's heartbeat... I went from wanting nothing to do with a baby, to wanting nothing more in the world than my wife and child.

I finished the rest of my wine, then nodded. "I'm happy for you, Trent. That's... really nice."

He shrugged. "It's just... real. Sometimes you have to fuck it all up first to see the beauty in what you had."

***

"HMMM, SO NOW YOU SEE *YOUR* MAN ISN'T THE ONLY one to have a bad reaction to an ultimatum. You women are gonna listen to that shit one day."

I threw a grape at Eddie, who caught it and threw it back, then took a seat across from me on the loveseat. He and I, along with Viv and Simone, were seated around my apartment, in what was, starting to seem like an intervention for me.

"Are you trying to say women don't listen?" Simone asked, eyeing Eddie over the rim of her margarita glass.

He lifted an eyebrow at her. "Hell yes. That's *exactly* what I'm saying. Every one of you has gone *left* after I've tried to steer you right. Except Miss Charlie. Shame I couldn't have attempted an intervention back then, so we wouldn't have to do it now."

"So this *is* an intervention?" I asked, picking up another handful of grapes.

"Yes."

Viv shook her head, tossing Eddie a frown. "*No.*"

"Well why the hell not?" Eddie looked between us three women, then took a long drag from his beer. "You're around here looking sad and lonely, *that fool* has been over there looking sick and sad, and the food hasn't been right at Pot Liquor since y'all bumped uglies. Your emotional bullshit is fucking with the sweet potato pie, I've had better mac and cheese from a box, and I don't appreciate it. So when are you and Nixon gonna stop acting stupid and get it together?"

I sucked my teeth. "My macaroni has *not* been bad, don't

compare it to that boxed crap. The better question is why you're hanging with us if you think women don't listen."

"It ain't been perfect lately, and I hang around beautiful women because it helps me *understand* beautiful women, which helps me *get* beautiful women."

"The macaroni has been fine."

"Has not."

"*Ya mama.*"

"Makes a better macaroni and cheese than you? Oh I know."

"Okay children," Viv interjected, waving her napkin in the air like a white flag. I rolled my eyes at Eddie, scrunching up my nose as I hit him with another grape. "Charlie... my darling cousin, I am so sorry to tell you that Eddie is right. It has been two weeks now since your little... incident with Nixon, and unfortunately, it is coming through in the food. That banana pudding you served yesterday was *slimy*, blech."

"Shut up." I threw a grape at Viv, and it bounced off her forehead. "I tasted that, and it was perfectly fine."

"Like those nasty ass sour grapes you're eating like they haven't been in that refrigerator since you moved in?" Eddie looked pointedly at the bag of grapes in my lap, and when I glanced down, they *were* looking a little... wrinkled.

"Whatever," I scoffed. "I will... look into what's going on with the food, but other than that, I'll have you know, ain't *nobody* around here looking sad and lonely, especially over cheating ass Nixon."

A collective hush went around the room, as everybody looked at each other, then back at me. Finally, Simone put her glass down on her coaster and sat up.

"So... I'm the newcomer, so I don't know the history, and these two,"— she pointed at Viv and Eddie — "Have been hush-hush. So that's what happened between the two of you? He cheated?"

"Yes," I said, at the same time that Eddie chimed in with a direct *"No"*. I angled my head to the side as I scowled. "Excuse me?"

"You're not hard of hearing. First of all, it was five years ago — let it *goooo*, let it go. Second... I contend that he didn't cheat on you. You gave him an ultimatum. For a man, that's *very* black and white. He chose the "end it" option after you pushed him into a corner. You handled the breakup by drowning yourself in tears. He handled the breakup by drowning himself in pussy and liquor — as his *single* ass was entitled to do. *Then*, once you realized he wasn't gonna give in, *you* gave in, went back, and decided you didn't wanna call it a breakup... even though that's exactly what the alternative to your little scenario was."

I rolled my eyes, ignoring the fact that they were pricking with tears. "Screw you, Eddie. It was more than that. We'd just lost a baby, not even two months before. He sat there and claimed to love me, and then not even a few hours later, he was giving himself to some bitch whose name he probably doesn't even remember. I waited on his ass for *six years,* and the minute we have a *real* disagreement, he runs to someone else. It's fucked up, no matter how long ago it was."

"So... does that one mistake overshadow everything else, from the six years before that?" Simone asked, in an optimistic voice. "I mean... he had to have some positive, redeeming qualities, right?"

Nodding, I reached for my own margarita. "I mean... yeah. He *did*. But he cheated."

"*No he didn't.*" Eddie muttered under his breath, and I picked up the whole bag of grapes and aimed.

"Just a moment, just a moment!" Viv said, scrambling to her feet to get between Eddie and me. "Charlie.... If you consider the situation logically... Eddie does have a point. I had not considered it this way, *but*... you did deliver two options. Marry me, or let's move on. So, if Nixon was very clear in his decision to not get married, the natural assumption is that you two were agreed on moving on, based on the conditions that *you* set."

I looked up at Viv with a sneer. "I thought family stuck together? You're supposed to be on *my* side!"

"I *am* on your side, *always*. What I am saying is... I know that you love Nixon. I know that Nixon loves you. And I know the kind of man Nixon is, and happen to think that he would do *anything* for you. Perhaps, if you can put aside your indignation of "he cheated on me", since *technically* he did not, that may put you in a place where you are open to forgiveness. I am absolutely not *excusing* him, and not suggesting that you should either. It was not okay to brush off your desire for marriage. It was not okay to not be sensitive to the recent loss of the baby. I understand the hurt of finding out that he slept with someone else so shortly after, I would be upset too. I get *all* of that, and I think you are entitled to those feelings... but it is obvious, to me, at least, that some part of you still wants to be with him. So maybe it is time to address those feelings and move past them, so that you can either... go ahead and be with Nixon, or find your happiness somewhere else."

"So I should what, just forget what he did to me?" I rolled my eyes. "Y'all are crazy."

Shaking his head, Eddie came to sit on the couch beside me, wrapping an arm over my shoulders to pull me close. "Charlie... that's just it right there. You're looking at it as something he *did to you*. Believe or not, all the stupid shit that men do isn't about hurting you. Have you ever given him a chance to explain *why* he did it?"

I ran my tongue over my lips. "No."

"See? Don't get me wrong, I absolutely think Nixon fucked up with you. Keeping you waiting six years, not calming your ass down instead of responding to that ultimatum, going to a bar instead of finding his homeboys, who would have made him keep his damned pants on, for giving you that ring so soon after, *telling* you he slept with that girl anyway... Lord, that man did some *stupid shit*. But, you're not innocent baby girl. You've thought a lot about your own feelings.... Have you thought about his? Maybe he was hurt about the baby and needed to work through that. Maybe he was hurt about you thinking he didn't love you, and needed to work through that too. When have you given this man a chance to work through his *own* shit instead of always catering to yours? When do you consider *him*? What would have been the problem with you saying "hey babe, I know you're feeling antsy about marriage, what do *we* need to do to calm those fears for you?""

I blinked hard a few times, then shook my head. "Nothing."

"Right. You've said yourself, he was nothing but good to you. Treated you like a queen. Since he brought you into my shop for you to talk him into that corny ass adorable macaroni and cheese tattoo, I've known that the two of you had something special. And look what happened... five years apart, over some shit you guys could have just talked through. It may not have been immediate, or pretty, or *perfect*, but... you would have been together."

Tears welled in my eyes as I considered Eddie's words. As much as I hated to admit it... he was... *right*. All these years, I'd been so focused on my own pain, on my own hurt, on my own anger, that I hadn't even considered *his*. Throughout our relationship, and even before, Nixon had always been just... *strong*. The idea that I had the power to hurt him seemed foreign, but now that I was looking through a different lens, I could *very* clearly remember the first and only time I'd ever seen Nixon shed tears.

When we lost the baby.

I'd been *so* diligent about my birth control pills, knowing that we were trying to wait until Pot Liquor had been open and running successfully for at least five years before kids became an option. Funny how we discussed *that*, but mention a ring, and Nixon blanked out.

In any case, a round of antibiotics that didn't play nicely with my birth control shot those plans to pieces. But... we were happy. Correction: *I* was happy. Nixon was *over the moon*. It was really the sweetest thing, how *he* would drag *me* to the baby section in stores, grinning at little bow tie embellished onesies for a boy, and tiny little tutus for a girl. He wanted to look at houses, and start a college fund, and... *God* his reaction to an "oops" baby was the kinda stuff dreams were made of. And he worked so hard. Many, *many* nights I had to trick Nixon into bed with made-up ailments. *Baby, my back aches, come lay in the bed with me and rub it until I fall asleep, please?* Only, *he* was always the one who passed out first, from pure exhaustion.

Before the pregnancy, I didn't think I could be more in love with him, but *man* was I wrong. That was one of the most truly beautiful times in our relationship, and unfortunately... led to the most devastating.

I'll never... *never* forget the day we went in for a normal appointment, just to check the baby's development, find out if it was a girl or a boy, since the positioning wasn't right at the appointment where we *should* have found out. We were both excited, and Nixon *could not* keep a grin off his face. He and the doctor carried on a conversation while I lay back, just listening.

And then the conversation stopped.

The doctor's entire mood changed, and when she looked at me and opened her mouth to speak, but couldn't seem to make anything come out... something in me broke. The doctor told me "he" had passed, and I called that bitch a liar. She was lying, *because I'd just felt him. Him. She shook her head no, and ... I'll never forget the day itself, but after that moment, the details were fuzzy. Nixon was walking me to the car, because the doctor said something about waiting until labor induced naturally, and then we were home. I woke up, and he was downstairs, in the kitchen, and his face was wet with tears. Then I was drinking every sugary drink I could find, because the baby just needed a little jolt, just a little bit of energy, and he would be moving again, and his heart would start, and he would be fine. And then Nixon had me by the wrists, and his face was still wet, and he was telling me to stop before I made myself sick, but I was* already *sick because our baby wouldn't wake up, and why the fuck didn't he understand?*

Then... I was at the hospital, hooked to machines, while they pumped something in my arm to make me go into labor. I woke up and my stomach was stapled closed, and I didn't have a baby anymore.

And I was gonna lose Nix too. I could tell by the way he looked at me, at my stomach sometimes. His refusal to get rid of the diapers, bottles, and toys we'd already started collecting. His seemingly constant *need to talk about the baby, the desire to pick a name, bombard me with reminders.... It was all soaked in his disdain for me, for losing his child, and I didn't want to talk about it. I* never *wanted to talk about it. I wanted to forget.*

But I couldn't.

I couldn't think of anything else — except how I was gonna lose Nix, because how could he still love me after that? He swore he did. Constantly reminding me that it wasn't my fault, bringing flowers, rubbing feet, all that jazz. He was just humoring me, until I was "well" again. So I got well.

And he continued, but I still didn't believe him.

If he wanted to convince me that the love hadn't changed... he had to do it with a ring.

I SHOOK MY HEAD. *NO WONDER* I COULDN'T SEE WHAT I was doing to Nix. I couldn't even see what I was doing to *myself*. It made me a little sick to my stomach to think of how I'd denied him the opportunity for us to grieve the loss of our child, then tried to force him into giving me a ring, then accused him of not loving me when he didn't kick up his heels at the idea. It *wasn't* fair. Not when I'd barely cared about a ring before.

I'd mentioned marriage, and knew his views... yet I stayed. I even teased him about it sometimes, just to get a reaction. Marriage was important to me, but our love was so much more than that. Because he made me so happy that it didn't matter, until I latched onto the idea as necessary proof that he loved me, and... it wasn't fair. Nixon made some mistakes, but when I stopped focusing on *his*... my God... what was the saying about sweeping around your own front door first?

Long after the crew left, I lay awake in my bed, thinking about the possibility of me and Nix... *macaroni and cheese* back together again. It made me smile a little, then a little more, until I started laughing, thinking about all of the good times Nix had shown me over nearly two decades of knowing each other, and six years of *loving* each other.

I laughed until I cried, because maybe.... that kind of pure, perfectly imperfect love was too far gone to get back.

chapter
fourteen

Charlie

SIRENS WOKE ME UP.

I knew they sounded closer than they actually were, but a prickle of goose bumps crossed my skin anyway, and I climbed out bed.

It was late, a little after midnight. None of the windows in Viv's apartment faced the right way to see anything other than residential streets, forestry, and a distant view of the water, so I reluctantly pulled on yoga pants and a tee-shirt over my panties and tank top, pulled on my fuzzy moccasins, and headed up to the roof.

There was smoke in the air, just faintly, but it hit me as soon as I opened the heavy metal door. I closed it behind me, then stepped out further, past the rows of vegetables that comprised the rooftop community garden, and out to where I could see.

It took my breath away.

Huge billows of smoke poured upward, in sharp contrast to the night sky, and I could see the lights of at least three different fire trucks reflecting off the windows along the street.

Wait a minute...

I took a staggering step back as I realized exactly where I was looking. That was *our* street, the same area of Urban Grind, the same area as... Pot Liquor. I looked down at my hands for my phone, and when I realized I'd left in my apartment, I bolted for the roof door, bounding down the stairs three or four at a time to get back.

Snatching my phone from the charger, the first thing I noticed were that there were no missed calls from Nix.

Things between us, since ... new apocalypse had been tense, but okay. We fell back into what we were doing before. Not lovers, not friends, but business partners, and it worked. If there were a fire at or near the restaurant, he would have called me. There was no chance he wouldn't know about it, because he *lived* there.

...unless... he *couldn't* call.

Oh God.

I called six times.

He didn't answer.

I stuffed my feet into a pair of tennis shoes, and strapped my phone into the zipper pocket on my pants. I think I locked the door behind me, but I didn't have time to think about it. I got my ass down the stairs, out of the building, and down to my restaurant.

I'D BARELY MADE IT PAST THE FLOWER SHOP WHEN MY lungs started burning from the smoke in the air. Despite the time, there were a lot of people out, either going in the direction of the fire or leaving. They were shaking their heads, talking about how sad it was, saying they'd never seen a building destroyed so badly by fire.

I walked faster.

When I got to the intersection in front of Urban Grind, it was completely blocked with fire trucks, police cars, and ambulances. Through the haze of smoke, I searched for a familiar face. When I saw none, I kept moving forward, getting as close as I could before I ran up on the barricade.

Shit.

I moved around, trying to avoid the eyes of any of the police working on keeping the crowd back. One of the fire trucks moved, causing a gust as it went, and once it passed, I could finally see.

The dry cleaner was on fire. Several different hoses still worked diligently to douse it with water, but the entire storefront of the building was gone. There was a gaping hole, where I could still see flames inside, but nothing remained to make it recognizable as the place it used to be. I could just barely recognize the businesses on either side of it. On the right was a small furniture store. Pot Liquor was on the left.

I felt sick to my stomach.

I could see straight through the side of the building, into the beautiful stainless steel kitchen. All the tables, all appliances were now shapeless masses of nothing. Above it, the apartment was burned nearly in half. The bedroom was right above the kitchen.

My chest heaved, and my ears began to close up as I turned around, searching the crowd with burning eyes for Nixon.

"*Nix!*" I screamed, repeatedly, even though the yelling fire-fighters and growing sounds of the crowd probably drowned me out.

A familiar face from high school walked past me, and I reached out and grabbed, connecting with a handful of his yellow firefight-er's jacket. "Grant! *Grant!*" He stopped, and instead of yanking away from me, stepped to the side as another group of firefighters hurried around the barricade.

"Charlie, what are you doing all the way up here? You need to get back! I know this is your business, but we need you to get where it's safe."

"I know, I know," I rushed out, grabbing his jacket again as he tried to walk away. "Have you seen Nix? He's not answering his phone, and he lives in the apartment upstairs, and I can't find him. I haven't seen him."

Normally cheerful, Grant's green eyes turned a little darker as his expression changed. "Ambulance." He said that one word, then pulled away, following his comrades toward the fire.

Why did he say it like that?

Feeling dazed, I turned in the direction of the ambulances, thinking that if he was still at the ambulance, that meant he wasn't at the hospital, which meant it wasn't that bad.

As I approached, I could see the EMTs rushing around a stretcher, so I headed that way. Right in front of me, they suddenly stopped their frantic movements, and started rolling a sheet over the person's head.

I stopped, because I couldn't move. I couldn't stand up either. I dropped to my knees, mouth open, lungs burning, chest heaving as they lifted the stretcher, sliding it into the back of ambulance. And then... they closed the door, and I couldn't feel anything. I started shaking my head, and laughed because... this shit wasn't real. This was a bad dream, and I was gonna wake up any second....
Now.

Now.

NOW.

I cupped my hand to my mouth as a sob escaped my throat. Squeezing my eyes shut, I doubled over as my chest erupted in pain.

No, no no no no no.

This isn't real, this isn't real, this isn't—

"Charlie?"

Opening my eyes, I looked up to see Roman standing over me, and before I could say anything he was kneeling down, pulling me back up to my feet.

"Are you okay?"

I couldn't manage to do anything except shake my head, and that deepened his frown of concern. He was in the middle of asking me if I was hurt, and already dragging me toward the EMTs when I finally found a voice through my tears to mutter Nixon's name.

"*Oh.* Have you not been able to find him?"

What?

Roman made a slight shift in his direction, pulled me around a throng of people, and there, *alive,* was Nixon. He was shirtless, barefoot, and streaked with soot and ash, but he'd never looked better to me. The heaviness in my chest lifted, and the tension in my shoulders melted away as a fresh round of tears — *grateful* tears — began to stream down my face.

Nixon sat at the edge of the open back of the ambulance, and the EMT next to him appeared to be checking his vitals. As Roman and I approached, he looked up, and the pure anguish in his eyes made my steps falter. His gaze dropped to the ground as the EMT stepped away, and it wasn't until we were right in front of him that he glanced up again, then focused on me, shaking his head.

"Baby.... I am *so* sorry."

I frowned. "Nix... what are you talking about?"

"This fool," Roman said, leaning over my shoulder, "Had to get pulled out of the building twice by the firefighters. He's crazy as hell, but he was quick with those fire extinguishers. Kept it from being a lot worse than it could have. I was heading to get him something to put on, and then I need you to take him home."

Roman stepped away, leaving us to stare at each other.

After a moment, Nixon shook his head again, pushing out a sigh as he looked toward the smoky sky. "I couldn't do anything," he said, his eyes focused upward. "By the time *our* smoke alarms went off, the fire was already too big. It was too late."

"But Roman said—"

Nixon scoffed. "Roman is being nice, because he sees how pitiful I am right now." He shook his head again, then finally looked toward me. "It's gone, baby. With the smoke damage, and the water damage... they're gonna call it a total loss."

I took a deep breath, then sat down on the edge of the ambulance beside him, looking out at the all the people still roaming around, staring at the remnants of the fire. When I turned my gaze to him, he was staring out as well, so I put my head on his shoulder. I was sure it would hit me later that the restaurant we'd worked to make a success for the last nine years was gone, but right then... the only feelings I could muster were ones of extreme gratitude that he wasn't the one laid out on that stretcher.

"Mr. Parker," Nixon said, answering my unspoken question. Garret Parker and his wife had opened their dry cleaner just a few years before us. She died the same year everything with Nix and me went to shit, and Garret became even more ornery and mean than he was before. Still, I hated knowing that he'd died.

Nixon grew quiet, and I could tell he was retreating into his thoughts, so I left him to that, but kept my head resting on his shoulder. Roman came and brought him some clothes, then walked us back down to Viv's building. He helped me drag him up the stairs, then made a quiet departure, leaving me to the work of getting Nixon into the shower, and the fresh set of extra clothes Roman left.

He was mostly silent, but pliant, and I couldn't help grinning at his willingness to let me shower him. We both knew he could do it himself, but for some reason... I just *wanted* to. I felt like he needed it. Or maybe *I* needed it, needed to take care of him, to assuage the guilt I felt over my revelations the night before, in my conversation with my friends.

I stripped down to my sports tank and boy short panties, stepping into the shower with him. He kept on his boxers, and said very little as I soaped and lathered him with my Dove body wash. He groaned in appreciation as I took my time over his back, chest, and arms, scrubbing away the black lines of soot and ash, leaving behind clean, golden-brown skin and the occasional tattoo. A few were newly acquired ones that he'd gotten since our breakup, but I didn't take the time to explore. It was late, and I was tired, so I knew Nix was probably *exhausted.*

After finishing all of his less intimate areas, I stepped out, leaving him to complete the rest while I changed into fresh sleep clothes of my own. His clothes were already in the bathroom with him, and after a brief moment of deliberation, I put out extras pillows and blankets for him on the couch. Not that I *wanted* him to sleep out there. Honestly, I wanted him close, but didn't feel right making an assumption my bed would be his choice. We hadn't talked about anything... he could still be angry for all I knew.

When I was done setting up for him, I climbed into bed, turned on the dimmer lamp, and lay in the semi-dark with my tablet while I listened to him finish his shower, pee, then wash his hands and brush his teeth. After that, I smiled at the various bumps and thumps of him getting dressed, then restoring the bathroom to order before he opened the door.

Those sounds, which I'd listened to almost every night for nearly four years of our relationship, were like music to me, so incredibly intimate and familiar it made warmth blossom in my chest and stay there. Instead of going into the living room, where I'd set up a place for him, Nixon climbed into bed beside me, and I had to suppress a smile. Close like this, I was inevitably drawn into looking into his eyes. His deep hazels were darker than usual, and filled with sadness, and hurt, and anger, and a whole host of other things that I wished I could take away.

But I couldn't.

As much as *I* loved Pot Liquor, Nixon loved it more. He was the one who'd been there nearly every day, while I was out in California, and before and after. PL was Nixon's home, and his life. And now it was gone.

I turned off the lamp and put my tablet on the bedside table, cuddling deep under the covers. We laid there, not saying anything, for what seemed like a long time. In the silence, there was an undercurrent of tension, where it almost felt like we were both waiting on the other to be the first to break, and then finally...

"Charlie."

There was something in his voice I couldn't ignore. A little raspier than usual, from the smoke in the air, and edged with pain, need, and... *passion*. My body still recognized it, and responded. The way he spoke my name... nothing else needed to be said.

My eyes were adjusted to the bit of moonlight streaming through the gap in the curtains, so I used that to find him, then straddled him in the semi dark. I lowered my face to his, touching foreheads, brushing my lips against his, little sucks, gentle bites, before I finally pressed my lips to his and kissed him.

I felt it immediately. That ever-present sense of rightness that occurred when I was with him, and that light shone even brighter now. I pushed my tongue into his mouth to gain entry, then sucked his, pulling an appreciative groan from him.

Nixon's hands slipped up my legs, then up my oversized tee shirt, gripping and kneading my ass before he slid them up to cup my breasts. As I reached behind me to free him from his boxers, the decision to skip panties suddenly felt prophetically *right*.

He sat up, capturing my mouth in another kiss as I slid down onto him, eliciting another, louder groan. In the dark, Nixon's hands touched and teased everything he could reach as I began to ride him, wrapping my arms around his neck to draw him close.

Damn he felt good. Heavy, and thick, and *right*, and *familiar*, and... like home.

I cupped his chin, tilting his head back so that he was looking at me in the shadowy light. "Tomorrow," I whispered, "we have to talk."

"And what about tonight?" He dropped his mouth to my neck, teasing the area with openmouthed kisses before he looked up at me again.

"Tonight... I love you."

Nixon's eyes widened for a moment, and then he gave me a little grin before pulling me into another kiss. "I love you too."

chapter
fifteen

Charlie

LUCKY.

That's how I felt when I woke up to the aroma of breakfast sausage and sweet potato pancakes.

Not because it meant that Nixon was cooking for me — that was a perk, of course — but because it meant that he was still *able* to. Because he was *here*.

Alive.

Out of nowhere, a sob built in my throat, and I rolled over, burying my face in my pillow. Somehow, even though he'd used *my* soap, the pillowcase, the sheets, everything, all of it smelled like him — a scent I could have easily never experienced again.

When I saw him last night, looking so out of it, so distraught, it was as if my own feelings were suspended, in favor of tending to him. Now, he was safe, and well enough to be up cooking my favorite breakfast, and I guess my body was tired of holding on to that well of relief, because it overflowed in a stream of uncontrollable tears.

I kept my face tucked into the pillow so Nixon wouldn't hear, and stayed there, hoping for eventual calm, but it didn't come before the door to the bedroom swung open. Nix came in humming under his breath, his footsteps padding across the floor as he approached my side of the bed. One of my heavy porcelain plates made a distinctive thump as he sat it down on the bedside table, then knelt beside the bed.

Neither of us said anything for a moment, until Nix reached up, running a hand across the small of my back. "You ignoring me this morning?"

At that, I turned my head toward him, and as soon as he saw the moisture on my face, his eyes brightened in understanding. He opened his mouth, but before he could say anything I was out of the bed and wrapping my arms around his neck, nearly knocking him to the floor. He righted himself quickly, chuckling as he returned my embrace.

I burrowed my face in his neck as I broke into a fresh round of sobs, and he squeezed me tighter, pulling me closer as he gently rubbed my back. It was surreal, thinking about the fact that I may have never felt this again. What if he *had* been lost in that fire, before we'd ever even talked it through?

But I didn't want to think about that.

As my tears subsided, I sat back to look at him. Run my fingers over his short hair, gently tug his beard, cup his face in my hands, and just *touch* him, because I could. Because he let me. Nixon endured my harassment, then planted a kiss on my forehead.

"You done?" he asked, a smile playing at the corners of his mouth.

I nodded. "For now."

For a long moment, I just stared at him, couldn't pull my eyes away. Then I reached to touch his face again, and pressed my forehead against his. "Nix... last night... I saw them putting Mr. Parker's body in that ambulance, and I thought it was you. I..." I stopped as a fresh round of tears bubbled forth, and Nixon pulled me back down to his shoulder. "I don't know what I would have done if that had been you. If I'd *lost* you, I—"

"*Shh*. You didn't though, right? I'm still here."

"I know, but—"

Nixon tipped up my chin and kissed me, effectively shutting me up. "But nothing. It was a long night... I want you to eat, okay? Can you do that for me?"

I gave him a reluctant nod, then accepted his help back up, and into the bed where he put a tray across my lap, then placed my plate in front of me.

"Eat," he gently commanded, then left me alone in the room. A few moments later, I heard his voice again, but no one else's, and concluded he was on the phone. I glanced over at the bedside table.

My phone.

My brow furrowed in confusion for a moment, wondering how he was able to use my phone, when it had a lock code on it. He certainly hadn't asked, and I hadn't told, but then I remembered that this was Nixon, who knew me like the back of his hand. It probably hadn't taken much to figure out that I still used the same randomly made up code I'd used when we were together.

I laughed a little, then began to eat, quickly realizing that I was hungrier than I thought I was. I finished my plate, took a shower, dressed in lounging shorts and a tee shirt, then changed the bed to fresh linens. When I was done, I went to find Nixon.

I found him in the kitchen, face contorted in pain as he stretched his shoulder. From where I was, he couldn't see me, so I continued watching as he cursed under his breath, then stopped the stretch to rotate his arm.

"Nix..."

When he heard my voice, he tried to shift his expression, but I'd already seen it. "What's wrong with your shoulder?"

"Nothing. Just feeling a little stiff this morning."

"Your expression didn't *seem* like it was nothing." I lifted an eyebrow at him as I ventured further into the kitchen, and placed my plate in the sink. I whipped around to face him when something occurred to me. "Nixon, did you hurt yourself last night?"

"Ah, damn, Charlie don't start fussing over—"

"You refused treatment, didn't you?"

"Baby—"

"Mmhmm." I tried to fight a smile as he reached up to scratch his head. "You want me to massage it for you?"

He grinned. "I mean... I'm not gonna refuse an opportunity to get rubbed on."

"Of course not. Come on," I said, leading him to the living room. I directed him to the floor in front of the couch, went and grabbed the coconut oil from my bathroom, then sat down with him between my legs.

I started with the left side, which was the one giving him problems. He talked to me about fire investigations and insurance claims while I kneaded and massaged until his grunts of pain disappeared. Nixon grabbed me by the leg, kissing the inside of my knee before he looked back, his eyes filled with gratitude.

But you said it was nothing. Men.

I simply smiled, then moved to his other shoulder. He was talking about how long it might take to know anything when my hands stilled over his skin. I tuned him out as I focused on the ink tattooed in his skin at that spot.

"Noah."

Nixon grew quiet, then wrapped an arm around my leg as he slowly turned around.

A lump formed in my throat as I met his gaze. "It's a good name." I ran my fingers over the tiny footprints, surrounded by angel wings. Below that, the date of the day he should have been born. Above it... his name. "Thank you, for naming him. He deserved that."

"Baby... come here."

Tears pricked my eyes as I moved down to the floor with Nix, and allowed him to pull me into his arms. He cupped my head against his chest, and I relaxed into his embrace, allowing both of us something we'd never had before: I let him hold me while I cried over our lost child.

Nixon said nothing, but kept me tight against him, gently stroking my back as I let out quiet sobs. After a few long moments, the tears stopped, and that's when he finally spoke.

"You know... this kinda feels like the same thing, you know?"

I pulled back, looking up at him with confusion. "What does?"

"Losing Pot Liquor. It's like losing another baby."

The glassiness in his eyes made my own well with tears again, but I swallowed them, in favor of listening.

"It's almost the same pain. The same sense of... disillusionment. The same feeling like... this shit can't be forreal, you know?

Even though you know it is, cause you saw it for yourself. Just doesn't even feel like reality."

I nodded. Pot Liquor wasn't just a business venture for us. It *was* kind of like a baby, and we referred to it as our love child often enough. Something beautiful, born of our desire to work, and grow, and build something *together*, based in the love we had for each other. Hell, we were still kids then ourselves. We were only 24 years old, with a little money in the bank, a little parental generosity, and a little, but still scary, small business loan.

The loan was long paid off, the parents' kindness returned, and our own bank accounts were replenished... but now the restaurant was gone.

"You know, the guys are gonna go by. Eddie, Roman, Carter, and Grant knows all of that building safety stuff, so he's gonna go with them. Get the stuff out of the safe for us, see if anything is salvageable. And I... I just can't make myself go. I want to, and I feel like I should, but that's just like...the final acknowledgement of this fucked up thing, and I don't want to do that again."

"Again?"

I watched his Adam's apple bob as he swallowed hard, looking away from me as he nodded. "Yeah. The day they... the day Noah was born. You were knocked out, and... they let me hold him." He shook his head, then ran his tongue over his lips. "I should have said no. But like I said, you were still unconscious, and I just felt like one of us should. You think doing a certain thing will make you feel better, until you're actually *doing* it, and you realize no... this made it a *lot* fucking worse."

Yeah.

I did.

He was telling me something I'd never known about those awful two days. There was a *lot* I didn't know, because the memories weren't there, either unformed, because of my mental state, or blocked by grief. Oh, and I wouldn't let him talk to me about it. I tried to just erase it all from my head, and by the time I realized that would never happen, Nixon and I were already broken up, and it no longer felt okay to ask.

As if he could hear the unformed question in my mind, Nixon

pulled me close, planting a kiss on my head before he spoke. "I was hurt. Worst pain I'd ever felt when the doctor told us Noah had passed away. But you flipped out, so I was just trying to get you home, since they said you would probably go into labor soon, and that would be easier on you than if they induced. I remember *not* wanting to take you home, because you were... just devastated, you know? I got you home and I tried to calm you down, but you didn't want me to touch you. You ended up crying yourself to sleep. While you were sleeping, I went downstairs, to... get myself together."

He paused there, to clear his throat. This was one of the parts I *did* remember, and I was so used to Nix being the "strong" one that it didn't surprise me at all for him to gloss over what "getting himself together" really meant.

"Anyway, I looked up, and you were there. I didn't even hear you come down, or know how long you'd been there, but the look on your face was like you were hurt, and confused, and just... out of it. You didn't say anything, just went back up to the apartment, and a few minutes later... something told me to go check on you. When I got up there.... It was a mess. You were in the kitchen, juice and soda everywhere, and while you were drinking, you kept saying *"I'll get him back for you,"* like you thought I was *blaming* you, or something."

He stopped again, shifting as if he was uncomfortable saying whatever happened next.

"Nix... what is it? Did... did something happen?" I pulled away, so that I could see his face, and he gave a heavy sigh as he dropped his eyes.

"You... uh... your eyes... it was like they were blank. Like you were in there, somewhere, but your body was on autopilot, and I guess... the grief just took over. You got a knife, and you started telling me that the baby was probably suffocating, and if you could just get him out, you could help... it was like something in you had just *snapped*. That's when I decided to take you back to the hospital."

I raised my hand to cover my mouth, trying to catch my suddenly short breath. "I... Nixon, are you *serious*?"

Almost reluctantly, he nodded. "When I got you to the hospital, your vitals were all over the place. They gave you something to calm you down, and once that worked, they decided to go ahead and induce labor. Then everything went wrong again. Your blood pressure dropped too low, and the labor wasn't progressing, and then your vitals went nuts again, and they told me they had to get the baby out *now*, so they gave you a C-section, and I couldn't go back there with you. Scariest fucking hour of my life, cause... shit, I thought maybe I was about to lose you too. Then... when it was all over... you just didn't want to talk about it. *None* of it. You would get so upset, and shut down, or kick me out of the room, so I finally just stopped *trying* to talk about it."

"And then... I started pretending like I was okay."

"Yeah." He drew me close again, tipping up my chin to kiss me. "Thank you, for not pushing me away again."

I shook my head, swallowing back tears as they threatened to start again. "You don't have to thank me for doing what I *should* do. I'm sorry for being selfish. You needed to grieve, and I was so busy just trying to get away from the pain that I didn't even consider you. And I'm *so* sorry for that."

Nixon kissed me again, reaching up to wipe away the stray tears that escaped down my cheeks. "You were distraught, baby. I didn't quite get it then, but I do now. I can't hold that against you. I'm *not* holding it against you... okay?"

"Okay," I agreed, managing a little smile through my tears as Nix cupped my face in his hands.

When I met his gaze, Nixon's expression turned serious again, the sadness in his eyes morphing into regret. "I'm the one who should be apologizing."

"For what?"

He scoffed, then used his thumb to caress my face. "You know what."

I did, but I looked away, leaning to rest my head on his shoulder. For a long moment, neither of us said anything, then finally, I cleared my throat. "Why, Nix? I mean... I get that I backed you into a corner, tried to force you into marriage but... you just walked away. Then slept with someone else. I can accept that I shouldn't have made a demand on you, forced you to make a choice... but I need you to help me understand why you did what *you* did."

Nixon sighed, then began stroking my arm. "Okay. You knew I loved you, right? Is that a fair statement to make?"

I nodded.

"And you knew that I would do pretty much anything for you, right? And that wasn't just talk, either. Anything you wanted that was within my power to give, I gave it to you, right?"

"Right."

"Okay. Baby... being with you, wasn't something I took lightly. I knew, without a doubt, that I wanted you in my life, forever. That night, when you were listing off all your positive qualities, I agreed with every single one. Charlie, you were — hell, *are* — it for me. The one person I could see my future with, clearly, so I made sure to fulfill my roles, protector, provider, friend, lover... whatever you needed me to give you, I gave. Whatever you needed me to do for you, I did. But that night... it was like none of that mattered. Despite everything else, all of sudden I had to give you a ring in order to prove it.

And... I'm not gonna lie, that pissed me off. Especially when you *knew* my views on marriage. How many times did you have to talk me outta running away from home? How many days did me, you, and Carter skip senior year because you were trying to cheer me up after my parents got into it? I grew up with that shit, my pops drilling into my head to never get married, it fucks everything up... that's what I *saw*. With my own eyes, I saw the clear difference. Before the wedding, they were happy. Afterwards, everything went to shit. I didn't want that for us, baby. *Never*. But you were forcing me to choose. Confirm that I loved you by condemning our relationship to fail, so we could end up hating each other, or break up now and save ourselves the trouble. *That's* what those choices sounded like to me.

So... I chose to walk away. I shouldn't have. I should have stayed, forced you to talk to me, refused to make a choice between two fucked up options. But I was pissed off. It's like... if a *ring* was the thing that proved my love, after I've spent six years doing my damndest to be the best man I could possibly be for you... what was the point anyway? You weren't asking for time, for attention, for more affection, for me to give you flowers more often, take you out more, hell, to clean up around the house. You needed a *thing*. And I *had* the "thing". I'd already bought the ring, before you got pregnant, because I knew you wanted it. I just had to figure if and how I could get around my own bullshit to give you what you wanted it. But then you *demanded* it. Everything I did wasn't good enough. *I* wasn't good enough, unless I gave you this *thing*. I mean... I know better *now*, after my mom talked some sense into my head, but back then, right in that moment, it just felt like it was over anyway."

Wow.

"So... you felt like just when we were *there*... when you were right at the finish line of proving you loved me... I threw a hurdle in your way."

He nodded. "Exactly like that. An *impossible* hurdle. I mean... you know me, Charlie. Know I don't give up easy. But... only a few months had passed after we lost the baby, you were still in recovery, so I was handling everything at the restaurant by myself, and then you dropped *that* on me, and baby.... I was just *tired*. So I took what seemed to be the path of least resistance. Physically, emotionally, mentally... I was just out of energy. I didn't leave you at our apartment to go out looking for somebody to cheat on you with. I was looking for my dad, because I knew he would reinforce me. He got it, he would see where I was coming from." Nixon stopped for a moment, then shrugged. "But I couldn't find him. So I started drinking a little bit, and then a little more."

He pulled me up, tipping my chin up so that I could meet his gaze. "Now... Charlie, I'm not about to sit here and insult you by telling the lie that I didn't know what I was doing. I knew what I was doing when I went to that girl's house. It was fucked up, I know that. But with that said, I need you to know that in my mind, you and I were broken up... I'd lost you. Not that it makes it okay. I should have been at home, fixing things with you, and instead I was out having a pity party for myself. I have no excuse for that, and *I'm sorry*. But I need you to know, baby, I would *never, ever* knowingly cheat on you. The *only* reason I went home with her, is because it was my understanding that you and I weren't together anymore. I was hurt, and I was angry, and ... whether or not it was right, that's how I chose to deal with it. And when I gave you the ring that day you came back? It had *nothing* to do with trying to cover anything up, and *everything* to do with not wanting to lose you again since I was lucky enough to get you back. If I wanted to conceal it, it could have stayed concealed. I was in another city, I used protection... I could have kept it to myself. Maybe I *should* have kept it to myself. But once you accepted the ring, I accepted the responsibility of making sure our marriage didn't end up like my mom and dad. I *wanted* to have a happy life with you, and I knew starting out with a secret wasn't the way to make it happen. So... I owned up to what I did. And... you already know the rest."

I gave him a little smile. "Yeah."

I tried not to let it show on my face, but my head was swimming with emotions. Grief and sadness over his recollection of the loss of the baby. Annoyance, bitterness, and anger over the way he characterized our breakup. Was he *really* trying to blame *me*? But then... that indignation gave way to understanding. Just as when Eddie and Viv tried to break it down to me, I could see where my own actions directly related to his. Hearing it from his mouth, from his point of view, gave me the opportunity to see his side. Once I stopped trying to place all of the blame on him, and accepted some of my own... it gave way to forgiveness.

Not just of him, but of myself too. For too long, I'd been shoving Noah's death behind a closed door, afraid that Nixon thought it was my fault, afraid that I was going to lose him too, when it turns out... he was worried about the same thing. It seemed like the loss of the baby, at the height of our happiness was just the beginning of the end. At a time when we should have been able to turn to each other for comfort, my inability to handle the heartache forced us away from each other. Everything else just hammered the wedge further.

"Hey," Nix said, pulling me into his lap. "Tell me... do you think that we can move forward from here? I mean... I know a lot has happened, and time has passed, but... you're the only person I really wanna be with."

I smiled, then leaned forward to touch my forehead to his. "Same."

Nixon's mouth spread in a grin, and then he drew me into a kiss. A sweet, passionate, deep, "nice to meet you again", clumsy kind of kiss, and it was perfect.

"Hey," he said again, when we finally separated. "One more thing."

Snuggling against his chest, I closed my eyes as he wrapped me in an embrace. "Yeah."

"I know this is moving kinda fast, since we just got back together, but... do you think I could move in with you? A brotha kinda needs a place to stay."

I lifted my head, and raised an eyebrow at him. "You're kidding, right?" His eyes went wide, and despite my overwhelming desire to burst out laughing, I kept a straight face. "Nix... you're kind of looking like a bum right now. Like... a real ass bum. No job, no home, and you're asking to move in with me. Does that even sound right to you?"

Nixon dropped his head, poking out his bottom lip before he started making loud, exaggerated wailing noises that sounded more like a wounded animal than crying. I gave in to that urge to laugh as I turned his face back up to mine.

"Boy, stop that," I teased, giggling as he pulled me so that I was straddling his lap. "You can stay, but you've gotta earn your keep."

He lifted an eyebrow. "Oh really? How's that?"

I grinned, then slowly ground my hips against his.

"I've got a few things in mind."

chapter
sixteen

Charlie

"So... does this make us like... groupies or something?"

Simone leaned back on the short, portable bleachers, stabbing her slushie with a spoon to get to the bottom. Summer was pretty much over, and it was almost a little too cool for the frozen treats, but I stabbed at mine too, then scooped a spoonful of the flavored ice into my mouth as I glanced across the blacktop toward the guys.

Across the park, the teenagers were doing whatever teenagers these days do when they get together. Behind us, the older kids engaged in a game of tag, and the younger ones played on the swings and playhouse. In front of us, the babies, including Roman and Simone's son RJ, and Zahra, his six-year-old daughter with Leah, played together on a blanket in the grass, and a little further out, shirtless, sweaty basketball was happening.

That's where *my* attention was, along with a good majority of the other women.

It was kind of an idyllic scene. Flawless end of summer weather to accompany the yearly community festival, the whole neighborhood out having fun, and good music filling the air, courtesy of Grown Folk's Music. It was perfect.

Except for that whole "business burned to the ground" thing.

I took a deep breath, then shoved another spoonful of fruity slush in my mouth. Not even a week had passed yet since the night of the fire, and it still felt surreal. The fire department hadn't finished their investigation, so the source of the fire remained a mystery. The insurance company wouldn't move until a cause was determined, so we couldn't start any type of clean-up effort either. It sucked, but... it wasn't all bad. All of that would eventually come together and be fine, and I was glad for that... but I was even more glad to have Nixon.

Behind me, Viv told Simone that she *couldn't* be a groupie, since she was actually married to the man she was lusting after. I grinned when she said that she and I were the groupies, since we'd locked neither Carter nor Nixon down. I was glad to hear her change in attitude from a few weeks ago, when she was ready to make the same mistake I had. She still didn't have a ring on her finger, but she seemed content, so obviously Carter had done a good job of easing her fears.

Leah was on a hosting break from the Grown Folk's Music table, and was sitting with us enjoying her own slush. I lifted an eyebrow when Simone and Viv started giggling in admiration over Grant, trying to pull her in with them.

"See, y'all are gonna get me in trouble, looking at that man. I'm about to take my butt back over to the radio table," she said, laughing.

Simone sucked her teeth. "Girl, please. You're married, not blind."

"This is true," Viv chimed in. Even without seeing her, I could *hear* the smile in her voice. "There is nothing wrong with simple admiration. I love Carter with everything I have, and would never disrespect him. But... Grant is... a *work of art*. Leah, you cannot tell me you do not see it."

I chuckled. "Oh, she sees it." When I glanced back at Leah, she was blushing, and seemed to be trying hard not to break into a grin. After a few more moments of ribbing, she finally shook her head.

"Okay, okay." She held up the hand that wasn't holding her slush. "So... maybe I do see it. I mean... he *does* have that pretty honey-brown skin... and that body."

"*Mmhmm.*", was Simone, Viv's and my collective response.

With a little sigh, Leah continued. "And those deep, emotional green eyes, like he's staring right into your soul."

"*Mmhmm.*"

"And that face, right? With that sculpted jawline, and that perfect nose, I mean, it's too masculine to call him beautiful, but my God! Right?"

"*Mmhmm.*"

"And with him all sweaty, and he's been playing all this time and doesn't even look tired! Can you imagine the *stamina* the man must have? And.... Okay, I'm thinking about this a little too hard, aren't I?"

"*Mmhmm.*"

All four of us burst into a laugh, which quickly dissipated when we looked up to see that the men had finished their game of 3-on-3. They weren't really looking at us as they approached where we were sitting, but *we* were certainly looking at them. Roman, Eddie, Nixon, Vaughn, Grant, and Carter.

"*Fine as hell in six different shades of brown. Sexy ass black man color spectrum,*" I muttered under my breath, and behind me, the other three ladies gave an affirmative *Mmhmm.*

Leah greeted everyone with a quick wave, then split, giving an excuse that she needed to get back to the radio table. Vaughn — her co-host— followed her. Simone and Viv both went to their men, but I stayed where I was. Nixon and Grant were talking, and I caught enough to know it was fire related, so I looked up at Eddie with a smile.

He stared at me for a second then shook his head before breaking into a grin as he sat down beside me. "So I see you've been fucking."

I brought my hand to my chest and drew back, pretending to be scandalized. "I can't believe you would say such a thing."

"Yeah, right." Eddie bumped my shoulder with his. "You look happy. Glowing and shit. That's how I can tell Nixon has been dicking you down now that you're what... roommates?"

Batting my eyelashes, I ate another spoonful of my slush, then said, "A lady never tells."

"Oh good, that means *your ass* can tell."

"You right," I said, joining him as he laughed. "But... no, in all seriousness... yeah. I'm really, really happy. Thank you for being real with me the other day."

"I'm real *every* day." Eddie kissed my forehead, then stood, shaking hands with the rest of the guys before he said his goodbyes and left. I walked over to watch the babies play while Nixon finished up with Grant. The sight and sound of babies always set off a bit of an ache in my head and heart, but not really in a sad way, more like... a dull longing.

I'd only been there a few moments before I felt strong arms around me, drawing me back. I squealed, wiggling and squirming to get away as Nixon pulled me against his sweaty chest, leaning over my shoulder to plant a kiss on my cheek.

"*Eww*, Nix! You're all... *gross*!"

"You know you like it. You ain't gotta pretend, baby," he said, swatting me on the butt once he'd released me from his hold.

"We're in front of the babies!" I wagged a finger at him to increase the weight of my scolding, since I really *couldn't* deny the fact that sweaty Nixon kind of... okay *definitely* turned me on. He wasn't smelly, just... wet, and hot, and friggin' *sexy*.

Nixon sucked his teeth. "Man, these babies know what it is. How you think they got here? It wasn't cause mommy and daddy were holding hands."

"*Nix*," I said, pressing my hands into him to push him back. I was trying to get him away from the kids, but instead of moving him, my fingers just slid in the slick ridges of his abs, and he stayed planted exactly where he was, without exerting any effort.

I yelped when he grabbed my waist again, dragging me against his chest and planting a juicy kiss on me. My first inclination was to push away, but when his tongue slipped into my mouth I gave that up, and leaned into the kiss.

"Get a room!" Roman teased, from somewhere beside us.

Nixon grinned when he pulled away, and a moment later, he'd picked me up and draped me over his shoulder. "That's sounds like a good plan, Rome. We'll catch y'all later."

I was glad I'd chosen to wear a bit longer dress than I'd originally planned, because my ass was in the air for the minute or so it took us to get across the street to our building, where he finally put me down. He spent the walk up to the apartment teasing and flirting, reminding me of what it was like between us before. It made me feel kinda silly for allowing five years of us being apart.

"You had a good time?" he asked, waiting for me to unlock the door.

I nodded. "Some much needed fun to balance out the investigations, and insurance claims, and all of that."

"Glad you enjoyed yourself baby."

In the apartment, he went straight to the kitchen, washing his hands before he pulled a bottle of water from the fridge. Looking over my shoulder, I shot him a scowl as I tossed my keys into the bowl on the counter. "I *was* enjoying myself, until you decided to come and spread your funk all over me."

Nixon stopped, holding the water bottle in mid-air as a sly smirk appeared on his face. "Charlie... baby... come on, now."

"Come on now *what*?" I quipped back, propping my hands on my hips.

"Acting like you wouldn't be down for a little bit of sweaty one-on-one."

He approached me slowly, a light sheen of sweat still beaded on his skin as he stepped in front of me. The heat in his gaze made warmth blossom between my legs as he placed his hands at my hips, drawing me close.

I bit my lip, playing coy as he lowered his mouth to my neck, sucking and biting until my knees felt weak. "Nixon, for real. Go get in the shower."

"This first."

His hands went up my dress, and I whimpered.

"This isn't sexy, boy."

"Then why are you *so* wet?" he asked, pulling a gasp from my lips as his fingers slipped past the waistband of my panties, and inside of me. He stroked and teased, wearing a wicked grin as he eased me backwards, against the pantry door.

I moaned powerlessly, parting my legs for him as he pushed

deeper, even while I searched my mind for a response. "I'm wet because... because I..."

"Because *you... can't... help it.*"

He spoke those words right against my lips, punctuating each one with a kiss before he moved his mouth back to my neck. I draped my arms over his shoulders, nails in his back as he continued to stroke. A moment later, he stopped, and I was about to protest but then my panties were pushed to the side, and *he* was inside me. Any little complaint died on my lips.

He drove into me with confidence, hooking my leg over his arm as he stroked, faster, deeper, harder until I couldn't stand on my own anymore. He picked me up, positioning me at the edge of the counter so he could enter me again. I wrapped my legs around his waist, rocking my hips against his, meeting him stroke for stroke.

"I should probably stop, right?" he breathed into my ear as I pulled him close, my arms tight around his neck so he couldn't pull back.

"What? You better not."

He chuckled. "Yeah, I mean... I'm all sweaty and shit... should probably take a shower so I don't gross you out." He stopped moving, then attempted to move away, but I dug my nails into his shoulders.

"Nixon, I will *kill* you."

He laughed louder, then slowly pushed into me again, burying himself as far as my body would allow. "Oh, you must be *close* if you're threatening my life." He kissed me, then drew my bottom lip between his teeth, nipping, then gently sucking it before he pulled away. "But I'm so damn disgusting right now, baby."

"*Plea—Ah!*"

He slammed into me hard, easily pulling out of my embrace, letting me know he really hadn't been trying that hard before. "Tell me you like it."

"*Mmm*, I like it," I moaned as he reached between us, teasing my clit as he stroked me again.

He shook his head, then plunged in again. "Not convincing. Tell me again."

"I *love* it."

He lifted an eyebrow, grinning in admiration as I shamelessly wound my hips against him. Grabbing the hem of my dress, which was already hiked around my waist, he snatched it over my head, tossing it onto the floor. He made quick work of my bra, but didn't bother with my panties. They stayed twisted haphazardly to the side as he lowered his mouth to my breasts, licking and nipping and sucking until my nipples were hard enough to cut glass.

My legs started to shake, and a hot, pleasant buzz began to spread over my skin. I was almost, *almost* there... and he stopped again. He bit his lip, flashed those *damned* dimples as he looked me right in the eyes and said, "*Sorry, baby.* But, you said you *love* it." He started a slow, easy stroke that felt good, but wasn't giving me what I needed. "I'm not feeling like you *love* it, you know? I think I need to hear it again, honeybun."

"Nixon Graham," I said, trying to keep the desperation out of my voice. "You are a *horrible* person for teasing me like this, but fine, I *love* your sweaty, fresh off the basketball court di— *oh my God!*"

I squeezed my eyes tight as he delved into me again, burrowing further, pounding harder, stroking faster, sending me rocketing toward release. We were *both* sweaty now, and he had one hand wrapped around my thigh, propping it up for deeper entry, while the other hand kept moving between my legs. I came with such intensity that I saw stars, and just barely felt Nixon still moving until he exploded as well.

When I finally caught my breath, I smacked him on the shoulder as he slowly pulled out. "Silly ass," I scolded, trying to fight against his contagious grin.

"What did I do?"

"You know what you did."

"Yeah, gave you the best sweaty dick of your life, that's what I did."

He helped me down from the counter, then smacked my butt again as he followed me to the shower. There, we made love again, then put on just enough clothes not to scandalize the delivery person when the food we ordered arrived.

"Hey," Nixon said, pulling me into his lap as we relaxed on the couch. "I've been thinking about it... and you know how you've been asking me for years about doing some rebranding for Pot Liquor, modernizing the logo, all of that?"

I nodded. "Yeah, of course. You've told me no like thirty times, because you're mean."

"I told you no like *fifty* times, because *you're* mean."

"I'm not—" I stopped, thinking about some of the things I'd said to him over the years, including that wish that he would fall into the deep dryer. "Okay, maybe I was a *little* mean."

Nixon grinned. "Uh huh. Well... since we're basically starting over anyway, maybe you should talk to a graphic designer about the logo. You wanted to do it, so... I'll let you take lead on that. We'll go with whatever you decide."

"You think we should be moving on something like that already?" I asked, resting against his shoulder. "The investigation isn't over, and we don't know what the insurance company is gonna do."

He shook his head. "Nah, we're moving forward regardless. I've got savings, I'll get another loan.... Whatever needs to happen. But when we can start cleaning up the space, clearing things out, I think we should be ready. So... we've gotta get this other stuff done."

"Okay." I nuzzled my face into his neck, breathing him in. "I'll talk to Simone, see if she can put me in touch with whoever she used." I kissed the space between his neck and shoulder, then brought my hand up to caress his ear.

"Yeah... sounds like a good idea," Nixon murmured absently, closing his eyes.

I kissed him again, then moved to straddle his lap. "You tired baby?"

"I am... and what you're doing feels good."

He opened his eyes, then gripped me at the hips, pulling me closer so I could feel his hardness.

"Again, Nix? Are you serious?"

He gave me a sleepy smile. "Hell yeah. We've got five years to catch up on."

***

"I *CANNOT* BELIEVE I AGREED TO THIS SHIT."

I smirked at the disgust on his face as Eddie looked around the graphic designer's office. He glanced warily at the "living wall" of green plants that lined the office, then around at the natural stone and wood tones that made up the rest of the office. It really was like stepping into a whole different realm.

The designer's office was located in one of the newer buildings on the block, so everything else had a very clean, modern look, in blacks, whites, and stainless steel. Simone had described the woman as "earthy", but I'd imagined more... *hippy* than "zen". Poor Eddie looked so out of his element. His style was eclectic enough — a perfectly pressed oxford paired with ripped jeans and shoes that looked fresh out of the box — but he still looked very... *misplaced* against such natural elements.

Her desk was empty when we walked in, so we sat down in the comfortable chairs in front of it.

"What's wrong, Eddie?" I asked, trying not to laugh at his scowl.

He turned to me with a raised eyebrow. "If this chick comes in here burning sage, I'm out."

Before I could respond to his silliness, a door opened behind the desk, and a girl with long twists walked in, the clunky heels of her boots clicking against the natural stone tile floor. In a word, she was... *cool.* Dark skinny jeans, white tank, tribal print blazer, tons of chunky wood jewelry and an extremely pretty, make-up free face in sable skin.

She brought a calm, pleasant energy into the room with her, and I couldn't help smiling as she rounded the desk and came right up to us.

"Hi, you must be Charlie?" she said, surprising me with the calm sensuality of her voice. I was expecting... perky, from this girl who barely looked older than twenty. She extended her hand, and I returned the gesture. "I'm Astrid Wilson... hopefully your new designer."

Eddie's deep tenor broke in. "I'm sorry, *you're* the designer? Little girl, quit playing. Is this bring your daughter to work day or something? Does your mama know you're playing in her office? Where is she?"

Astrid's face spread into a smile. There was no trace of annoyance as she turned to Eddie, sweeping him with a gaze before she returned to his face. I *knew* that "hey boo" look in her eyes, and fought my own smile.

"I have no idea where my mother is at the moment, but this is *my* place of business, and I'm perfectly capable of handling it — and my clients — without her assistance. I have no children, and I'm not one myself. I'm twenty-five years old, brother. A grown ass woman... I *assure you*."

Holy shit.

I didn't think a day would ever come where I saw a man or woman knock Eddie off balance, but there he was, eyes wide with interest and attraction, lips slightly parted like he didn't know what to say.

With a little grin playing at her lips, Astrid turned to me, winked, then said, "Alright Ms. Bennett. Let's talk about what I can do for you today."

chapter
seventeen

Nixon

I would never get tired of waking up next to Charlie.

Even though it had been the norm for the six years we were together, all of a sudden it felt like a novelty. Like a prize I'd won for completing a challenge. Only... now I knew that without proper care, my privileges could be easily revoked. *That* wouldn't happen again. Not as long as I could help it.

The sun wasn't quite up, but light was starting to filter in through the curtains. With her eyes still closed, and her bare breasts gently rising and falling with her breath, Charlie seemed at peace. I reached out to touch her, not to wake her up, but because I just couldn't help it.

She stirred a little, reacting to the impact of my hand at her waist, caressing her skin. Her eyes stayed closed, so I pulled away, leaving her to sleep while I climbed out of bed and headed for the shower.

Under the spray of the hot water, I closed my eyes. Today marked two weeks since the loss of the restaurant, and it still... just didn't quite feel real. We'd been to the site, had the damage assessed, ruled out foul play, all of that... and *still*... it just kind of felt like something that... happened.

I grinned as soft hands circled my waist.

Charlie stepped into the shower then pulled the curtain closed behind her, smiling as I turned around. I kissed my honeybun, morning breath and all, and she giggled when I drew her closer, lowering my hands to squeeze handfuls of her butt. We stayed in the shower, touching and playing and cleaning each other until the water ran cold, then stood side by side in front of the sink to brush our teeth.

Unreal.

This was like... an alternate reality or something. Waking up with Charlie. Showering with Charlie. Brushing teeth with Charlie. Such a difference from not even six months ago, when she made no effort to hide her continued disdain for me.

And all it took was a damned conversation.

I made a mental note of that, tucking it with the other things I'd learned during our separation. *Just talk shit out. No excuses. Just sit down, and say what you have to say.* That went right beside *make sure it's really a breakup*, and *don't keep the girl waiting six years for a ring.*

While I got dressed to leave, she pulled on a little dress that barely skimmed the tops of her thighs and left the room. I hadn't even gotten my shirt over my head, but I followed, my attention stuck to the easy sway of her hips. She giggled when I reached out to grab the hem of her dress, smacking my hand away as she went into the kitchen. I sat down on the other side of the counter, at the bar.

"So, what's on the agenda for today?" Charlie asked, looking up at me as she pulled a basket of eggs from the refrigerator, followed shortly by a variety of vegetables.

I scratched at my eyebrow, cringing a little before I gave her an answer. "Another meeting with the contractor, remember?"

Charlie paused mid egg-crack to roll her eyes at me, then went back to what she was doing without saying a word. She had a long standing bias against construction contractors — and a long standing ban against participating in meetings with them — since she tried to put a screwdriver through one's hand when we first opened Pot Liquor.

To her credit, that guy was a complete asshole, at least to her. He never started shit around me, but when she would go and check on the site, it was always condescending "let's wait until the boss man is around" or "I don't think you know what you're talking about, little lady". What burned Charlie up the most was, "are you sure you have the authority to make a decision like that?" as if she hadn't put up half the money to pay his crew in the first place. But him *touching* her was the final straw, and his crew had to pull Charlie off him. The only things that kept me from killing him: I wasn't there when it happened, and Charlie begging me to *please keep your ass out of jail, don't you dare leave me saddled with a half-finished restaurant and this big-assed loan.*

In any case, she had no interest in dealing with contractors anymore. Even when we fired ole boy, and had to hire someone new, she shifted that responsibility to me, and found another way to help.

"So have they given you any estimates on how long it will take?" She pushed the whisked eggs to the side so she could chop the vegetables while they warmed to room temperature.

I sighed a bit as I thought about yesterday's meetings, one with Grant about the fire, the other with the new contractor. Charlie had a late meeting with the graphic designer, and by the time we were both back at the apartment, we were too tired to do anything except sleep.

"About eighteen months."

Charlie put her knife down, staring across the counter at me with her lips parted. "*Eighteen* months? Are you serious?"

I drew my shoulders up, then nodded. "Unfortunately, yeah. The site has to be completely cleared, the rest of the building torn down because they've gotta do some stuff with the foundation. Then we can actually start rebuilding, and it has to be done carefully, because Urban Grind is on the other side, and we don't want to cause any damage there. Not to mention the shit-ton of building inspections we're gonna have to pass."

"Why so many inspections?"

"Grant told me yesterday that the fire was caused by electrical issues. I mean... I wasn't *too* surprised, because I knew some of the buildings still had the old original wiring. Roman updated UG, we updated Pot Liquor, and we were trying to talk to the other owners about updating theirs too— precisely so this kinda shit *wouldn't* happen—, plus some other remodeling stuff just to make the block look better in general. We even offered to help offset the costs, since it would benefit everybody. Everybody was on board except Mr. Parker. Come to find out, his ass had been paying off the inspector. The other businesses with the old wiring were getting citations and shit for it, while *his* ass was skinning and grinning talking about he passed. If he hadn't died in the fire, I would've punched him in his damn face."

Charlie's mouth dropped open. "*Nixon!*"

"What?! Charlie, he didn't even have connected smoke detectors, sprinkler system not working, just... wild ass negligence, and was *smug* about it. We put *everything* into that place for almost ten years, and it's gone because he couldn't buy a hundred dollars' worth of smoke detectors? Hell *I* would've bought the things. So yeah, I would've punched his old ass, with no regrets."

Shaking her head, Charlie finished chopping her veggies, and finally turned on the stove. "I don't know about punching anybody."

"Says the girl that tried to separate a man's finger from his body."

"Well, he should have kept his damned hands to himself." Charlie tossed me a little grin, then reached to grab her omelet pan from the rack. "Anyway... eighteen months is a long time. Everybody will have forgotten about us by then."

I shook my head. "Not so. I mean... that was the whole point of the meeting with Astrid yesterday, right? To talk about building a website, doing the cooking videos on YouTube, keeping our name in front of people..."

"Right. But... we still have bills to pay in the meantime. And what about our employees? I mean, it was a *great* plan to keep a surplus in the payroll account so we could still pay them for the last two weeks, but that's *ten* people, Nix. We can't pay them indefinitely with no income, and the website and YouTube channel aren't gonna cut it. Neither is the cookbook."

Pushing out a heavy breath, I laid my forehead on the counter. "I know, I know babe. I'm still figuring that part out."

For a moment, neither of us spoke. Then, Charlie looked up from her skillet and gave me a bright smile. She leaned over the counter, grabbing my face in her hands to kiss me, then went back to the stove. "Brighten up, Nix," she said, glancing at me over her shoulder as she poured eggs into the pan. "Remember what we said, no negativity, right? We'll figure things with the restaurant out, and it'll be fine. *You* almost weren't. *We* almost weren't. But we are. *You* are. And that's the most important part. We have *plenty* to smile about."

"And pity parties don't make payroll."

Grinning, Charlie turned again, pointing her silicone spatula at me. "O-*kay*?!"

I got up, moving around the counter to get into the kitchen, where I approached her from behind and wrapped her in my arms. She was absolutely right. Of course it hurt to lose something we'd worked so hard to build, for such a large part of our life. But when it came down to it… being able to hold the love of my life in my arms again was what really mattered.

***

"Man you still haven't given her that damned ring?"

I scowled at Carter in the passenger seat before I turned my eyes back to the road. I'd brought him along with me to the meeting with the contractor, then to another meeting I'd set up after my conversation with Charlie that morning. I *had* been feeling good until this fool told me he still hadn't proposed to Viv. Months had gone by since that day in the barbershop. What the hell was he doing?

Across the car, Carter sighed. "I'm trying to figure out the right time to do it. We're *just now* coming up on a year together. Isn't that too soon?"

"Man, I knew I wanted to spend my life with Charlie before we ever went on a date, so… I'm probably the wrong person to ask." I chuckled, thinking of the crush I'd had on Charlie since we were little kids. She was pretty, and smart, and funny, and she could hang with the guys. And I don't mean she was hanging around trying to be seen, either. She would play any sport we played, talk about anything we talked about, watch any movie we wanted to see, and actually enjoy what she was doing. And she had a potty mouth to be reckoned with. It was love at first "fuck you".

"So what the hell do I do?"

"Give her the damn ring, genius." I laughed at Carter's deadpan expression. "Look... when is the actual day of your anniversary? And *please* tell me you know that shit."

He gave me a wry smile. "It's next Saturday."

"Same day as Charlie's birthday?"

"Yeah."

I nodded. "Okay. So we're doing the birthday dinner thing at Honeybee, right? You bring Viv, everybody is feeling good, having fun. After dinner, take her somewhere nice, with a view of the water, and propose. Keep it simple."

"Is that what you would do for Charlie?"

"Nah. I would go even simpler than that for her, because I know that's what she would prefer. Cook her favorite meal, take her to the bedroom and tire her out, then put the ring on her finger. Done."

Carter looked out the window, chin cupped in his hand like he was deep in thought. Finally, he turned back and nodded. "Yeah. I think I'm gonna do that. I mean... I've gotta do something. About a month ago, she kinda freaked out, wondering what we were doing... I let her know I wasn't going anywhere."

"Good... but you know it's still on her mind, right?"

"Yeah. That's why I'm ready to go ahead and make a move. What about you and Charlie? I see you're back to being neighborhood sweethearts again."

I chuckled. "Yeah... we're just taking it easy though, you know? It's like the honeymoon phase again right now, we're feeling each other out. I know *one* thing I'm not gonna do."

"Yeah? What's that?"

Shaking my head, I pulled into the parking lot behind our building. "Wait another six damned years to lock her down."

***

"I T   W A S   A   B L A C K ,   F R O Z E N ,   S N O W Y   N I G H T   I N   19...
whatever makes it 34 years ago. A blizzard, up in the Spanish Pyre-
nees, and I was stuck at the ski lodge. It was a luxury resort, in
Baqueira, but *still*... stuck is stuck. A beautiful, tragically stranded
expat meets a handsome stranger with an Italian accent but tawny,
olive-toned skin. *That* is how the story begins. I was sitting at the
bar..."

Charlie tapped me on the shoulder, her expression a mixture of
horrified and confused as she leaned to speak into my ear. "Is my
mother *really* telling the story of my conception to a room full of
people?"

I chuckled, then kissed her cheek. "Looks like it, baby."

Melissa Bennet was by no means sloppy drunk, but the slight
drag in her words certainly indicated a bit of tipsiness. But it was all
good. It was a celebration, with friends and family. Everybody,
including Melissa, was having fun.

Roman and Simone, with their two kids, with Leah looking a
little... uncomfortable with her husband beside them. Eddie was
there with a guy I assumed was his date, but he kept shooting
glances at Astrid, who was ignoring the shit out of him to pay
attention to her own date. *That* was funny. Viv and Carter were
there as well, along with Rod, Carter's little brother.

We listened and laughed along as she weaved a *very* entertaining tale of seducing some maybe Italian/maybe Spanish man,
then making a "narrow" escape down a mountain in the middle of
a blizzard after he'd declared his love. Afterwards, she stood up,
took a bow, declared the story entirely fictional, then took *another*
bow.

We sang happy birthday, had cake, and when Lorenzo walked
in to bring Charlie a gift, Melissa — as expected — disappeared. In
the excitement of opening gifts, Carter slipped out with Viv,

tipping up his head at me as they left. I mouthed "good luck" to him, then turned back to Charlie just as she was slamming the top back on a box from her Aunt Morgan.

"What's up?" I asked, confused by the flush of red crossing her skin.

She lifted an eyebrow at me, then raised the corner of the box, showing me the contents — a big pile of sex toys.

"That's from both of us, my love," her Aunt Morgan said from across the table, pointing between herself and Melissa's empty seat with a smile. "You kids have lots and lots of fun, okay?"

I grinned. "Oh, we *certainly* will."

Charlie smacked me on the leg, and I chuckled as she went through the rest of the pile. To open in front of everyone, I gave her a few ingredient books she'd been wanting, along with a good camera she could use to take pictures and film video for the site. Later, when the party was over, and we were back home, showered, and relaxing in bed, I put a flat square box into her hands.

"What is this?" she asked, smiling as I sat up beside her.

"Just open it."

She raised an eyebrow, chewing at her lip as she lifted the top off the box, then pulled out a set of keys. Her fingers went immediately to the key ring, custom made into the new Pot Liquor logo she'd worked on with Astrid.

"Nix... are you gonna explain?"

I grinned, then turned her to face me. "You know a couple of weeks ago, when we talked about how long it was gonna take to get the restaurant open, and there was some concern about income during that time, right?"

She nodded. "Right."

"Well..."— I gestured toward the keys— "Problem solved. You are holding the keys to Pot Liquor's new food truck."

I got a little tense for a moment, wondering how she would react. She could get really pissed that I'd moved forward on something like that without her, but I *hoped* her eyes would light up with happiness, well up with tears... something like that.

Hopefully.

Charlie threw her arms around my neck in a tight hug, then

pulled back to plant a kiss on my lips. "Nixon, are you serious? A *food truck*? That is... so friggin' *cool!*"

Yes!

"When did... when have you had time for this?" she asked, grinning down at the keys in her hand as she sat back.

Shaking my head, I placed my hand over hers. "Well, it's not ready to operate yet. All we have is the truck right now, but it's ours. Astrid is working on the signage and stuff for us, and everybody has agreed to advertise, put out flyers, tell their customers, all of that."

"So everybody knew about this? Everybody is helping?"

I chuckled a little, reaching up to wipe away a stray tear that escaped the corner of her eye. "Yeah. We're family, right? You would do the same thing, wouldn't you?'

She nodded, then sniffled, trying not to break into full on tears. "And the website... all of that... that helps drive interest, and now we'll actually have a place to send people."

"Exactly, baby. We'll adjust the menu, start offering breakfast. I've already applied for permits for a good spot to reach the corporate people for breakfast, lunch, and dinner... it'll take a couple of months to be ready, but we'll be back in business, baby. Then we won't have to worry about rushing to get the restaurant ready. We can make it even better."

Charlie smiled, then reached to pull me into another embrace. "Nix... I am *so* happy... and all of this sounds really good, but... I know the insurance hasn't released any money yet. How is this getting paid for? I haven't seen any money come out of the restaurant accounts for something like this."

"That's cause I didn't use *restaurant* money."

She narrowed her eyes for a moment, then a moment later they widened with understanding. "No. *No.* You used your personal savings for this?"

"Charlie, listen to me. It's okay."

Shaking her head, she opened her mouth to give a rebuttal, but I covered it with my hand.

"*Stop*. It's fine. I invested that money in the food truck because I believe in us. If something goes bad, yeah, I'll take it back from the restaurant, but until then, we're good. I *promise* you, okay. I told you I would figure it out, right?"

She nodded. "I knew you would, it's just... I don't understand how you've always managed to make sure things were taken care of."

I shrugged. "Because I always wanna see you happy. Make you smile. Not having to fire our employees because we couldn't pay them makes *both* of us smile. Makes *everybody* happy."

Charlie smiled, then leaned in to kiss me again. "I love you *so* much."

"I love you too honeybun," I said, drawing her into my arms. "Happy birthday."

chapter
eighteen

Charlie

I KINDA WANTED TO THROW UP.

I was *tired.* Like, *real ass* tired. Friggin' *exhausted*, after staying up late and waking up early this entire week, trying to put together a good-sized database of recipes for the site, including step-by-step pictures.

Exhausted.

And disgusted by the thought of looking at, smelling, tasting, touching, or cooking any more food. I'd done enough taste-testing in the past week to last a lifetime — or at least until it was time to start developing the menu for the food truck.

The food truck.

Just the thought of that lifted my spirits. It was the perfect way to expand our business, and bring in some income while the restaurant was rebuilt, and an idea I wouldn't have even thought of. But my man did.

I sighed, then stood up from the computer.

My man.

Why the hell did it feel so easy and natural to refer to Nixon as *my man* when it had barely even been a month? Maybe... because deep down, I'd always considered him mine. I mean, you don't love someone the way I loved him for *six years* and then just... forget. And honestly, it was more like eleven years. I was kidding myself if I thought those five years of harsh words and snarky comebacks were anything other than an attempt to deflect. As soon as I was back in close proximity with him, my ability to be cold — and honestly *mean* — to him had evaporated.

Voodoo dick, girl. You couldn't help it.

Damned right I couldn't. There was actually a hitch in my step now, accommodating the pleasant soreness between my legs from the night before, when a sleepy-sex quickie turned into an all-night thing, with us passing out asleep between sessions, then waking up every few hours to try a different position. It was very "new relationship" of us, but like he'd said before... we had a lot to catch up on.

I clutched my hand to my mouth, trying to hold back a dry heave as I stepped into the bathroom. The pistachio cream scent of my body wash still filled the room from my shower a while before. Then, the aroma had been fine, but now... *gag*.

Thinking back, if I didn't know better, I would think I was pregnant.

Wait... *did* I know better?

I pulled my phone from the pocket of my shorts, then logged into my app to check the *exact* date of my last period.

Almost five weeks ago.

Which was really nothing to panic about.

Nothing to panic about.

Nothing to panic about.

So... I panicked.

I dropped to my knees in front of the bathroom counter, flinging the door open and digging frantically through the contents. In my head, I cursed myself for throwing away all of those pregnancy tests that last day in Cali. I *really* could have used one right now, but if I were a lucky girl, Viv would have one... somewhere.

Please Viv, have one somewhere.

Just when I was about to give up, I spotted a familiar white foil wrapper, with pink and black lettering. *Hell yes*, I thought, reaching all the way to the back of the cabinet for the stray test, which must have fallen out of a box of several.

My hands shook as I tore it open, then shoved my shorts away from my hips and sat down on the toilet. A minute later, I was washing my hands while the test rested on the counter, waiting for those two minutes to pass.

It was kinda like deja-vu. This scene was a repeat of three months ago, when I was taking that test before I got on my flight, praying that it gave me a reading of negative. Only this time... I wasn't quite sure *what* I wanted that test to say.

Wait.

That's a lie.

I wanted it to be positive.

Was that even okay, to want that?

Again... Nixon and I had only been back together a month. We had a lot of history, sure, but we didn't even really know if *we* were gonna work out. We were still stuck in kind of a... second honeymoon phase. What if once the newness wore off, we discovered that breaking up wasn't the mistake... getting back together was?

In any case, we hadn't exactly been *preventing* pregnancy. We'd been having sex like it was going out of style, without a thought of contraception. And I was a pretty firm believer that if you weren't trying *not* to get pregnant... you were *trying* to get pregnant. Nixon hadn't once mentioned birth control, never pulled out a condom to use with me... so it that what happened? We were *trying* to have a baby?

The timer on my phone went off, indicating that the requisite two minutes had gone by. I took a deep breath, but couldn't make myself look at the test.

What if I *was* pregnant, and I lost it again? What if it was already gone? I drank quite a bit at my birthday party a couple of weeks ago... if I was pregnant now, it meant I was pregnant *then* and alcohol is one of the biggest no-no's. What if I hadn't even given the baby a damned *chance*?

The phone chimed again, because I didn't respond the first time. I turned the alarm off, took another deep breath, then picked up the test and held it in front of my eyes.

Two pink lines.

I gasped, and tears immediately sprang to my eyes. I covered my mouth with my hand, and just kept staring at the test... hoping it wasn't gonna change in front of my eyes.

Positive.

Meaning *pregnant*.

By Nixon.

Holy shit.

I lifted my gaze to the mirror, not realizing until I was looking at myself that I was smiling. I couldn't *stop* smiling. Or glowing. I was... damn, I was already *glowing*. Or maybe it was just because I was so damned happy.

Yeah.

Happy.

I almost tripped over my own feet getting into the bedroom to change clothes. I pulled on a pair of jeans, a light sweater, and shoved my feet into flats. I had to tell Nix we were having a *baby*, and a phone call wouldn't do.

His reaction was something I didn't second-guess for a moment.

I pushed the laptop closed as I passed by, grabbed my keys, checked my back pocket for my phone, flipped off the lights, and opened the door.

I expected to step into the hall, closing and locking the door behind me, but there, standing in front of my door with a huge bouquet of roses was someone I'd hoped I was done with. His hand was raised to knock, and he was dressed as impeccably as ever. When he caught my gaze, his handsome face spread into a smile.

"Charlie... that gorgeous face of yours is a sight for sore eyes. I have missed the hell out of you girl."

Heart racing, I managed to pull my lips into a tight smile, because I could *not* say the same.

"Hello Adrian."

***

REALLY, *REALLY* AWKWARD.

If there's ever a question about how it feels to invite the man who is legally your husband into the home you're currently sharing with your ex-boo who became your *next* boo once it didn't work out with the *first* guy you dated after aforementioned husband went to jail...

Friggin' awkward.

That's the answer.

Since that crazy weekend which seemed so long ago now, where I'd slept with Nixon, fought with Nixon, then gotten dumped by Trent, I'd been ignoring Adrian's calls. After about a week, they stopped. Anything he needed to say to me could go through my lawyer, and *she* hadn't called.

It seemed crazy now, but really... it had been very, *very* easy to simply pretend he didn't exist. Just a little blip from the past, which I stored away, along with thoughts of the money and bank accounts I'd lost because of him. With so much going on, between the fire, and getting back with Nixon, and starting the food truck and the website, I realized I hadn't even been pretending. I just didn't have room in my mind — or my life — for Adrian and his nonsense.

Adrian sat down on the couch, and I sat across from him in one of the armchairs, warily eying the bouquet of roses he brought.

I *hated* roses.

But Adrian wouldn't know that. Because really, he didn't know me. Three, almost four years married, and the man didn't even know what flowers I liked.

"So," I said, breaking the uncomfortable silence. "What... are you doing here?"

Adrian smiled, tipping his head to the side. "What do you mean, what am I doing here? I came to see my wife."

"You *know* what I mean. How did you get out of prison, and why didn't you call first? I could have saved you the trouble of coming by."

He sat forward, propping his elbows on his knees. "Well, I've said from the beginning that I was innocent, I just needed to be able to prove that. Brandon — you know him, Brandon Jensen, the consulting firm we moved to Cali for? — he had a hookup with a guy he knew back in New Orleans. A guy that can get into anybody's computer system, anywhere."

"So, a hacker. Is that how you know where I live?"

Adrian nodded. "Yeah, a hacker. And no, my lawyer figured out your address for me. But anyway, the hacker thing... it could have backfired... *if* it didn't turn out so awesomely well. He was able to find the money trails, emails, *everything*, proving that I was not, have not ever been, and do not ever plan to be, intentionally involved with any kind of securities fraud. One of the higher-ups from a company that tried to get me to come and work for them set me up! But... ol' boy packaged it up in a neat little file, sent a copy to everybody who needed to see it, and I am *free*, baby!"

He clapped his hands, and my face spread into a full-on smile. When he stood up, and pulled me up with him, I accepted it, allowing him to pull me into an embrace. But then, he drew back, aiming his lips toward mine, and I put a hand between us and wiggled out of his arms.

Adrian lifted an eyebrow, running his tongue over his lips as he slipped his hands into his pockets. "Seriously, Charlie? Even now, after you see me here in front of you, I'm telling you I'm innocent, and have *proof*, and still you act like this with me? What is the problem?"

"Adrian... I've tried to talk to you about this, while you were still in prison. I am *genuinely* happy for you. I'm glad you've been vindicated. I was hoping, even when it didn't seem like it made sense, that you really hadn't done the things they said. And it looks like that's the case. I think that's *excellent*. But..."

He shook his head as he scoffed. "Ah, the infamous *but*. What is it?"

"This marriage, Adrian. It past the expiration date a long time ago, and we both know that. We didn't get married for love, we got married because it was convenient... but I'm ready for love now."

"Okay, so let's work on that. We can build. I know you stopped answering my calls because of the stress of the case against me, but that's over now. We can focus on *us*."

Pushing out a heavy sigh, I crossed my arms over my chest. "I didn't stop answering your calls because of the case, Adrian. I stopped answering because I wanted you to leave me alone. I wanted you to stop holding up the divorce, and let me move on. I don't understand why you can't do that."

"Because I love you."

"No, you don't." I shook my head. "You don't know enough about me to *love* me. You may love having a wife, but you don't love *me*. If you did, this isn't something that would be suddenly popping up, now that I want a divorce. Not when you've made no effort to know me beyond a friend with benefits. Not when you were cashing in additional benefits somewhere else as well."

His mouth dropped open in a hint of shock, and he stuttered over his next words. "Now, Charlie. We talked about me having a little more freedom, since we weren't... cashing in benefits very often this last year. I wanted that, you wanted a baby."

"You are absolutely right. Now tell me, what married couple who *loves* each other, sees the other person as their soul mate, their forever partner, the other half of their *life*, agrees to something like that? I mean... I'm sure there are couples who do, and good for them, I don't mean to bash their lifestyle, but... that's not what I want for *me*, Adrian. We had an agreement. Dissolving the marriage if either of us wanted out *was* a part of it. I knew you to be a man of your word... so I need you to honor that."

Adrian looked at me for a long moment, then plopped down on the couch, resting his head in his hands. When he looked up at me again, his eyes were glossy, and that snatched the indignation right out of my chest.

"Charlie... come on, baby. I was accused, and almost convicted of a crime I had nothing to do with. I lost my job, lost my house, lost my money... you're the only thing I have left."

I shook my head, then sat down beside him on the couch. "That's not true, Adrian. You said Brandon helped you out, so he must have believed in you. You may have to do some major first aid to your reputation, but I'm sure he would probably hire you back, now that you've been exonerated. And you can buy another house, with the money that I'm sure they've reimbursed, now that your innocence is proven. Right?"

Reluctantly, he nodded his head. "Right."

"See? And... Adrian, I swear I don't mean to be unkind... but... as far as *me* ... you can't lose something you never had."

He tipped his head to the side. "What are you saying?"

"Well," I said, lowering my gaze to my hands. "You know when we first met, I was trying to do some investing, so I could get my restaurant away from my business partner, because we had a falling out. As you know, that never happened, and we were able to run the business amicably, from a distance. But... what you don't know is that he and I dated for six years. We came fairly close to getting married, but we broke up, right before you and I met."

"So *that* was the falling out?"

I nodded. "Yeah. But... we never really got any closure there. Never really talked it out. As much as I thought I hated him, all this time... it turns out that really wasn't the case. I'm sorry, Adrian, for even... bringing you into this. I should have sat my ass down, and waited until I got over it — if that ever happened — and *then* tried to pursue dating. Instead, I used my relationship with you as a rebound, and that really wasn't fair. Yes, we were in agreement that we weren't looking for anything serious, but I was nursing a broken heart. I didn't want to do anything that even resembled love, and I took advantage of my friendship with you. Again... I'm *sorry* for that."

Adrian shook his head. "Okay, apology accepted... but what does this have to do with now?"

"Um... well... since I've been back, some things have... changed. Nixon and I have talked through some things, and... we've decided to give it another chance. I understand that you'd like to be able to work on a love relationship between us, and turn this marriage into something real, but Adrian... I can't do that. I can't give you my heart, because it's still with the same person who's had it for the past eleven years."

With a little snort of derision, Adrian sat back into the pillows, casting his gaze on the ceiling. "So that's just... it, huh?" he asked, not even looking at me. "Just like that... I don't even have a *chance*?"

"I'm sorry. I really do think you're a good guy, Adrian, and I'm not just saying that. You're smart, handsome, and when the FBI gives you your money back, rich. I'm sure you'll find the person who's a good fit for you. Someone whose heart is available to give. Someone who is actually down with your *no exclusivity* thing."

Adrian chuckled. "I was bullshitting about that. I didn't even know you knew."

"Oh, I know," I laughed. "And I appreciate that you were discreet, even though you didn't have to be. It seemed like she made you happy, and by the end, right before you told me about the investigations and all of that... I just wanted the baby, so I was glad she was keeping you occupied. Maybe *that's* where your attention would be better received. Have you talked to her at all?"

He gave a noncommittal shrug, then sat up again. "I guess it doesn't hurt anything to tell you yeah, I have. Since you're dumping me now anyway," he laughed. "She's come to visit a few times."

My face balled up in a scowl. "Negro... she's been coming to visit your ass in federal prison — *real ass prison*— and you're stressing me out over this damned divorce? Are you *crazy*? Wait, no, don't answer that. Your ass is definitely crazy."

"You think so? I don't know... I kinda feel like she only wants me *because* I'm married."

I lifted an eyebrow. "Um... well... why don't you *ask*? Best way to get an answer to a question— wait a minute... mofo, is *that* why you're coming to me with this "I love you so much please don't leave me" crap!? So your damned sidepiece who *likes* being a sidepiece won't leave you?"

Adrian's eyes went wide, and he hesitated a little bit too long before he answered. "Uh... no?"

Heat flared in my chest, and my hands twitched, itching to be drawn into fists. "Adrian... get your ass out of my apartment. And you'd *better* sign those damned papers, or you're gonna have some more legal troubles on your hands. And make sure somebody from the FBI calls me about my damned money too."

"*Okay, okay!*" He said, chuckling as he lifted his hands in defense. "I'm sorry, okay? I... look, I'll see what I can do about the divorce, okay? Talk to my lawyer, see what I can make happen."

"Oh, you *better*."

"I *will*."

Adrian stood, reaching for another hug.

"I'm gonna go ahead and get out of here…are we good?"

With a raised eyebrow, I allowed the hug, then grudgingly told him we were good. I mean… I really just wanted this to be over. If that's what it took, *fine*.

Once he left, I breathed a sigh of relief, and felt a weight lift off my shoulders that I hadn't even realized was there. But I was *so* glad it was gone.

I was so glad *he* was gone.

He hadn't even been on my mind before, but now that he was there, he was *on* it, and the first place my thoughts landed were with Nixon. I was sure that he, along with everyone else, assumed that I was divorced before I even came back to the city… and I hadn't exactly been transparent. Most people don't really want to ask you about a divorce, and I'd been capitalizing on that. No one had asked, so I simply hadn't told, which was fair.

Right?

Wrong.

I closed my eyes, and pushed out a heavy sigh. I didn't need this. This was supposed to be a happy time. I shook my shoulders, trying to brush off any negative energy, and focused my mind on *that*. I needed to let Nixon know that if all went as it should — and I was praying like hell that it *would* — in about nine months, he was gonna be a daddy.

chapter
nineteen

Charlie

I FLINCHED WHEN THE FRONT DOOR OPENED.

"Babe, you won't *believe* how well the food truck is coming along. You busy? I want you to come with me when I head back down there."

Damn.

I hadn't even had a chance to catch my breath from Adrian's visit before Nixon came breezing through the door, chatting about the latest happenings with the food truck. I wasn't even expecting him home.

If he'd been ten minutes earlier...

"Charlie?"

I looked up at Nixon's handsome face, smiling from the kitchen as he lifted a bottle of water to his mouth.

"Yeah?" I answered, trying not give in to the anxiety creeping up my spine.

Nixon grinned, tipping his head to the side. "I asked you a question... what, you still feeling tired from last night?"

I wanted to smile at that. I *really* did. But... I couldn't. As much as I wanted to just be bubbly, and happy, and share good news about the baby... guilt was at the forefront of my emotions.

"I need to you tell something."

Eyebrow lifted, Nixon moved toward me from the kitchen.

"What's going on? Are you okay?" His eyes fell on the bouquet on the table. "What's up with the flowers? You *hate* roses."

"Um... I do. They're from Adrian."

I swallowed hard, waiting for Nixon to recognize the name. "Adrian... as in your ex-husband, currently sitting in prison, on trial for fraud?"

"Adrian as in... my *current* husband, cleared of all charges."

At first, he chuckled, then looked at me, waiting for me to laugh along, or at least crack a smile. When I didn't, his expression changed to confusion.

"Charlie... what the hell are you talking about?"

I took a deep breath, then clasped my hands in front of me, planting my feet to combat my sudden lightheadedness. "Um... well... right before I moved back here, I filed for divorce. And... I talked to him, and explained that I was ready to move on, but he wouldn't sign the papers. I was asking, and asking, and *asking*, but he insisted that he wanted to try to work it out... so he wouldn't approve it."

Nixon scratched his head, running his tongue over his lips. "So... you're telling me that we've been living together... *sleeping* together... for the last month... but you're still married?"

"Technically, yes, but—"

"You're telling me... it never fucking occurred to you that this was the type of shit you should probably tell me?"

"Nixon, I know it looks bad, but if let me explain—"

"*Explain what*, Charlie? We *just* got back together, *just now* moved past a major fail in communication. I would think this is the type of thing you'd be falling over yourself to *let me know.*"

I shook my head, blinking back tears as a dizzying wave of nausea made me sway on my feet. "I wasn't even thinking about him, Nix. With everything that was happening, the fire...It wasn't even on my mind. I was just focused on rebuilding."

"You *should* have been focused on getting a damned divorce!" Nixon gave a dry laugh, then shoved a hand into his short hair. "I can't believe this shit... I'm out here bending over backwards trying to prove myself to you, make sure you see that I'm a better man than I was, trying to show that you can trust me... and you're still married... *wow.*"

"Nixon—"

He raised his hand to stop me. "Just... save it, Charlie. I... I've gotta go."

Tears pricked my eyes as he headed toward the door, and I turned away, not really wanting to see him leave. Just *knowing* that he was walking away gave me the same heart-wrenching sensation as when he'd left me at that table five years ago, not knowing where he was going or if he was coming back.

What could I say? I *was* wrong. It didn't matter that I didn't have feelings for Adrian, didn't matter that I *wanted* a divorce... I should have told Nixon.

His heavy footsteps reached the door, and stopped. He turned the knob, but I never heard it close behind him. Just when I was about to turn around, he spoke, in a voice edged with ire, disdain, and hurt. "Are there any other secrets you need to tell me, Charlie? Anything else I need to know?"

My hand drifted up to my stomach, and I considered saying nothing. This wasn't the way I wanted to let him know. *This* wasn't the tone I wanted to set at all. But would it just upset him further if I *didn't* say anything now? If I waited until the "right" time... was that something he would see as a manipulation? Or even worse, as another deception?

He gave what I could only interpret as a disgusted snort, then I heard his footsteps again, and the door began to creak closed.

"I'm pregnant."

The door stopped, and then I heard footsteps again as it swung back open.

"What did you say?"

A sob built in my throat, but I pushed it away, clutching my arms around my stomach. "I'm pregnant," I repeated, a little louder, and what felt like barely a moment later, Nixon's hand was against my back, and he was turning me around to face him.

I didn't want to look in him in the face, but he cupped my chin, forcing my gaze upward. His expression was harsh, but warmth, excitement, hope filled his eyes... absent of the adoration I usually saw.

"Are you serious? Are you *sure*?"

I nodded, then pulled away from his touch. "Yeah. I was feeling sick, and my cycle is a little late, so I took a test this morning. I was... coming to find you when Adrian showed up."

Wrapping my arms around myself again, I stepped back, overwhelmed with the sick feeling coursing through my stomach. It wasn't morning sickness. It was the sudden absence of affection making me feel ill.

Whenever I was around Nixon, he didn't have to *say* he loved me. He *radiated* it. But not now. He was interested in the fact that I was pregnant... hopeful, even happy. But the only emotion I felt for *me* was... coldness.

He was angry.

I got that.

It was... it was fine.

"That's... Charlie, that's... amazing. And you're sure it's...?"

I dropped my gaze to the ground as those words hit me like a blow to the chest. "Yeah, Nix. The baby is yours."

"I don't mean to imply—"

"No. No, it's fine. I understand." I nodded, then gave him a dry smile.

"Okay. Well... I'm gonna head back to check on the progress at the truck. And... I might crash at Vaughn's tonight."

Another wave of pain gripped my chest.

"Yeah. Okay."

Neither of us said anything else before he left, and as soon as the door closed behind him I broke down. A dozen questions swarmed my mind. Was he *really* going to Vaughn's? When he came back, would it just be to get the stuff he'd accumulated? Were we *already* over again?

I wrapped my arms around my knees and cried, until nausea drove me into the bathroom, where I stayed there on the floor.

Maybe this really was just a mistake.

***

THAT NIGHT, NIXON CAME HOME.

Instead of staying with Vaughn, as he'd said, he came back to the apartment.

It was awkward.

He wouldn't *really* look at me, just at my stomach, as if I was magically going to sprout a baby bump at five weeks pregnant. We exchanged very few words, and instead of joining me in the bed, he slept on the couch.

For two days this went on, with us talking about things for the foot truck and website, and him asking several times a day how I was feeling. I was *feeling* like my heart was breaking again. I was *feeling* miserable, because of the tension that had replaced the happy peace we had at home. I was *feeling* anxious, wondering when one of us was finally going to say we'd messed up by trying to do this again.

But I knew he was just asking about the baby.

I found myself at the barbershop zoned out, my mind on a whole other plane as Carter gave a desperately needed trim and edge up to my short, tapered fro. He had me in the "private" chair, tucked out of sight, but I could see almost everyone else. He chattered to me about all sorts of random things, and even though I appreciated the effort, I wished he would shut up. Between Nixon and Viv, I was sure he'd heard about my epic fail, and was doing what he could to bolster my mood.

Thanks, but no thanks, future Cuz.

At least he wasn't bombarding me with tidbits about wedding plans, as Viv had over the phone. She wasn't even in the country, but I knew she was just excited, and trying to take my mind off my own problems. But... when I called her, concerned that Nix and I were already over, when we'd barely gotten started... I didn't want to hear about a winter wedding.

Instead of being rude to Carter, I tuned him out, letting the chatter of the other patrons at the shop fill my ears. Just a few feet away sat Lorenzo and Walter, Nixon's dad. Lorenzo had the men around him riveted as he told the tale of a woman — the most beautiful he'd *ever* seen — he'd met in Spain, at a luxury ski resort.

Why does that sound so familiar?

I kept listening, even as I searched my mind for why the hell his story sounded like something I'd heard before. The other guys laughed, calling him a punk when he spoke quietly about the woman stealing his heart, but Lorenzo declared he was unashamed.

I smiled a little. His mystery lady had to be *quite* a woman to keep a man like him interested for the number of years he spoke about in his story. Lorenzo was an incredibly handsome older man, with dark olive skin, thick wavy hair that he kept neatly cut, and a healthy amount of the confident arrogance that drove most women — myself included — wild, when paired with a good personality and a kind heart. If I was in the market for a sugar daddy, Lorenzo maybe could have been the chosen one.

I wrinkled my nose.

Or not.

I'd known him way too long, since I was a little girl, to think of him like that. Besides... *Melissa* was the only Bennet girl Lorenzo wanted. The smile returned to my face, thinking of how my mother had wasted no time getting herself out of dodge when he slipped into my birthday party to give me my gift. You would think *he* was the handsome foreigner she'd had to escape from on a snowy mountain.

But that was... crazy.

Wait.

Luckily, Carter was already pulling the clippers away from my head, because I stepped down, not caring about crooked lines as I moved into the center of the shop to stand right in front of Lorenzo. He flinched when he saw me, but quickly recovered, flashing me a smile.

"Pretty girl! I didn't know you were—"

"How long ago?"

He ran his tongue over his lips, glancing nervously around before he smiled again. "How long ago for what, baby girl?"

"The *story*, Lorenzo. How long ago did this happen?"

"Aww, Charlie. You know you can't trust an old man's memory. It's been so long that--"

"*How long*? Give or take thirty-four years?"

He didn't even have to respond. His sheepish expression said everything.

I snatched the barber's cape from my shoulders and tossed it into Lorenzo's lap as tears welled in my eyes. *Goddamn*, I was *so* sick of crying. I turned to Carter, who looked confused, and said, "I'll pay you later. Right now... I've just gotta get out of here." He still seemed baffled, but he nodded. Ignoring Lorenzo's pleas for me to wait, I stormed out of the shop.

Lorenzo followed right behind me, jogging to catch up and grab my elbow.

"Charlie, would you wait a moment?"

I snatched my arm away, shaking my head. "For what? What could you possibly have to say to me?"

"Not to be mad with your momma."

I scowled, turning on my heels to face him. "Why the hell not? She's been *sitting* on this information for thirty-four years! And so have you! What kind of sick shit is this? You've been around me my whole life. I've *never* felt like I was lacking anything because I didn't have a dad, partially because *you* were there. I've talked to you... confided in you... and you couldn't tell me this? All this time, and ... you couldn't just tell me?"

"It's not that simple, Charlene."

"Oh, but it is," I scoffed. "Trust me, I know. You don't withhold the truth from people you care about. Not when it's something they have a *right* to know. I'm learning that lesson now, so you should too."

"I'm *sorry*."

Rolling my eyes, I stepped away from the embrace he offered with open arms. "I believe you... but it doesn't make it okay. Just... just leave me alone."

"And what about your mom?"

With a hand on my hip, I turned back toward him. "What about her? She's jet setting right now, I'll talk to her when she gets back. What in the world did she put on you? Why are you so concerned about how I react to her? She was wrong as hell too!"

Lorenzo shook his head. "I wasn't... I wasn't a good man, Charlie. I loved your mother from the first time I saw her, but I wasn't ready to settle. I followed her here after our affair, and for a short time, while she was pregnant with you... we were very happy. But... I messed that up."

"You mean you had women around, stressing my mother out while she was pregnant?"

Again, his lack of an answer spoke for him. I turned, intending to head down the street when he grabbed my arm again. "Listen, sweetheart. Your mother was just trying to protect you. She didn't want you looking up to me, thinking you had to do the kind of stuff those women were doing to keep *my* attention to hang onto the affections of any man. I respected that, and kept my distance, but made sure you were well taken care of."

"And I guess *not* being a whore was something you never considered?"

"I tried, but—"

"Nope. Nuh uh. Don't even want to hear it." Shaking my head, I pulled away, holding up my hands in warning for him to keep his distance. "I... I don't *hate* you. I'm just pissed right now. I need some time."

He nodded, then took a step back as I turned away. As if I didn't have *enough* going on between Adrian and Nixon, now *this*? I didn't understand why I just couldn't seem to keep it together. Failed relationship *twice* now with Nixon. A failed marriage. One failed pregnancy, and now a new one I was terrified would go the same way. And a father who had been in my face my whole life without me knowing.

Awesome.

Really. Freaking. Awesome.

chapter
twenty

Nixon

"HEY BABE, YOU GOT SOMETHING IN THE MAIL!"

I flipped the lights on, then closed the door behind me as I walked in, pausing mid step to wait for a response. When I didn't receive one, I looked around as I tossed the mail onto the table.

Where was she?

The sunny early fall weather had given way to rain halfway through the day, and I was halfway surprised that there weren't candles lit all over the apartment. Charlie *loved* rain, and it was rare for her not to take the time to "set the mood". Lights off, candles, and 90s R&B were all part of what she consider the "proper" atmosphere for a rainy day. And no clothes, because *why the hell are we wearing clothes when it's raining?*

I never understood the logic in that, no matter how many times she explained, so I let it ride, and just went along. Nakedness, smooth music, and candles usually led to adult activity, so who was I to complain?

I left my wet boots and jacket by the door, then went exploring. I couldn't *see* Charlie, but I could feel her presence, so she was definitely in the apartment. In the bedroom, the lights were off, but the bed was empty, and so was the bathroom. On a whim, I glanced into the closets.

Still no Charlie.

I glanced over the darkened bedroom again as I reached for the light switch, spotting her just before I flipped it up.

Charlie was on the floor, tucked into the corner of the room by the window. She had her forehead pressed against the glass, her gaze pointed outward to stare at the rain. Wrapped in a soft blanket, with nothing showing except her pretty face, she looked so innocent and adorable that it was hard to stay mad, but really... I was tired of that anyway.

Especially knowing that she was having my baby.

I called her name, and she didn't respond. No flinch, no hard blink, nothing. I approached her slowly, then knelt in front of her and touched her leg. That time, she looked up, and it was then I noticed the tears streaking her face. Her eyes were red and puffy, like she'd been crying for a while, and now that I was closer, the pink cords on either side of her face answered my curiosity of why she wasn't responding to my attempts to get her attention.

I tugged the earbuds from her ears, then reached up to wipe her face. "Charlie... what's wrong?"

"Nothing."

She moved away from my touch, then pulled her earbuds away from me, lifting to return them to her ears.

"Wait a minute now," I said, grabbing her hands. "You're in here crying. You can't say nothing is wrong."

"As far as I know, the baby is fine, Nixon. I'm still pregnant, so... you can get back to whatever you *want* to be doing."

She was trying to sound nonchalant, and confident, but I recognized the hitch of pain in her voice. *Get back to whatever you want to be doing...*

"Charlie... you know I care about more than just the baby, right?"

"Okay Nix."

Giving up on getting the earbuds back, she drew her knees away from me, and pressed her forehead against the window again as a flash of lightning illuminated her face in the dark. I pushed out a heavy sigh, then reached forward, turning her back to my direction.

"I'm *not* about to let you push me away again," I said, trying to meet her gaze.

She scoffed. "Nixon... I'm not the one who's been acting cold. I'm not the one who said they might need to go stay with a friend. You haven't touched me in two days, and the only things you've bothered to try to talk to me about are the business and the baby. So... who's pushing who away?"

I dropped my head.

Yeah... I guess she was right, but how the hell did she *expect* me to react to news that my girlfriend was still married? Thing was, I didn't even give a shit about Adrian. Or Trent, for that matter. Neither would've kept me from pursuing a reconciliation with Charlie, once I'd gotten that "I love you" out of her, that first inkling that I had a chance at winning her back. What I *didn't* like was being kept in the dark that for nearly a month, I was sleeping with a man's wife.

It's the kind of shit that could earn a man a bullet to the head.

After my own personal revelation that communication was key, it was hard to swallow that she'd kept something like that from me for so long. I understood where she was coming from. It *had* been a busy month. We *did* have a lot going on. We *were* so wrapped up in each other that besides the business, pretty much everything else got forgotten.

But it didn't make the shit feel any better.

I was pissed. I was mad as hell that he'd been in her place, mad as hell that he'd brought her flowers, mad as hell that his ass *existed*, to be honest. There wouldn't be a need for a divorce if she hadn't run off and married him in the first place, and *maybe* I was still a little upset about *that* too.

Maybe.

Anyway, yeah, I was mad that she waited a whole damned month to tell me, and... I was mad that this bullshit overshadowed the news of her pregnancy. We were supposed to be happy right now, celebrating. Sharing secret smiles while we were out with our friends, and figuring out how to deliver the news to our parents.

Instead, she was shrinking away from being touched, and feeling like all I cared about was the baby, which was... *so* far from the case.

"Baby..." Against her protests, I pulled her into my arms, and after a few moments, she relaxed.

"I *hate* you being mad at me," she mumbled, burying her face against my neck. "I feel like shit."

I chuckled, then kissed her forehead. "So now you know how it feels, huh?"

"Yeah." She pulled back, her eyes glossy with tears. "I'm really, *really* sorry for not telling you."

Nodding, I wiped her face, then kissed her again. "Apology accepted... crybaby. You see how I didn't hold it against you for years? Or go get married, and move across the country?"

"Okay, now you're pushing it. And don't call me a crybaby," she said, sniffling, but smiling. "I can't help it."

"Oh, I know. I should have known you were pregnant. You were a crybaby the first time too."

Charlie swatted me on the shoulder as she giggled. "Shut up. I've had a really crappy last few days."

"I'm sorry, honeybun. What happened?"

She lifted an eyebrow. "Well... they started out really great. I found out I was pregnant, by a man I love with all my heart. But then, the bastard who wouldn't give me a divorce showed up. And I had to tell that man I loved I was still married, and he was upset with me. And then, this morning... I go in for a haircut, which should be relaxing, but instead... I accidentally figure out that *Lorenzo* is my dad."

Immediately, my face dropped into a scowl. "Wait a minute... what?"

She gave me a wry smile, then nodded. "Yeah. Exactly. You know that story my mom told at my birthday?"

"The one she made up?"

"You mean the one that's absolutely *not* made up, because I heard Lorenzo telling his side of it to his little cronies at the barbershop?"

"*Wow.*"

Sitting back, she leaned her head against the side of the window again. "Wow is right. He gave me some bullshit about my mother thinking he was a bad role model or something, which... I guess it makes sense, but he was always around anyway. Never at the same time *she* was, but he's always been inserting himself into my life. I just... thought it was because he liked her, but turns out... he was trying to have a relationship with his daughter."

I reached under her blanket to stroke her leg, and got a pleasant surprise when my hands met bare skin. She closed her eyes, letting out a low moan that told me she'd missed this kind of contact just as much as I had. I wanted to scoot my hand up a little further, but knew it wasn't the right time. Instead, I satisfied my need to touch her by moving a hand on to each leg as I moved in front of her, then mirrored her position against the window.

"How do you feel about knowing this?"

She shrugged, then turned to meet my gaze. "I dunno. I mean... it's not like I've had... daddy issues or anything, I don't think. I had male figures around me, so I can't remember feeling like I was missing anything. I had my uncle when they were in America, and your dad, and... Lorenzo. So... I know that I'm angry, but I think what I'm most heated about is that they didn't tell me. They just let me live with this assumption, and... it kinda makes me see why you were so upset. Not that I didn't understand it before, but now... I *get* it. And I'm sorry."

"Stop apologizing," I said, taking the liberty of pulling her into my lap. She snuggled close to me, still wrapped in her blanket as the rain continued to come down. "I accepted your apology, right?"

She burrowed her face against my neck, breathing deep as she nodded.

"*I'm* sorry." I stroked her shoulder, then brought my hand up to push my fingers into her curly hair. "I was pissed off, but I didn't mean to make you feel like I only cared about the baby. I... shit, I didn't know what to say to you without saying something stupid, so I stuck to what I assumed were safe topics. The business and the baby. The business doesn't mean shit to me if you aren't a part of it, and I don't know if science has come far enough for the baby to get here without you. And I don't know shit about taking care of a baby anyway," I laughed.

Charlie turned her face up toward me, locking her eyes with mine. "Nix..."

"Yeah?"

She swallowed hard, then rested her head against my shoulder again, flinching a little in response to a clap of thunder. "I'm... I'm kind of scared."

"About what, Beautiful?"

The baby... and us."

I smiled, then lowered my head to peck her on the lips. "Join the club. You wanna know the name of it?"

"Yeah."

"The *I don't know why our crazy asses think we can do this, but I'm damned sure willing to try* club."

Giggling, she swatted me on the shoulder. "Silly ass."

"You love it."

"I do."

Now that the mood had shifted, I felt free to help myself of a generous caress of her thighs, and a healthy handful of ass. "*Why* are you naked under here?"

With a sheepish smile, she shrugged again. "Cause, it's raining. And besides... I just didn't have the energy to put anything on. I'm *exhausted*, already."

I moved my hand up to slide over her stomach. "You feeling sick?"

She nodded. "A little. Not as much as I was at this point with Noah."

"That's good, right?"

"Too early to tell. I'm hungry."

I burst into laughter at the helpless look she gave me after that, like the *only* way she would eat again was if I fed her. I gave her a gentle smack on the bare bottom, then maneuvered us to our feet.

"Tell you what... you put some clothes on, and I'll see what I can whip up for us, okay?"

She gave me a little grin, then dropped the blanket, showing off that sexy curvy body that I loved. "Why I gotta put on clothes?"

"Cause you said you were hungry... if you wanna work out a different arrangement now.., I can handle that." I reached for her, turning her around as I pulled her against me, slipping a hand between her thighs. "Do you *want* to do something different?"

"*Mmmm*, I do... after you feed me."

I chuckled again, releasing her from my hold. "*After* I feed you, okay honeybun. If that's the order we're working in, you've gotta put on some clothes."

She let out an exasperated sigh. "*Fiiine.*"

Charlie headed for the bathroom, and I headed for the kitchen, where I washed my hands to see what we had. A few minutes later, I heard Charlie's bare footsteps padding across the hardwood floor.

"Hey," I called out. "There was something for you in the mail."

When I looked up from seasoning our pork chops, Charlie was already at the table, reaching into the basket. She gave the thick envelope with her name on it a quizzical look, then opened it and pulled the contents from inside. A few moments later, her face broke into a big smile.

"What is it babe?"

Her grin was huge as she turned a letter toward me. "This is from Adrian. He is vacationing in Guam — unincorporated territory of the United States — for the next week, which satisfies their residency requirement, and he will then file for a dissolution of our marriage — which only takes a few weeks there. Then, we will be officially divorced, I will be a single woman again, *and* my money is waiting in an escrow account. He sent confirmations from his lawyer, bank account numbers, everything!" I smiled at the happy little dance she did, moving her way into the kitchen to place a kiss on my lips.

I was relieved that she was gonna be officially divorced too, because I didn't want to have to knock Adrian's throat into his back. I was happy for her to have her money returned, because shit, it was *hers*. She earned it.

But this *single woman* bullshit?

I would have to do something about that.

***

"So after everything that happened before... you're really gonna take that chance again, son?" My dad took a long swig from his coke, then turned back to his task of unraveling tangled fishing line from his reel. I tried to make it down to my dad's boat with him at least once a month when the weather was good, but this time I was almost wishing I hadn't.

He asked about Charlie and me, and I told him, because... he was my dad. I *should* be able to tell him about the good news that she and I were together again, and I was happy, but not even a full minute after I told him I was thinking about making it permanent... he was already on this bullshit again.

"Come on, Pops. Give it a rest. You know damn well that *marriage* isn't what ruined your relationship with Mom."

"Says *who*?"

"*Says her*," I exclaimed, cursing as I pricked myself with one of the hooks I was preparing for the lines. "Dad... it's over. It's done. Your cover is blown."

"*My* cover? Son... I don't answer to *anybody*, let alone a nagging ass wife. Now, I love that sweet little lady of yours like my own. Hated it when it you two broke up, cause I know it hurt you. But I am *telling* you... you're in for a world of trouble if you ask that girl to be your wife. Just enjoy being young, being together. You're working on your business, just date each other, and focus on that. What's the rush?"

I sighed. "The *rush* is that I lost her last time. I don't want that to happen again."

"She stuck around six years last time."

"Yeah," I scoffed, "And I highly doubt she's interested in a repeat performance. I'm not looking for your blessing here dad, I just want you to be happy for us. And I would *love* to hear you admit that you just... you messed up, man. I did too, it's not a big deal, Pops. You have no idea how *freeing* it is to just admit you fucked up."

Pops laughed, a deep, hearty chuckle as he began stringing his fishing pole with the newly untangled line. "I'll let you have that, youngin'."

"*Come on*, man. Mom is happy. She's married again now, she moved on. And they are *beautiful* together. He treats her like gold. I grew up in the house with you, Pops... I know you weren't doing that for her. Why is it so hard for you to say you were wrong?"

"Why do you need to hear it so bad?"

I sat back on my stool, taking a deep sigh as I thought carefully about the question before I answered. Why *did* I need to hear that?

"Because you fucked me up, man." My dad lifted an eyebrow in surprise, but surprisingly said nothing — his nonverbal permission to continue. "Man... you hammered that "don't get married" crap into my head as soon as I was old enough to date, and I bought it. I had Charlie... and I was ready to give her the world, but I kept hearing your voice in my head, telling me it was a mistake. And even though I *knew* what she wanted, I listened to you, because... dude, you're my dad. I'm supposed to be able to follow your lead, live by your example, but doing that cost me the woman I love. Then, when Mom finally speaks up, I find out that you were full of shit, Pops. I mean... I know it was ultimately my own responsibility to do right by Charlie, and I'm not trying to pin that on you. But man you know that shit was wrong. Even if you didn't back then, you're sober *now*. You're telling me that you look back on that time with mom and really think *taking vows* was the problem?"

Pops was still for a moment, then laid his fishing reel across the table and turned to me with a groan. He drained the last of his coke, then tossed the can into the trash, where it clinked against the other dozen cans already there —reminders that his addictive personality had to replace the alcohol with *something*.

"Okay, son."

My eyes went *wide*.

"I can say that maybe it was a mistake to tell you those things. You were young and impressionable. I should have let you find your own path. You know what... you want my blessing to marry Charlie, you've got it. But when," — he raised his hands in defense — "*if* it goes bad... I'ma walk around you, holding up a big ass "I told you so" sign, everywhere you go, son. Deal?"

I chuckled a little, scratching my head. "I guess that's as good as I'm gonna get from you, dad. So yeah, deal."

"Alright now!"

Laughing, we shook hands, then returned to our task of getting our fishing gear ready to go out on the water. "Hey," I said, glancing over at my dad as he leaned over the tackle box. "Did you know Lorenzo was Charlie's dad?"

He went still for a moment, then looked up, giving me a subtle nod. "I still don't know why they never told that girl, but wasn't none of my business. I just made sure Lorenzo kept his ass in line, and saw about his baby for him when he couldn't."

"You know she's pissed right?"

Pops grimaced. "She knows?"

"Yeah," I nodded, placing the tubs of bloody chicken livers we were using as bait in the cooler. "She found out a few days ago."

He shook his head. "Ah damn. She alright?"

"She's alright," I confirmed. A few seconds passed, and then I smiled. "She's pregnant."

My dad let out a shout of laughter, standing up straight as he tossed his head back. "Girl hasn't even back in town a full season! Boy, you ain't waste no time did you?"

"No sir, I didn't." I smiled at him again, then turned toward the water. "I did that last time. Not again."

He wiped his hands on his pants, then approached me, reaching to shake my hand. I returned the gesture, then pulled him into a hug.

"You know... back in my day, you were supposed to marry a girl before you knocked her up, not the other way around."

I twisted up the corner of my mouth. "Dad... I was ring-bearer at your wedding."

"That's my point son. Graham men, doing shit backwards," he chuckled. "Apple don't fall far from the tree."

I clapped my dad on the shoulder, then turned back to finish gathering our supplies. "I don't mean any disrespect Pops... but when it comes to relationships, I hope my apple fell as far from your tree as possible."

chapter
twenty-one

Charlie

It didn't take Viv long to start looking a little misty.

Between us, we'd already established that she and I must have been the vessels our mothers squeezed all of their emotional sensitivity into. We'd barely been in the room together for ten minutes, and already, both of us were blinking back tears.

I'd talked to, but really hadn't seen Viv since the night of my birthday party — the night she and Carter got engaged. They'd gotten on a plane to France the next day, and while Carter had returned to handle an important meeting for his budding software firm — and ended up working in the shop that *awful* day I found out about Lorenzo — Viv had stayed a few more days to let her mother drag her around French bridal shops.

Now, she was back, and she was glowing. While I'd already done plenty of squealing about it with her over the phone, I wanted to hear the full details again, live and in color.

"Well," she said, pulling a folded piece of paper from her purse. "You know after your party, he took me to Ivory for drinks. It was *such* a clear, beautiful night that afterwards, he took me over to that little park, by the pier."

I brought a hand up to my chest. "Ohhh, did they have the lights out?" I asked, referring to the thousands of tiny white lights they strung in the trees, making it *so* perfectly romantic.

Viv nodded. "Yeah. It was beautiful. He took me over to a bench, and pulled this paper out and handed it to me. He said it was not really a poetry piece, just some thoughts... and he wanted me to read it out loud."

She took a deep breath, then cleared her throat as she unfolded the paper and began reading it to me. "Who knew that one heart could hold the key to unlocking *four* loves you didn't even know you were missing? Buried by hurt from my mother, unfairly withheld from my brother. I pushed hers away because I was terrified, and for myself, I just wasn't that sure I deserved it. But *she* loved me back to a part of life I was scared to live. Effortlessly. Beautifully. She erased the fears, and loved me to a place where my perceived inadequacies didn't exist. Carried me, on her back, to a place with the freedom not only to give love, but to receive it as well. Not just little portions either. Love in abundance, and I'm abundantly grateful to her. This time, I hope *she* accepts *my* gift."

By the time she finished, Viv's face was wet with tears. "And then... when I looked up, he was on one knee, and he was holding out the ring."

She held up her hand, showing me the gorgeous white gold ring, with a diamond in the middle, surrounded by a halo of smaller chocolate diamonds.

"Oh, he did so good, this is *beautiful* Viv! And *chocolate* diamonds? I mean, come the hell on," I said, taking her hand as I smiled down at the ring. "I'm *so* happy for you, cousin. Carter is such a good man, and you deserve somebody like that."

"Thank you Charlie." She threw her arms around me, pulling me into a hug before we sat back on the couch. "So... what has been happening with you and Nixon? Is everything still good?"

I nodded. Just a week ago, we'd made up from the whole "still married" thing, and with my divorce coming soon... we were free to just *be*. It felt beautiful.

"I have something else to tell you," I said, grabbing her hands again.

She raised a wary eyebrow. "You have not discovered another auxiliary parent, have you?"

"No, fortunately." I laughed, then shook my head.

Viv had been *pissed* when I shared the news about Lorenzo with her. Over the phone, I heard her break into a string of French curses, and I suspected that the only reason she was back stateside was because of disgust with her mother for being in on the secret. *My* mother was still bouncing around Europe and Asia, avoiding coming home, probably because she *knew* I would want to talk.

Viv smiled. "Okay, well lay it on me, then."

I took a deep breath, then bit my bottom lip, trying to quell the extreme urge to break into a huge smile. "Well... in about a week and a half, I have a really important appointment."

"Alright..."

"With a doctor."

"Uh-huh."

"And Nixon is coming with me..."

Viv's eyes went wide, and her hand flew up to cover her mouth as it dropped open. "Oh my goodness, you are having a baby?!" When I nodded, Viv threw her arms around me again, drawing me close and squeezing me tight. "Charlie that is such beautiful news! How are you feeling? Is Nixon excited? I *know* he is excited!"

"He is," I confirmed. "We haven't really started telling people yet, but I think he told his dad. Try not to tell Carter yet though, I think Nixon wants to be the one to tell him."

"My lips are sealed... as long as you zip yours as well."

I tipped my head to the side in confusion. "Viv... what do you mean?"

She leaned forward, giving me a conspiratorial smile. "Well... Carter does not know yet, but... me too."

***

"What if there isn't a heartbeat?"

I posed that question staring straight up at the ceiling as I traced imaginary patterns on the textured surface. All morning, my hands had been shaking, my nerves on edge... and now that we were in the obstetrician's office, and I was sitting on the exam chair waiting for the doctor… it wasn't any better.

Nixon had already dragged his chair close to sit beside me, but now he stood, taking my trembling hand in his. "Don't think like that, baby." He lifted my hand to his mouth, kissing my fingers. "It's fine. We'll be okay. No matter what… we'll be okay."

I nodded, even though I didn't agree. Who were we kidding? We would both be a wreck if—

"Good morning," the doctor sang as she came into the room. The fact that she was a black woman somewhat alleviated my anxiety. Somehow, she already just felt… familiar. "I'm Dr. Portia Morris, and I'll be looking after mom and baby." She looked between Nixon and I with a smile. "Okay… so which one of you is Charlie, and which one is Nixon?"

I grinned. "I'm Charlie, he's Nixon."

Dr. Morris winked at me, then reached to shake my hand, then his.

"Let's get started, shall we?"

We'd already done the paperwork, checked vitals, and all of that, so the last thing to do was what I was most scared to do. Listening for the heartbeat.

Dr. Morris spread the warm liquid over my stomach, then pressed the wand of the fetal Doppler to my skin. A few seconds of staticy white noise passed, but no heartbeat. I was about two seconds away from bursting into tears when she shifted the wand, and pressed something on the machine, and suddenly the rhythmic sound of a heartbeat filled the room. Tears of relief immediately sprang to my eyes, but that relief was short-lived when I glanced up at the Dr's face. Her face creased with what appeared to be concern, she shook her head as she pulled the wand away from my belly, bathing the room in silence.

"Dr. Morris, is something wrong?"

Nixon asked the question that I couldn't, because of the lump of terror wedged in my throat. *His* voice held a hint of panic as well, but Dr. Morris was calm and collected as she switched the on screen of the larger machine in the room.

"We're going to find out," she said in a soothing voice, smiling between Nixon and I again as she pulled out a different wand. This time, she connected to the ultrasound machine, and Nix's and my eyes were glued to the monitor as she pressed the wand to my stomach.

It took a moment or so of poking around, but suddenly the screen filled with the grainy black and white image of the inside of my uterus. It was an image Nix and I had seen before, several times. We were used to the greyish field that covered most of the screen, punctuated by a bubble of black — the amniotic sac — which held another little mound of grey — the baby.

Only... there were *two* bubbles of black, each holding a little mound of grey.

"I *thought* things sounded a little noisy in there," Dr. Morris said, glancing at us with a big smile. "Congratulations guys. Twins."

She said some other stuff. I'm *sure* she did. Confirmations that I was eight weeks along, that the babies were the right size, reminders to take my prenatal vitamins, all of that. She said it, and I heard it, but it was like her words were being filtered through a screen of disbelief that the first thing, that *twin* thing that she'd said... was real.

Twins.

Twins.

I finally breathed.

I didn't even realize I was holding my breath, but when I released it, a flood of tears came with it, and Nixon wrapped me in his arms. When he pulled back, he kissed me deep, not caring that the doctor was still in the room, watching.

"Twins, huh?" He said, his own eyes a little glossy, and shining with happiness as he met my gaze. "Where the hell did *that* come from?"

I shrugged, then smiled. "Blame Morgan and Mellissa."

***

"I KNOW YOU'RE IN THERE OLD WOMAN!"

I suppressed a grin, pushing past my mother into the door once she flung it open it open with a flourish, her face set into a scowl.

"Who the hell are you calling an old woman, little girl?" she asked, following me into her kitchen.

I grew up in this townhouse with her, and knew it well enough to know that if she was just getting back from another trip around the world, her counters and fridge would be full of treats. I grabbed a handful of Japanese White Rabbit candies, taking a seat at her counter to unwrap one and pop it into my mouth.

"You," I said, once I'd finished that candy and started unwrapping another. "I knew it would get you to stop ignoring me and open the door."

She rolled her eyes, then went back to her task of restoring order to her kitchen.

"You look good. Well rested. Did you have a good time?" I asked, watching as she arranged exotic teas into decorative tins. My mother was a woman of expensive tastes, and no shortage of hopeful suitors to fund her extravagant habits. *But*, thanks to her inheritance from my grandparents, and the boutique hotels she owned around the world — a habit picked up after I moved out — she had the means to do whatever she wanted without asking a man for a thing.

Nevertheless, *her* attitude was "Why spend *my* money when he wants to spend *his*?" in reference to whomever her international flavor of the quarter was.

"You don't have to pretend to be interested in my trip, Charlie. I've already spoken to Morgan, and I guess you're here to talk about that nasty rumor Lorenzo has spread, hmm?"

"Rumor? Give it a rest, momma. You had a few too many at my birthday party, and told a story I wasn't supposed to hear. You're caught."

"Caught? Little girl, I was a grown woman when I went up that mountain, and I'm even more grown *now*. There wasn't any *catching* to do."

"Lorenzo caught you." I lifted an eyebrow, waiting for her response.

"You are *not* too old for me to go get a belt, Charlene."

I tipped my head to the side. "Yeah, but you wouldn't risk hurting your grandbabies, now would you?" I asked, grinning at the expression on her face as I patted my belly.

"You won't be pregnant forev— wait a minute...did you... did you say *grandbabies*?! As in *more than one*?!"

"Sure did... and you would have known when I found out three days ago, if you hadn't been running around foreign countries trying to hide. You could have at least come on home so I could confront you about not telling me my father has been *right in front of me* my whole life."

"Oh hush," she said, smiling as she batted my hand out of the way to rest hers against my stomach. "You're stressing my grandbabies with this nonsense."

With a heavy sigh, I shook my head. "Okay, so let's put it to rest. We aren't just brushing this under the rug, momma. This stuff with Lorenzo... is that why you were pushing so hard for me to settle down, get married, all of that? Because you never had it?"

She looked up at me and smiled. "Yes. That is *exactly* why. I saw how happy your Aunt Morgan has been with Martin, and I wanted that for you. Don't get me wrong... I have a *great* life... but I've never had a great love."

"Never? Not even Lorenzo?"

My mother laughed, throwing her head back as she sat down at the counter. "Child, he *wishes*." She propped her elbow in her hand, then shook her head. "Yes... I met your father up there in the mountains. I was twenty years old, and beautiful. He was twenty-five, and foreign, and *fine*, okay? He asked to buy me a mug of cocoa, and we sat in front of a big fire. Talked and laughed for hours and hours... and then we shared a night. The *promises* he made would make your head spin. The next morning, his wife and his girlfriend came knocking on *my* door looking for him, and I got my ass out of there."

"Yikes." I cringed, pushing away the rest of the pile of candy. "Are you serious?"

"As a heart attack. I had *no* interest in anything like that. I left, and moved on to the next country. A month later, I found out that I was pregnant, and I had to cut my globetrotting short. I moved back to the states. Settled right in this very townhouse, and a few months later... Lorenzo showed up at my door."

"So... he followed you here?"

She smiled. "He sure did. Showed me his divorce decree and all. See, I messed up and told him my real name. Should've told him my name was Carmen San Diego. He wouldn't have gotten very far with *that*, would he?"

"That's mean!"

"No it's not," she scoffed. "Girl, your daddy moved his ass in *my* house, sucking up *my* air, wearing down the cushions on *my* couch while he was screwing every Mary Sue and Sarah Jane on the block. *While* I was pregnant. Honey... your mama is too pretty for *that* nonsense. I kicked his ass to the curb, and he's been sniffing behind me ever since."

I nodded. "Okay... so I can understand why you wouldn't want him as a partner, momma, I really do. But do you think it was fair to not tell me he was my father? You're lucky you weren't around the day I found out, cause I let *his* ass have it." I paused for a moment, breathing a heavy sigh. "I think I'm past the anger now. I'm just really disappointed. I lost a baby, momma. It's possible that it could have been prevented, if I'd known my heritage, could have given the doctor that information to screen for certain genetic abnormalities and things like that. Instead, I'm putting "unknown" in the father's medical history section on those forms. But I *could* have known. I *should* have known. I'm not saying that's what happened to Noah. We never got answers there, it was just... a tragedy. But what *if* momma? And you withheld this information from me because my dad was a *hoe*? Newsflash, ma, it's not that uncommon."

"It wasn't because he was a "hoe"," she said, using air quotes. "It was because I didn't want my little girl growing up thinking a man like that was the norm. Have the first man you love be one that uses and disposes of women like rags, making them do all of that craziness, keeping up in drama? No, not if I could help it. I was fine with him being "the nice old guy that likes your mama", but being a *real* influence on you? Uh-uh."

I sighed heavily, then laid myself out on the counter. "I... I guess that makes sense. I still think you could have told me once I was grown though."

"I'll concede that," she said, reaching forward to run a hand over my hair. "Are we good now? You've found your peace with it?"

Shrugging, I looked up to meet her gaze. "I guess. I mean... I was at peace with not having a dad, until I found out that I *did*. Now... it just kinda... is what it is. I already made nice with Lorenzo, so we're good."

"Good. He's been a great secret father to you," she laughed. "Where do you think the money I gave you to help open Pot Liquor came from?"

I sat up, surprised. "*He* did that?"

My mother nodded. "Sure did. Made sure you had great birthdays, made sure you could pay your tuition...you can consider him something of a... silent partner in your parenting."

"Wow." I shook my head. "So... it seems like if he was so... *secretly* involved, you two would have spent a lot of time together. So why was he always asking me "where ya fine ass momma?""

She smiled. "Oh, sweetheart. I may have communicated with him, but I made sure to not be *around* him when I could avoid it."

"Why?"

Leaning forward, she kissed my forehead, then patted me on the shoulder as she stood. "Sweetie... your daddy could sweet talk the panties off a first lady. Once I got delivered from the voodoo dick on that man... I was *not* interested in going back."

***

I woke up to kisses on the back of my neck more often than I liked.

Not that I *minded* getting kissed on the neck. I actually *loved* it, but kisses on the neck in the morning meant that Nixon was taking the quickest possible path to get me aroused, so that I was already wet when he put his fingers between my legs, which meant it would only take a few strokes before I was ready for him to be inside me.

For yet another quickie.

Nothing against quickies, but damn... quickies was all we did anymore. With everything going on, the website, the rebuilding, the food truck, the pregnancy... between the two of us, no matter what time we tried, it seemed like neither of us ever had the time or energy for more than that. I couldn't remember the last time we'd made the kind of slow, intense, sheet-scorching love that had gotten me pregnant in the first place. I *missed* that.

But under *no* circumstances would I complain.

Not when Nixon was doing *so* much, working *so* hard, so he could provide for me and these babies. I wouldn't dare open my mouth to ask him to do more, when what he was doing was already more than enough. *He* was more than enough.

Every once in a while, that conversation from after the fire would ring in my head. Him reminding me that he did and sacrificed so much for me... it wasn't a request for a pat on the back, or a suggestion that I crown him king, or bow at his feet, nothing like that. He just needed me to recognize that he was willing to work his fingers to the bone to make me happy... and I *did*.

So... no, I wasn't gonna complain. Even when in the middle of dinner, he stopped eating and stared at me over his plate. "Baby... are you okay?"

Quickly — maybe *too* quickly — I nodded. "Yeah. Just... tired. The formal divorce decree came in the mail today. So, it's official now."

His eyes lit up. "*Good*. I didn't want to have to fight anybody about it."

Shaking my head, I ran my fingers down the condensation on my water glass. "You know I hit eighteen weeks today?"

"Yeah," he smiled. "I get the updates on my phone."

I grinned at that. Just like last time, Nixon was *so* into this pregnancy. He'd fallen asleep with his head pressed to my belly more times than I could count, and kept up with appointment dates and such better than I did. Then... my smile dropped. Just like last time, I was concerned he was going to work himself into an early grave.

"*Baby...*"

When I returned my gaze to his face, his expression was concerned, and his shoulders were tense, like he was ready to spring out of his seat and attack danger at any second.

"Nix, I'm *fine*. Finish your dinner, and I'm gonna go run a bath."

Before he could respond, I'd maneuvered myself and my baby bump away from the table. The landlord had installed new, wider bathtubs just a week ago, and I hadn't taken a long soak yet.

When I came back from filling the tub, the kitchen was clean, and Nixon was sitting down in front of the computer, undoubtedly to work.

"Uh-uh," I said, pulling him back up. "You're gonna come and get in the bathtub with me instead."

With a regretful smile, Nixon leaned forward, kissing my forehead. "I'm sorry, babe, but I have to—"

"No you don't." With a pointed look, I closed the laptop, then tugged at his arm. "Whatever it is... it can wait. You need to relax."

"Charlie, seriously. This expense report needs to get done."

"Or what?"

He lifted an eyebrow. "What do you mean *or what*?"

"Exactly what I said. What, exactly, is gonna happen if you *don't* do that expense report, or the dozen other things you were going to do tonight?"

Tipping his head to the side, Nixon considered my question, but it took him too long to respond.

"See," I asked, gripping fistfuls of his shirt. "If you don't do it tonight... it just doesn't get done. Right?"

He scratched his head. "Yeah... I guess you're right."

"You guess?"

"Okay," he grinned, grabbing me at the waist to draw me closer. "You're right."

"Mmhmm. And... we should probably hire some help." Nixon started to shake his head, but I reached up, stilling it. "Baby, listen to me," I said. "We don't have to run ourselves in the ground. The food truck is doing great. I have money from my savings. The insurance covered the rebuilding, and the restaurant will be finished and back open before we know it. We can afford it, Nixon. I can't have you stressing and working yourself into a stroke or a heart attack before you're even thirty-five because you won't hire somebody to help us with all of this. These babies are gonna need you. And I'm not *complaining*, but... I need you too. *Now*. It's not that I need you to do more, I need you to do...*less*. We barely spend any time together anymore, Nix."

Nixon sighed, then scrubbed a hand over his face. "Babe... you know I'm doing this for you and the twins, right?"

"I do," I quickly assured him, with a smile. "I *know* that. But... you know the saying, work smarter, not harder? *Listen* to what I'm telling you I need from you, instead of doing what you *think* I need from you... isn't that the whole purpose of this communication thing?"

Pulling me close, Nixon enveloped me in his arms. "It is... you're right."

"I'm sorry, if this feels like me nagging you, or like I'm never satisfied. I just... I guess I don't want to leave anything unsaid."

"I get that, baby."

I smiled. "Good. So... come on. Let's get in this tub, before the water gets cold."

Chuckling, Nixon gave in to my tugging and followed me into the bathroom, where we lowered the lights and climbed in together, with me resting my back against his chest. I'd put in one of my bath bombs, so we stayed there, soaking, kissing, touching, and caressing, until the water turned from hot to warm, and we climbed out.

We let the tub drain, then got into the shower to rinse off. Once we were dry, I stripped the duvet and covers from the bed, then laid one of my bath sheets out.

I directed Nixon to lay on his stomach across the bed, and I took my time to rub him down, warming oil between my hands before massaging it into his skin. His feet, legs, butt, back, shoulders, arms.... I lavished attention on my hard working man until I'd touched everything I could reach, then directed him to turn over.

He did so lazily, and when he made it onto his back I straddled his legs, grinning down at him as I rubbed his chest and stomach.

"You're not falling asleep on me, are you?"

He grunted, then peeled his eyes open with a smile. "I'm not trying to, but this feels damned good. Didn't realize I needed it."

I paused over his chest, leaning to press a kiss against his lips. "I know."

I turned around, bending forward to rub oil into the fronts of his legs and thighs. The feeling of Nixon's hands, moving over my ass, down to my thighs, up to my waist, then back down to my thighs pulled a little moan from my throat. I stayed in the position as he slipped a first, then second finger inside of me.

"This is a sexy ass view," he said. His voice was edged with fatigue, but his fingers were wide awake, and a moment later, I found out his mouth was as well. He eased me forward, onto all fours as he maneuvered his legs from between mine, putting his face there instead. I gasped as his mouth covered me, licking and sucking and kissing and biting and devouring me like I was a last meal before execution.

"W-*wait* a minute," I breathed, moaning again as his tongue slipped and slid between my legs. "This is supposed to be about you. I wanted... I wanted to...*ah.*"

Shit.

I couldn't *think* straight with his fingers and tongue everywhere, and his — *oh my God.* His fingers were still inside me, mouth still full of me when my head went fuzzy, vision exploded into a sea of stars, body tensed, then released as I came. I was still throbbing, still wanted more, when I pushed him onto his back, eliciting a groan of pleasure when I covered him with my mouth.

I curled my tongue around him, sucking hard, then again with lighter pressure as I moved over him, lifting my gaze to watch him watch me through half-lidded eyes. Gently, he gripped my hair as he raised off the bed in response to my attention, grunting a rough, "*Goddamn*, honeybun," before he clenched my hair a little harder.

The more he pushed upward, in gentle back and forth motions to stroke my mouth, the more those harsh grunts and whispers escaped his throat, the more aroused *I* became. I loved this, savoring the taste and feel of him in my mouth, knowing that I was the only one he allowed to control his body in this way.

"*Baby*," he groaned, and I knew what that meant, but I kept him in my mouth, pulling him deeper, and deeper, until he let go.

Before I could wipe my mouth and catch my breath, Nixon had turned me onto my back again, propping pillows under me so I wasn't flat. His hungry gaze raked over me, so intense that I felt it, like wind whispering over my skin, before his eyes landed on my breasts. He positioned himself over me, carefully avoiding putting his weight on my belly. His hands drifted down to my now sensitive nipples, lightly teasing until they adjusted to his touch enough for him to gently take one his mouth. He watched my face, gauging my reactions, knowing that his tongue needed to be easy and slow, to prime me up before he could finally suck. I watched one arousal-darkened nipple, then the other disappear into his mouth, and I arched away from the pillows as his fingers entered me again.

"Charlie," he murmured against my chest, raising his eyes again to meet my gaze.

"Yeah?"

He closed his eyes, groaning a little as his hardness replaced his fingers inside me. When he opened them again, he gave me a lazy grin, flashing his dimples.

"I love the hell out of you, girl."

He started stroking me then, deep, long, and intentionally slow, so it took me a moment to respond. My body clenched around him, and he pushed back, sliding through my slick, wet heat to build that familiar pressure in my core.

"I love you too Nix," I whispered, digging my nails into his shoulders as he pushed deeper, riding the line between pain and pleasure, but it was so *blissfully* good feeling him like this, taking his time, leading me slowly to my peak that it didn't matter. He pushed my legs up beside my stomach to burrow deeper still, as far as he could.

He kissed me, gently nipping my bottom lip before he drug it into his mouth and sucked. A moment later, our tongues were united, tasting and massaging as we made love. The buildup was slow, and then suddenly the coil of pressure wound as tight as it would go. I gave in, and released, melting back onto the pillows with my hands gripping Nixon's arms as he kept driving forward, until he exploded as well.

He collapsed beside me to avoid my stomach, then immediately drew me close, kissing my shoulder. Not even two minutes later, I heard his subtle snores, and I laughed quietly. Maneuvering out of his arms, I used a warm towel to clean him and the sheets up the best I could, then took another shower.

When I emerged from the bathroom, he was still passed out, his lips slightly parted.

"Sleep tight," I whispered, pulling the sheets up to cover both of us as I settled in beside him. Because he was a sound sleeper, I turned on my side, taking advantage of the opportunity to just study his face.

Nixon didn't look *that* much different from before, except for the subtle lines of age and stress in his face. I took a mental note, to hire an assistant for him, if he wouldn't do it for himself. He was always so in tune with my needs — just like tonight, when I'd said everything *except* "I need more than a quickie", and he'd somehow figured out that's what I meant anyway. I wanted him to feel the same overwhelming love I felt when he put himself aside.

I decided, right then, to *always* make sure he was well taken care of, just like he took care of me.

chapter
twenty-two

Nixon

CHARLIE WAS STRESSED.

She hadn't said anything to me about it, and I doubted that she would, but every once in a while, I would catch her staring at the calendar in her phone, with a far off expression in her eyes. Sometimes, if she was rubbing my back, her hands would linger, fingers faltering over the date on Noah's tattoo.

Every year, I felt the weight of that day. Over time, it got lighter, but I certainly remembered. Every year, I wondered what *she* was doing. If she was still mourning... still hurting. This year... I didn't have to wonder.

I could see for myself she was getting more and more anxious, and I suspected it had a lot to do with her current pregnancy. She was approaching twenty weeks, and the day of that appointment, the one where we'd find out the genders, was the day after the one we'd lost Noah.

She was more than just stressed. She was... kind of freaking out.

Obsessive about what she ate, who touched her belly, going up and down stairs, everything was a big deal this week, when the week before... it wasn't.

I didn't know what to do for her.

I *hated* not knowing what to do for her.

Charlie wanted me to hire an assistant, so I did. Turned out, she was right. The salary I paid Ava — originally a lawyer, but now freshly graduated with a BA and an interest in restaurant management— was more than worth the drastic decrease in stress, and instant increase in the time I got to spend with Charlie. Some of it was just a shift in where the time was spent. Now, I could help with recipe development for the food truck *and* the website, both of which were big hits. Some was time spent alone, just being quiet, or watching a movie while I rubbed her butt until she fell asleep. Other times, like now, were times spent with our friends, which I didn't realize I missed so much until we had it back.

Heavy construction happened next door during the daylight hours, as the crew worked to bring Pot Liquor back. There was no trace of that now at Urban Grind, only the ever-present aroma of coffee, and the smooth, easy guitar melodies from the live band on stage.

In our little booth, Viv was speaking animatedly about something, moving her hands for emphasis. I watched Charlie watch her hands. Specifically — Charlie was staring at Viv's engagement ring. Out of curiosity, I continued watching, waiting on some emotion to cross her face... and finally, it did.

She smiled.

She looked from Viv, to Carter, then back to Viv, dropping her head as a *huge* grin that had nothing to do with what Viv was fussing about overtook her mouth. She shook her head, straightened up, and then... she looked back at me, still wearing a smile.

For that little moment, Charlie's eyes were absent of the anxiety and fear I'd been seeing for the last few days. When she realized I was looking at her, her smile brightened even more, and she leaned into me, resting her head against my shoulder.

I checked my pocket, then kissed her on the head. Dropping my mouth to her ear, I asked, "What are you smiling about so hard?"

"*Them,*" she whispered, snuggling closer. "They *needed* each other. It's just really beautiful."

You're really beautiful.

I wasn't sure why I her happiness for Viv struck me so hard.

There was no jealously that her cousin had a ring and she didn't, only... *love.*

Thinking about it, I realized that even once Charlie was officially divorced, she hadn't mentioned getting married. No sideways comments about when it would be her turn, no dropping of little hints. Except for the tension about the babies, she was just... cool. Living in the moment, allowing me to prove myself, without any prodding. Maybe this time... she was letting *me* decide when it was time.

"Hey... why don't we go on and head home?"

She lifted her head to look at me, and then smiled, curiosity brimming in her eyes just before they darkened with desire. "Sure."

We excused ourselves with handshakes and hugs, leaving the rest of the group to their conversation. Outside, the early fall air carried a little chill, so I kept Charlie tucked close as we headed down the street. She was quiet. So quiet I suspected that now that we were out of the loud, lively environment of the coffee shop, her mind had wandered back to *that* day.

I wished I could take that pain from her.

"Charlie..."

I stopped walking, pulling her to a stop with me before I turned to face her. Her nose was starting to turn a little red from the cold, and with her kitten-eared hat — which she *swore* she didn't get from the kid's section — pulled low on her head, she looked so sweet and beautiful that it made me smile.

"What's up?"

I took a deep breath, then cleared my throat. A car drove past, honking their horn, with the passenger yelling something out the window about the sweet potato pancakes from the food truck. We laughed and waved, and when I turned back to Charlie, her face was still pulled into a mid-giggle smile.

"Marry me," I said, grabbing her hand. "On Wednesday. Let's get married Wednesday."

At first, her brow wrinkled in confusion, and she looked around as if she were expecting something to pop out at her. When nothing did, she turned her attention back to me, her face pulled into what was almost a scowl.

"Wednesday… you know what day that is, right? Why…?"

I cupped her face in my hands, planting a soft kiss on her lips. "Let's make a new memory for that day. A *happy* memory."

She said nothing for a moment, as tears glossed her eyes, but then she gave me a little smile. "I like that idea a lot, Nix. But… are you sure? I'm not going anywhere… not this time."

I shook my head. "Charlie," I said, reaching into the pocket of my jacket and pulling out the little blue box. In front of her, I dropped to one knee and opened it. "Marry me, this Wednesday… please?"

Charlie clapped her hand to her mouth, eyes wide at the sight of the ring. She ran a hand through her hair, then dropped both of them, wringing them in front of her as her fingers trembled. She ran her tongue over her lips, then let out a labored breath. "Yes," she finally said, her voice shaking as she frantically nodded her head.

The *feeling* that coursed through my chest… a rush of excitement, and happiness, and *love* for this girl.

Just… *love.*

I pushed the ring onto her finger, then stood just in time for her to throw her arms around my neck in an awkward hug. There were a few people out on the street, and they clapped, speaking congratulations as they passed. I heard it all, but the only thing I registered was the "I love you so much." Charlie mumbled into my ear, her voice cracking with tears just before she seized my face in her hands and kissed me.

Eventually, we stopped making out in the middle of the sidewalk and started for home again, as the night air grew cold.

"You know…" Charlie said, as I opened the door for her to enter the building, "This is… not at all how I expected things to be when I moved back here. I never, *ever* imagined I'd be getting *married*, to *you*. Hell, I would have bet money against the chances that I would fall in love again… with… *you*."

I sucked my teeth, smacking her on the butt as I headed up the stairs behind her. "*Again*? Stop playing, Charlie. We both know damn well… neither of us ever stopped."

***

"I haven't felt the babies all morning."

My heart plummeted with those words, heaviness gripping my chest. That wasn't the type of shit you expected to hear mentioned randomly at breakfast. Charlie stopped mid-bite, dropping her sausage back onto her plate. She looked up at me with wide eyes, hands shaking, chin trembling as she tried to stand up.

I shot out my own seat and rushed to her side, easing her back down into her chair. "Relax," I insisted, even though I was struggling not to panic myself.

With one hand stroking her hair, I used the other to reach under her gown and press a hand to her stomach. For a moment, I felt nothing, but I pressed a little harder, and then at least one of the babies began to move. A few moments later, they both seemed to be active, and Charlie screwed up her face, shifting positions as I watched.

When she noticed my confused expression, she smiled. "They're on my bladder and it *hurts*. Guess they want to make sure I know they're fine."

I relaxed my shoulders as I returned her smile, then pressed my head to her stomach. It was the morning of our "big" appointment, with all of the screenings, and tests, and ultrasounds, and to say that we were a little on edge was an understatement.

Charlie had barely slept the night before. I knew because I was up with her, tossing and turning, trying to push my own lingering fears away. Obviously, I wanted to be realistic. We'd lost a baby before. It wasn't impossible for it to happen again, but... damn, it would be nice to not have to live with those kinds of fears. I'd always found comfort in the thought that maybe losing Noah was a part of God's larger plan — I just hoped that *keeping* these babies was a part of the same agenda.

But... they were fine right now. They were alive, and well, and kicking me in the head through their mother's stomach. So... things were good.

Perfect, actually.

Today, we would find out the gender of the twins. Tomorrow, Charlie would become my wife.

We wanted to stick with something small — as in nonexistent — for the wedding. Truth be told, we just weren't interested in that, but as soon as Charlie's mom saw the ring on her finger, she threatened my life about not having *any* event — Charlie's was only spared because she was carrying the grandbabies — and we agreed to a small reception to appease the wishes of our parents. We decided not to mention that *they* were a little responsible for some of the crazy ideas we had about marriage, part of the reason we wanted to just *do* it, with no fuss. The past was exactly that, the past. We were moving on.

After a few moments to catch our breaths, Charlie and I got ready for our appointment. Two hours later, we were sitting in the waiting room.

Beside me, Charlie absently turned an empty plastic bottle in her hands. A while ago, it held what she'd described to me as "nasty orange soda" she had to drink, then have her blood taken, then wait, and have it taken again, and now... we were waiting. It felt like we'd been waiting all day.

Charlie was... tense. She'd look down at her engagement ring with a sigh, and relax for a few minutes, but then it was right back to that deeply contemplative expression, letting me know where her mind was: a place of fear. But, I was reasonably sure she wouldn't freak out again, unless something big happened. We'd already had our angst episode for that morning.

"Hey babe," I said, clapping her on the knee.

She looked up, pulling her face into a smile. "Yeah?"

"What are you thinking about?"

Her smile faltered, then she looked back down at the bottle in her hands. "Noah."

I wanted to pull her into my arms, do something to ease the apprehension etched into her face, but before I could say anything, the nurse was at the door to the waiting room, calling Charlie's name.

A few minutes later, we were back in a room that felt a little too familiar for comfort. We'd purposely chosen a different doctor, at a different office, so we wouldn't be reminded, but... I guess all ultrasound rooms look pretty much the same.

Dr. Morris breezed in with a big smile on her face and a folder in her hand. "Good news, guys. Charlie, your blood results look absolutely perfect, so no worries there. You ready to take a look at these babies?"

Charlie nodded, reaching out to grab my hand as Dr. Morris lifted her shirt, covering her belly with the ultrasound gel. She picked up the wand and flipped on the sound for the monitor, and moments later, the room filled the galloping sound of the babies' heartbeats. We were transfixed, absorbing it all as she showed us properly developed fingers, toes, lungs, spines, and all kinds of other things that little by little lessened our worries about their health.

"And now... for the good part," Dr. Morris said, tossing a grin over her shoulders. "If we look over *here*... see where I just put the mouse pointer? That lack of a penis between the legs indicates that you have at least one little girl."— Charlie gripped my hand tighter — "And over here... the *presence* of a penis indicates a little boy. Brother and sister both look to be developing *just* fine."

With happy tears shining in her eyes, Charlie looked up, bringing a hand to stroke my face. "You hear that? Another chance to give you a son."

"And a daughter too," I said, chuckling. "How you gonna play our baby girl out like that?"

She shook her head. "No... *no*, I don't mean it like that. I'm *thrilled* that we'll have a little girl too, but I'm grateful to be able to give you back what you— what *we* — lost. I know Noah can't be replaced, but it just feels like... I don't know how to describe it."

I didn't know how to describe it either, but I think I knew what she meant. These babies were a blessing, absolutely, but they weren't a substitute for Noah. His presence was a piece of our lives that would always be missing, but somehow, that made the gift of his brother and sister seem even more precious.

charlie.

"AT LEAST THIS ONE HAS GOOD TASTE," MY AUNT Morgan said, gazing lovingly at my ring with a contemplative sigh. "Gorgeous platinum band, beautiful pavé-set halo... good enough size on the center stone. Beautifully cut diamonds. A nice *elegant* ring."

With a smug little smile, my mother glanced over at my aunt. "Come on, now Morgan. Carter did good with Vivi's ring, it's just... *quirky*."

"It's *gaudy*."

"Y'all are *bougie*," I interjected, pulling my hand away from my mom. "Viv's ring is absolutely gorgeous, and it fits her personality perfectly. It's damn near the same as mine, just with a little color." With a chastising glare, I stood up from the table and looked around, trying to spot my husband.

My *husband*.

Unlike with Adrian, when I used that title for Nixon, my heart swelled with a mixture of happiness, and pride, and love, and... *desire*.

Damn he looks good.

We didn't have many occasions to dress up, and really go all out, but what better day than the one where you'd just married the person you loved? We dressed normally, in jeans in sweaters for the non-event at the courthouse that left us officially married, but neither of us wanted to risk the family's wrath by showing up at the reception that way. Nixon looked delicious in his dark charcoal suit, and although I'd agonized over my own attire, I felt beautiful in my flowy royal blue maternity gown, thanks to the wonder twins.

They'd pulled together a beautiful reception for us in just three days. Roman had agreed to close early to the public, and with a generous gift of flowers from Simone's shop, they'd turned the trendy, urban coffee shop into something out of a bridal magazine. Way more than Nixon and I needed, but... this wasn't really for us anyway. It was for *them*. All of our family — including Lorenzo—

and all of our friends had taken the time to celebrate us, on a *Wednesday* night. I definitely felt the love.

Nixon looked up from his conversation with Carter and Grant as I approached, and his mouth spread into a grin.

"Excuse me, fellas," I said, putting a hand on both men's shoulder. "Can I borrow my husband for a moment?"

I accepted congratulations and kisses on the cheek from each before they departed, then slid into Nixon's open arms, smiling when he pulled me close.

"I *really* like how that sounds," he said, lowering his mouth to mine.

I opened my mouth for him to slip in his tongue and kissed him deep, not caring about the crowd. I was *married. I* was married, and to a man that I madly, deeply, *truly* loved. Like... real ass love. They would just have to accept this public display of affection.

"You like how *what* sounds?" I giggled as he lowered his mouth to my neck, discreetly peppering kisses along my throat. "When I call you my *husband*?"

"Hell yeah. Say it again."

"My *husband*," I repeated in a low, seductive voice, biting my lip after.

"Ooh," Nixon said, sucking in a breath as he lowered his eyes. "Charlie... don't start any shit. You know I'll take you in the bathroom and—"

"If we can get the newlyweds to stop acting like horny teenagers..."

Laughing, Nixon and I turned toward the sound of Leah's voice coming over the mic. She was up on the stage, grinning at us as she directed the spotlight to where we were.

"We'd like you guys to come up on stage," she continued in her "radio" voice, waving her hands encouragingly at the small crowd, to get them to clap and cheer. "Lead us in your newlywed toast, say a few words, all of that."

I looked up at Nixon and he nodded, grabbing my hand to lead me to the front of the room. He accepted the mic from Leah, keeping my palm tucked in his as he turned to address the crowd.

"Uh... first of all... thank you everybody for coming to cele-brate with us. I don't really have much to say, because the longer I'm holding this mic, the more likely it is I'm gonna say something to get my ass in trouble with my lovely new wife."

"*Stop cursing, there are kids here,*" I whispered.

"See? I'm already in trouble now. Y'all are messing up my chances of losing my virginity tonight."

Our friends erupted in laughter, and I smacked Nix on the butt, holding up a scolding finger as I tried — and failed — not to burst into laughter myself.

"Okay, okay. In all seriousness... I really do appreciate each and every one of you. Everybody here... y'all have been more like a family to us than friends, and we are *so* grateful. Um... six months ago, I did *not* think that I would be standing next to the woman I thought I'd lost forever, with the privilege and the *honor*, to call her not only my wife, but the mother of my children — *again*. In the course of our relationship, she and I have lost a lot. But, by the grace of God, we've gained even more." He paused, his eyes shining as he raised my hand to his mouth and kissed my fingers. "I married the love of my life today... and this is a day that I am proud to share."

He nodded at the crowd, then looked back at me with a smile as he cleared his throat. I accepted the mic, then swallowed hard, tearing my eyes away from him long enough to look out at the crowd as they finished their applause.

"Well," I started, squeezing his hand. "Your boy Nix here stole all of my thunder, and said everything already, but... I want to reit-erate my thanks... *our* thanks, for all of the love and support you've shown us. We've known many of you our whole lives, and like Nix said, you're all more like family than just friends. Even when I left, you kept up with me, and when I came back... you embraced me as if I was never gone, and it means the world. I um... I've learned a lot... grown a lot... and I'm just *thankful* for the way that my crazy, convoluted path led me not only back home, but back to this man. I *love* you, Nixon Graham. And I am delighted to stand in front of our family as your wife."

Nixon just stared at me for a moment, with such intensity that it made me blush. A second later, I half screamed, half giggled as Nixon swept me into his arms, second-trimester belly and all, giving me a deep, absolutely inappropriate, absolutely perfect kiss as the crowd cheered. When we came down from the stage, there were a few moments where we were bombarded with congratulations, but then Viv, in her gorgeous purple maternity gown pulled me to the side, rescuing me from the crowd.

"I hate you," she said, dragging me to an empty table to sit down. I was so grateful to be off my feet that I moaned a little, taking a moment to close my eyes before I responded.

"Why do you hate me, cousin?"

I opened my eyes, really looking at her as I waited for her answer, realizing then that her face was streaked with tears.

"That was *so sweet*," she said, her voice cracking with tears as she pulled a handkerchief from her clutch, carefully dabbing her face and eyes. "And I have ruined my makeup now because of you and your husband being so damned... *adorable.*"

I placed a hand on Viv's knee. "I'm so *sorry* for messing up your makeup at *my* reception."

"Oh," she said, giving me a sheepish grin. "I suppose you have a point there."

We shared a laugh, and then I looked around, making sure neither Morgan nor Melissa was near. "So...your appointment was earlier today, right?"

"It was." Viv took her own moment to look around, then lowered her head to mine. "A girl."

I started to squeal, then clapped a hand over my mouth, trying not to draw attention. *Not* knowing the genders of our babies until birth — or as long as we could keep it a secret — was part of the older adults' punishment for not telling me about Lorenzo. Turns out, *all* of their asses knew, even Nix's parents. Everybody was excited to be grandparents, so not knowing the gender in advance was proving to be a sufficient bit of torture.

A few moments later, I said my goodbyes to Viv as Nixon whisked me away to our waiting limo. We were spending our wedding night at a five-star hotel in the city, and in the morning, we were boarding a flight to get us to the Maldives for a short honeymoon.

In the limo, I rested my head against Nixon's shoulder and closed my eyes. Neither of us said anything, and I really wasn't sure we had to. Between us, we'd already shared so much, good and bad, that even in silence, many things were spoken.

Nixon draped his arm over my shoulder so that I could cuddle closer, then rested his hand against my belly. One of the twins kicked, and we laughed, then fell into silence again. Leaning forward, Nix kissed my forehead, then settled back against the seat for the hour long ride into the heart of the city. I opened my eyes just long enough to find his lips and share a kiss, then closed them again and settled in, feeling an almost overwhelming sense of serenity and love — a blissful level of contentment only Nixon could provide.

***

It was too soon.

There was nothing I could do about it. Nothing my doctor *would* do, as I'd found out when I went to the hospital hours ago, when the first signs of labor started, but still...it was too soon.

I closed my eyes, gripping the side of the bathroom counter as another wave of pain coursed through my pelvis. I focused on *not* biting my way through my lip and counted.

One. Two. Three.

On I went, up to forty-six seconds before the pain finally dissipated. With my heart still racing, I looked up at myself in the mirror and shook my head.

Don't panic. Don't panic. Don't panic.

I stayed there for several minutes, calming myself, breathing deep, doing anything I could not to spazz out. I took a deep breath, then made my way into the room, cringing as each step brought another gush of warm liquid down my legs.

But I was only thirty seven weeks.

My water was broken, and I was thirty-seven weeks.

I wasn't sure at first, because I had woken up to pee. There was nothing abnormal about that, because I did it five or six times a night, but *this* time, when I went to stand up from the toilet there was a surge of pain — real ass, hot, *excruciating* pain — radiating from my pelvis to my back, and then, when I tried to move... another gush of liquid.

But I'd already peed.

I was ready to write it off as sciatic pain, a symptom of being late in my third trimester with twins, but then another gush of liquid made me think twice. In other words... shit got real.

Just as I made it to Nixon's sleeping form, spread awkwardly over the pull out couch, another contraction wracked my body and I fell clumsily to my knees, shooting my arms out for balance so I wouldn't land on my stomach. Already feeling weak from the pain, I closed the distance to get to Nixon, and reached up, grabbed whatever I could and *squeezed* to counter-balance the agony.

"Charlie, Charlie, *Charlie*, goddamn, baby, you're cutting off my circulation." Was the first thing I heard when I came out of that contraction, fifty-two seconds later. "Baby... tell me what's happening."

Immediately, tears that had nothing to do with the physical pain sprang to my eyes. "Babies coming. My water just broke, but it's too soon. Their little lungs and stuff, they need more time to develop, and—"

"Baby... *baby*," Nixon said, putting his hands on my shoulders. "Be easy. *Relax*, if you can. Dr. Morris told us this, remember? That twins come a little early sometimes. Everything is okay. How much time between contractions?"

I shook my head. "I don't know."

"Just think, how long ago was the one before the one you just had."

Ugh.

"I don't know... seven minutes? Maybe? Not ten...longer than five."

Nixon nodded. "Okay... let's call Dr. Morris then."

He pulled his phone from the charger and got on the floor with me, massaging my aching back as he waited to speak to the Dr. A few moments later, another contraction hit, and I tuned him out as he answered her questions, focusing instead breathing my way through the pain.

We were already *at* the hospital, already admitted because I'd gone into labor earlier that morning then... just *stalled*.

I was grateful for that stall.

I just wanted the babies to be as healthy as they could possibly be. Livid didn't even begin to describe how I felt when Dr. Morris told me they wouldn't stop the labor, because they were "full" term. *Technically*.

But... I had to just breathe. If they said it was fine... it was fine. That's what I had to believe. I couldn't... I couldn't think about Noah. I couldn't focus on that. I had to *breathe*, because if I freaked out... I would miss it again. I missed the labor process the first time, and I didn't want that again. Not for me, and not for Nix.

Breathe.

"Baby, let me help you up onto the bed."

I nodded, holding on to Nix for balance as he helped me to my feet, then onto the bed, where I laid back just in time for another contraction. I grabbed Nixon's arms, tugging him close as pain enveloped me again.

"*Ahh*, shit. Charlie, I think you're breaking my skin."

I didn't let him go until the pain passed. Nixon stepped away as soon as he could, scowling as he rubbed his arm. "Who *are* you?" he asked, lifting an eyebrow. "Fucking... maternity ward Barbie, with the kung fu grip?"

"*You* did this to me. You can take a little pain, don't be a baby."

Nixon playfully poked out his lip, then pulled a chair up beside the bed. "I'm messing with you baby. Squeeze away."

"Uh-huh. What did Dr. Morris say?"

"A nurse is gonna bring some pads and stuff for the bed, and for us to call back if your contractions hit four or five minutes apart."

"Four or five? Which one?"

He drew his eyebrow up further. "Four... or five. Shit, I don't know, I'm telling you what she said."

"I knew I should have let my mother stay instead of you."

Nixon scoffed. "What, so she could show you the most fashionable labor positions?"

I laughed, then closed my eyes as Nixon pressed a kiss to my forehead.

"You look so beautiful right now."

Opening my eyes, I fixed him with a scowl. "Negro, I just saw myself in the mirror in the bathroom, and it was *not* cute. Stop lying."

"I'm not," he chuckled. "No, you don't look *polished*, but... you're about to have my babies soon. So... you look beautiful. Don't fight it, just embrace it."

Smiling, I reached to stroke his beard. "Thank you, Nix."

"You're welcome. And something else... baby, your titties... I've been trying not to say anything but they are... like two big creamy toasted marshmallows. So plush, and soft, and—"

"Nix!"

"What? I just wanna bite you right now, girl. You look sexy in your little fancy custom maternity gown. Cleavage all out."

"Would you *stop*?" I giggled, swatting his hand away as he reached for one of the ties on my kimono-style gown.

"For what? I'm saying... you're turning me on right now... but I guess we can't do anything now that your water is broken, huh?"

I raised an eyebrow. "No, I would think not."

"*Damn*," he muttered, leaning back. The nurse came in to change the bedding, and put down padding, and as soon as she left, Nixon leaned forward again, with a little grin on his face. "Hey... I wonder what it's gonna be like down there... once you've pushed *two* babies out."

I laughed. "Are you worried it'll be loose or something, Nix? I'll get a vaginal rejuvenation if it is."

"You'll get a *what*?" he asked, tipping his head to the side.

"A vaginal rejuvenation. They go down there, and it's like a little surgery, where—"

"Wait a minute, *hell no*," Nix said, his face drawn into a frown. "I'm good on this vaginal rejuvenation shit. Leave *my* pussy alone."

"*Your* pussy?"

Nixon licked his lips, then smiled. "Yeah... *mine*."

I sucked my teeth. "Whatever. Last I checked, *I* was the one with the vagina."

"That's not what you were saying the other night. *Oh my God Nix. Beat it up Nix. It's yours Nix. This pus*—"

"Will you *stop*," I gasped, mortified as I glanced toward the door of the hospital room. "One of those nurses could have been walking in and overheard!"

He shrugged. "I don't care. Let the world know, I'll tear it up. That's probably how your water—"

Shit.

Nixon's words got lost in static as another contraction took hold, and before I could say anything, I felt one of his hands in mine, the other rubbing my back.

"*Just breathe, baby,*" he encouraged in a low, soothing voice that I latched on to, focusing on his loving words to get me through the contraction.

When it passed, he smiled at me, then wiped my forehead.

"You okay?"

"Yeah."

He sat down next to me, on the edge of the bed, drawing me against his chest. A few minutes later, another contraction came. Once it was done, Nix lowered his face to mine.

"That's only *three* minutes baby..."

I nodded, then found the strength to return his smile. "Yeah... show time."

epilogue

WHAT THE HELL DID I WALK IN ON?

That was my first thought upon entering our apartment over the restaurant, which was clean when I left, but now looked like a miniature baby bomb had gone off, leaving behind stray diapers, pacifiers, breasts pads, and a laundry basket full of onesies.

I'd only been gone long enough to grab a new box of baby wipes from the store.

I stepped further in, looking around for Nixon and/or my babies. I spotted them in the middle of the living room, contained in a makeshift fortress of the couch, chair, loveseat, and all of the pillows. Nixon was in the middle of the floor, and seven month old Mackenzie and Micah were crawling all over him.

My baby girl grinned up at me, then turned back to Nixon, smacking him in the face like she was playing a drum. Baby boy Micah just watched, and daddy didn't move. Right when I was about to grow concerned, Nixon suddenly sat up with a fierce growl, and both babies screamed and laughed as they took off, crawling across the floor to get away from him.

"Is *this* what you've been doing all day?" I asked, pretending to scowl as I reached for Mackenzie, who was motioning for me to pick her up.

Nixon smiled. "Of *course* not, baby. I've been working on something else too. Watch."

I lifted an eyebrow as he began creating a beat with his hands on the floor, with Micah mimicking his moves beside him. He made a sound with his mouth like he was scratching a record, then turned to my baby... who blew a spit bubble, then laughed.

In my arms, Mackenzie blew a spit bubble too, sprinkling my face before she lifted her chubby little hands in a clumsy applause for her brother. "*Nix...*"

"What?" he shrugged. "A man can't teach his babies to beatbox?"

Both babies turned to look at me, their expressions serious as if they knew what was happening. I rolled my eyes at Nixon, then earned a giggle from Mackenzie by kissing her chubby cheek.

Nixon brought Micah to me, tossing him in the air before holding him up to get his kiss. Then, he stepped over the pillows, wrapping an arm around me to get a kiss for himself.

"My mother will be here in like... ten minutes to get the kids." I murmured against his lips. "What do you wanna do once they're gone with grandma?"

Nixon grinned, reaching down to slide his free hand over my ass. "I wanna do what we did to make these babies."

I giggled, letting out a playful scream as I dodged his attempt for a second grope, then put Mackenzie back down in their circle. While Nix watched the twins, I made sure they had plenty of pumped breast milk, clothes, diapers, and full instructions for everything.

Right on time, my mother knocked on the door, with Morgan — carrying Viv and Carter's baby girl Bellamy — in tow. Behind them was... *Lorenzo.* I lifted an eyebrow, but neither Nix nor I said anything about *that*, just handed their grandbabies off to them and locked the door.

As soon as we were alone, I collapsed into a chair with a heavy sigh.

"What's with all the heavy sighing, woman?" Nix asked, kneeling in front of me and undoing the button and zipper of my jeans.

"Nothing really," I said, lifting my hips so he could slide the pants off. "Just wondering if we can go back to bed already."

Nixon chuckled. "Baby... it's ten o'clock in the morning."

"What's your point?" I moaned as he kissed the inside of my knee, then began making his way up my thigh.

"My point," he said, skipping to my other leg, "Is that if we start now... we could technically have sex all *day*, without having to stop to change a diaper, or breastfeed, or any of that."

I smiled. "Well... Mr. Graham... I think I like the sound of that."

"Well... Mrs. Graham." He looked up at me with a grin. "Sounds like we've got a plan."

— the end —

Thank you for reading Fall In Love Again.
To continue the series, go straight to The Way Love Goes - Sean & Fallon's story!

Keep reading for a sneak peak!

One

Fallon

IT'S A LITTLE BIT INSANE HOW WHEN YOU'RE PISSED, your body redirects your energy. Hot tea streamed over my fingers because my hand was shaking so bad, but I didn't even register any pain. Logically, I understood that doing nothing about the scalding liquid would later present itself as a regret, but I kept on clutching that cup, trying to keep my tears in check.

Other emotions would come later, but right now, I was angry. I was very, *very* angry, and I was very, *very* hurt, because what the hell did he mean, *he wasn't coming?*

"Ray... the only reason I'm here is because of you. You were the one being transferred here. *You* started talking about getting engaged. You asked me to come with you."

His deep rumble on the other end of the phone line only high-lighted the pain. How dare he break my heart in a bedroom voice? "I understand that, Fallon. And please, I want *you* to understand that I appreciated that. I appreciate you."

"Then *why*?"

He let out a sigh that was so heavy *I* felt it in my chest, and I could imagine him shaking his head. "This just isn't working anymore."

"How so?" I snapped, finally releasing the teacup onto my desk with a *plop* that sent a puddle of tea dripping to the desktop. "It was working when I was flying up here to secure space for my store. It was working when I *moved* six months ago. It was working when I was spending every bit of spare time I had looking for, and then *buying a house*, Ray. You've given me no indication that anything was wrong, and now you're ready to break up? Tell me, please, when did you realize it *wasn't working anymore*?"

Silence, only punctuated by the subtle sounds of his breath ruled the air between us for a few moments before he answered. "Right before you moved."

I let out a bark of laughter. "Right before I—right be—are you *kidding*, Ray? I put my business's reputation on the line opening this second location. My financial security, and my credit. My name is on a mortgage now, because I was so in love with your trifling ass that I *moved here for you*. And motherfucker... you're going to sit on this goddamned phone and tell me that you knew, six fucking months ago, *before* I completely uprooted my life, when I still had a chance to back out of this shit, that you weren't even really feeling it like that anymore? After you all but promised me a proposal. After I've been with your ass for *three years*?"

I stopped to giggle again, and I was sure I sounded like a complete maniac, but at that moment, I didn't really care. "Oh, Ray. Ray, Ray, Ray... you know... I am really, *really* glad, for both of our sakes, that you didn't get on that plane this morning. Because if you'd told me this shit in person... I would fucking kill you."

I pulled the phone from my ear, then pressed the button to end the call.

Breathe, Fallon. Breathe, breathe, breathe, I told myself.

So I did.

I took deep breaths in and out until I felt my heart stop racing. I closed my eyes, willing calm to wash over me, replacing anger with peace. Pushing out negativity, breathing in positive energy, and then... I snatched up my teacup and launched it at the wall.

There were several reasons that was a bad idea, the first being that the cup wasn't empty, so now I was going to have to clean tea from my bedroom floor. Second – though the cup hit the wall with a *thump* and remained intact, once it hit the floor, it shattered into pieces. Another thing to clean up. The third, and definitely largest reason I shouldn't have thrown the cup, didn't present itself until a couple of moments later, when a fine crack appeared on the wall where I'd hit it. Right in front of my eyes, that crack traveled and spread until it reached the prized Rashad Martin photo print on my wall.

It fell at the same moment I stepped forward, intending to grab it.

But... *ha-ha...* the photo wasn't the only thing. When the heavy frame came down, it brought a whole section of drywall crashing to the floor with it.

So I did the only thing that seemed to make any semblance of sense in that moment.

I sat down on the floor and cried.

THE HOUSE WAS SUPPOSED TO BE AN ADVENTURE.

Before I moved, Ray and I would spend lazy Saturday mornings together watching HGTV, looking around the Chicago condo we leased, trying to see what we could do. We hit yard sales together, to decorate our home in the modern eclectic design aesthetic we shared, and dreamed about rehabilitating a house. Purchase something run-down, barely fit to live in at all, let alone call it a home, and then together, restoring it to its former beauty, bringing it back to life while he built his political career and I built my business... but now... I guess that dream was dead.

Along with my relationship.

My phone rang again, and Ray's handsome face flashed on my screen. I wanted so badly to ignore it, but my thumb slid across the screen anyway.

"What do you want?"

"To apologize," Ray said, and I rolled my eyes. *Of course* he wanted to apologize. "You just... you were so excited about moving, and you'd already gone through so much to set up the new location for your store. I didn't want to ruin that for you."

A surge of annoyance spiked in my chest. Was this fool dense? "With *you*, Ray. I was excited about moving with you, excited about building our life. A year ago, you came home and told me your boss wanted you in charge of the office out here, that you'd have to be here to accept the job, and you needed a first lady. I didn't want to move. I wanted *you*. So I took these chances, for *you*. While you were training, and preparing, I was putting everything on the line to expand my business, and find a home for us. I left my friends, left my family, left the life I knew to build a new one for us. It was never about being *here*. It was about being here with *you*."

"I'm sorry, Fallon," Ray insisted, after another long moment had passed. It bothered me that he actually sounded sincere.

I shook my head, then roughly swiped tears from my face with the back of my hand. "Yeah. You really are."

I hung up, and was about to toss the phone away when it started ringing, yet again.

"*What?!*" I growled into the receiver after swiping the screen to answer, and my combative greeting was met with sucked teeth.

"Um, *ugh*," Ayden said. "What's with you this morning?"

"Sorry," I mumbled, pressing a hand to my forehead. "Thought you were Ray."

"And you answered like *that*? What's the story there?"

I blew a quick puff of air through my lips as I shook my head. "Way too long to tell right now. What's on the agenda today?"

"Adjusting your attitude."

"What *else,* Ayden?"

There was a short pause, and a second later, she began rambling off shipments and purchase orders and window display designs. I listened while I pulled myself up from the floor, taking mental notes about what I needed to handle myself, and what to delegate to her, even though I was pretty sure she already had it down.

That's why I liked Ayden. She always had her shit together, even when *I* didn't.

"So do you want to tell me what's going on?" she asked, as I surveyed my appearance in the mirror. If nothing else, at least I looked good today. The weather was agreeing nicely with my skin, and my two-day-old twist-out looked better than it had on day one.

"Not particularly." I pulled my toothbrush out of the cup, and turned on the water to rinse it off. "I would actually like to pretend this morning didn't really happen."

My phone rang at 5:13am, right before Ray's scheduled flight. We'd planned this well in advance, that he would call me when he was about to board the plane for the two hour flight that would get him here. I was supposed to be picking him up from the airport, and the advance call would give me an idea of what time he'd arrive, so I could plan my day accordingly.

What *really* happened is that he waited until the last possible minute to tell me he wasn't getting on that plane at all. That he'd requested the position that required the move go to someone else.

That not only was he *not* coming... he didn't even want me to come back.

A sob built in my throat as I really considered that. How delusional I had to have been, how utterly blind not to see that the man I'd been with for *three goddamn years*... was considering putting me off the team. How stupid I was to uproot my life for someone who didn't even have the decency to tell me in advance that he wasn't taking the flight that would have connected us again after living apart for six months. How pitiful, to go to such great pains over someone who'd promised me nothing.

So, yeah... delusional, stupid, pitiful.

Sounds about right.

I lifted my toothbrush, and just before I put it in my mouth, I caught a whiff of a strange metallic smell. My face pulled into a scowl as I sniffed around for the source of the odor. Raising my toothbrush to my nose, I nearly gagged at the rusty chemical smell. Still frowning, I turned the water back on, then lowered my face toward the stream.

Ugh.

Definitely the culprit.

"Fallon, are you still there?"

Ayden's voice on the other end of the line nearly made me jump out of my skin. I'd forgotten that I was holding the phone at all, let alone that she was still there.

"Yeah," I said, flipping the faucet down to turn off the water, and tossing the toothbrush into the trashcan. "I need you find me a contractor, so some progress can get made on the massive list of shit wrong with this house."

The little brownstone building I'd found, a diamond in the rough, was perfect – as long as one kept in mind that "perfect" was pretty damned subjective. It had a lot of problems, but really, that made it *just right* for what Ray and I had wanted in a home.

Ayden, the home inspector, and my realtor, Jada, had all looked at me like I was crazy, and the mortgage broker seemed uncertain. But restored to its former glory, it could rival any of the other newly restored places on the block. I had the vision, determination, and good enough credit to make it happen.

I hired an exterminator to make sure I was bug-free, and an electrician to make sure I wasn't going to die in an electrical fire. I hired a crew to go in and clean it up as best they could. And then... I moved in. I hadn't touched anything, hadn't started a single project, because I was waiting.

"A contractor? Really? I thought you and Ray were going to be doing everything DIY? Won't he want to have a say in the selection process?"

I stepped out of the bathroom, heading downstairs to get a bottle of water and a fresh toothbrush to brush my teeth. "If Ray was actually leaving Chicago that would be a consideration. However, he's not, so really... I no longer *have* a 'boo'." As I passed through the bedroom, my ruined photo print and the gaping hole in the wall caught my attention again. "Add *raggedy ass drywall* to the list of things to tell the contractor, and don't forget *funky ass water*."

"Done and done. But wait a minute... no longer have a boo? Ray *not* leaving Chicago? What the hell is going on?"

I paused on the stairs and pushed out a breath. As my personal assistant – and ride or die bestie— Ayden was so connected to me that she would find out soon enough anyway about the drama with Ray, so it really didn't make a ton of sense not to just tell her now.

So I did.

And when I was done, she was silent for a long moment before she launched into a tirade. "That sorry, no-good motherfucker. How *dare* he wait until you— why the hell would he— *UGH*, I can't stand his ass! What is wrong with him?!"

"I don't know, Ayden. Wish I did."

"Everything you've been planning centered on *him*. If he's out of the picture now... what are you going to do?"

Ah, the question of the hour. What *was* I going to do?

My lingerie store, *Scantilily*, was successful in Chicago. We had a retail area, where customers could just stop in and purchase, but our bread and butter, what set us apart, was the *Scantilily* experience. No stick-thin, ribcage bearing models plastered the walls in my store. Upscale décor, accessible pricing, and a sales experience modeled after bridal shopping were the cornerstones of my business model. Women of all sizes came in with their friends or lover, or whatever combination in between. They told us what they were looking for, and we delivered. They sipped champagne and modeled, and joked, and laughed, and left with a great memory and bags full of things that made them feel sexy.

It was a great business... I just wasn't that sure I could replicate that success.

But I stepped out anyway. Ray said he was moving to further his political career, and he wanted me to come with. It was just the push I needed to take the chance on a second location, in what was honestly a beautiful, up-and-coming area. The costs, though, were *huge*. The deposit on the building space we were leasing, the costs to have it built out to fit our business model, hiring employees, advertisement, licensing, insurance... it was a lot.

I couldn't open a new store from a distance – well, I *could*, but I didn't want to. The *Scantilily* brand was my baby, my everything. I needed to be hands on. My mother damn near disowned me for moving away from the city where I'd been conceived, raised, and still loved, to "chase behind a rusty ass man". Turns out, she was right. But obviously, I didn't know that then.

All I knew was that he was talking about getting married once we were relocated, and mulling over a rough outline for a five-year plan that included kids. I was about to turn thirty-four, so even though I wasn't even sure I *wanted* kids... time was ticking. And I loved him, and I believed he loved me. We were young, vibrant, and making our way – this was the time to do these things!

I just really wish he'd broken up with me before I bought the house.

Of all the mistakes, of everything... that was definitely the most idiotic one. It was supposed to be my *"Look, I wasn't just playing along with you when we talked about this, I'm not too cute to break a nail or use a saw!"* gift to him when he got here. It was going to be a surprise, because that was something we'd always done with each other, back when things were less... roommate-like. Competing to see who could outdo the other, who could deliver the best bombshell.

Ha.

Ray *definitely* won this time.

"Guess what? I know you made all these huge decisions thinking we would be together forever, and this was going to be this great adventure with each other, but... SURPRISE, don't nobody want your ass, bitch! HAHAHA!"

That wasn't really what he said, of course, but by my estimation, it may as well have been. I was standing frozen, on stairs of questionable structural integrity, wondering what the hell I was going to do now. He was probably snuggled comfortably in bed, beside my replacement. He would move on with his life, because that was what men did. They broke hearts and then skipped away, finding the next woman to be too enthralled by a handsome, straight, ambitious black man with no kids to realize that with all those qualities, he *still* wasn't worth shit.

And while he was doing that... what would I do?

With everything in an upheaval, my heart broken, and me embarrassed beyond belief that I'd done all of this to be with him... what would *I* do?

Come on, Fallon... what are you going to do now? What are you going to do with your life?"

I...

I would...

"I'm going to make it work." I straightened my shoulders, and stopped allowing my head to droop as I looked around *my* new house. "Ray didn't make me. He was just... a season. That season is over, apparently, so I'll move forward. I'm going to be just fine without him."

If you enjoyed this book, please consider leaving a review at your retailer of choice. It doesn't have to be long - just a line or two about why you enjoyed the book, or even a simple star rating can be very helpful for any author!

Want to stay connected? Text 'CCJRomance' to 74121 or sign up for my newsletter. I'll keep you looped into what I'm doing!

Check out CCJROMANCE.COM for first access to all my new releases, signed paperbacks, merch, and more!

I'm all over the social mediasphere - find me everywhere @beingmrsjones

For a full listing of titles by Christina C Jones, visit www.beingmrsjones.com/books

about the author

Christina C. Jones is a best-selling romance novelist and digital media creator. A timeless storyteller, she is lauded by readers for her ability to seamlessly weave the complexities of modern life into captivating tales of Black characters in nearly every romance subgenre. In addition to her full-time writing career, she co-founded Girl, Have You Read – a popular digital platform that amplifies Black romance authors and their stories. Christina has a passion for making beautiful things, and be found crafting, cooking, and designing and building a (literal) home with her husband in her spare time.